A PLACE FOR CONNIE

Alison Rundle

Some of the characters and names mentioned in this book are real. The incidents and events are the work of the author's imagination.

The place names mentioned are real, but the descriptions are an

amalgamation of all the beautiful places I have visited over the years, in both Crete and Corfu.

ISBN 9781982908454

Beau Publishing

2018

Thank you to my husband Stephen, for his patience and constant kindness

Thank you to my daughter Bobbie, for just being her beautiful and extraordinary self – all the time and without fail.

Thank you to my daughter Jenny (1984 – 2009). Her loss changed our live and taught me that life is indeed what you make it. We miss her every day.

Thank you to my friend Richard – my catalyst.

Many thanks to Dimitri and his family who own The Brouklis Taverna in Arillas, Corfu. Thank you for giving me so many delicious meals and allowing me to use a photograph of your beautiful restaurant.

Thank you to all the people of Arillas, Corfu who never fail to provide a warm welcome and an interesting story or two.

A Place for Connie

Prologue
Makrigialos, Crete 1977

It was greyer today, the sun shrouded with wisps of cloud, the air damp. It would be hot later. Once the sun had shed that misty cloak of his, he would split the trees with his heat.

She sat under the ancient pine tree at Papou's back door, her long legs stretched out, holding the baby's hands tight as he balanced on her knees. His big green eyes were locked on her - listen, she said to him, can you hear the sea? I love the sea. Will you like the sea? Yes, you will.

He pulled her hair, pushed his sticky little-baby hands onto her face and she dropped her mother-kisses onto his rosy cheeks. She loved him. She did. She had never felt such love, never. How lucky she was to be sitting here with her gorgeous boy, sheltered under her favourite tree on this gentle and soft morning. Oh, this lovely child all of her own. There they were, just the two of them, a mother and her baby enjoying their love with no one to disrupt it. Come on you, she murmured into his ear, time for a little walk. She stood up and wrapped herself in the stripy carrying cloth, he sat on the sand and he jiggled his chubby legs,
wanting his mother's arms around him again.

What was that floating out there? Rising and falling and as grey as the waves that pushed at it. She squinted to see. What was it? The baby squealed, her attention shifted to him again and she laughed and picked him up, sat him astride her hip, pulled the cloth taught under his bottom. There it was again, getting closer, bobbing gently up and down with the swell. She tied the ends of the wrap tightly behind her back and took a couple of steps towards the wet shore-line. The baby bounced up and down. Wait, baby, wait. There. Some blue in the sky now as the sun began to shine. The thing rolled and lolled. Arms outstretched.

Papou was wide awake, sitting on the edge of his bed and ready to start his day. He scratched his moth-eaten old chest and wondered where his spectacles were. What was that? Someone was shouting. He hitched his pyjamas up and shuffled to the window. The English girl was out there, her mouth open and a horrible screaming coming from her. He hurried to open his door. She was lurching across the beach, the baby bouncing with every stride as she struggled through the sand to get to him. What was she saying? Papou, Papou. Someone. Dead. He couldn't understand, she was puffing and panting too much and speaking English. A dead? A dead what?

Oh, my goodness. There was something there, riding on the ridge of pebbles left on the shore by the rippling sea. Something big, caught there between the sand and the sea, slowly turning in the ebb and flow of each wave.

Oh, my goodness. He went closer; the girl kept on screaming and the baby cried and cried. It was a man. Lying there on the sand. Dead. Arms akimbo and undulating lazily as the sea rocked him in its swell. His grey sweater full and fat with water. He pushed the seaweed and hair from the face.

They ran to the café and banged and banged and banged on the door until Vaso came downstairs rubbing the sleep from her eyes.

THE BEGINNING, NEWCASTLE – UPON - TYNE 1980

It was too hot. Time for fresh lipstick and a spray of perfume. She pressed her forehead against the mirror. Cool. Nice. She wanted to go home. She smoothed her dress down and smiled at her reflection - best face forward.

Linda and Katie were watching her coming out of the toilets. Connie knew they didn't really like her anymore. Not since she'd come back home from London. They'd both come in when she was in the loo and she'd heard what they said - that bloody Connie is too clever for her own good, too far up her own backside. All that jet-black hair and eyeliner, who the hell did she think she was anyway - Siouxsie bloody Sioux? Queen of punk? Lady - bloody - Muck more like, she's so stuck-up. And they had sniggered and giggled. Connie had imagined herself coming out of the loo and looking them straight in the eyes - yes, I'm Lady Muck and don't you forget it, she would say and leave them

standing there with red faces and open mouths. But she didn't, she waited till the door opened and their voices had been drowned out by the blast of music that flooded in and then she crept out of the cubicle. She thought they were her friends. What would her mother have said? Oh Connie, take no notice. Honestly, I don't know why you waste your time worrying what such low-class people think – that's what she'd have said.

Someone else was watching her too. Entranced. This girl, who didn't even glance his way, had all his attention. His eyes were blue. His hair was red, not carrot or strawberry, but the red of a Titian beauty or a drowning Ophelia. Thick and long, curling like a girl's past his
shoulders and almost to his waist. He was skinny. Shirt undone, hairless chest pale and skinny. Drunk.

She's a funny one, he thought. Too thin and spiky. Her eyes were green. Her hair was black. She was as tall as him. Not drunk. And as for that dress - all those loose threads hanging around the hem as if she'd hacked a lump off with kitchen scissors. And that whatever it was she'd got wrapped round her shoulders, well, that looked like an old tablecloth - he was sure his Nan had one. No shoes. She had no bloody shoes on. It was like she couldn't be bothered, like she didn't care less.

He couldn't stop looking at her. He walked up to her, weaving slightly, preparing himself to shout in her ear over the loud music. She was watching him come closer. She didn't lower her gaze, didn't smile. He felt his face getting hot. She took away his bravado in an instant with that green gaze fixed on him. His lips quivered. Please God his breath didn't stink.

'Your eyes look sort of blue……like proper bright blue…..but with leaves in….' Shit. Stupid.

'Green. And you're an idiot.' Now she smiled at him. Well. A kind of smile. Maybe she only bared her teeth. He felt a shiver go through his whole body. And end up in his pants.

'I know. Sorry. I just wanted to say something so you wouldn't wander off.

Sorry. Sorry.' Christ, how many times. 'Sorry. Where's your shoes?'

'Lost.' She moved closer. Her hip bone on his. The smell of her. God. The heat of her. Oh God.

'C'mon. Let's go.' she took his hand and lead him away. Like a lamb.

He never left her side again. Every day he thanked his lucky stars and couldn't believe this strange, almost wild creature was his girl. His lovely girl. He thought his heart would burst clean out of his skinny ribs when he looked at her, because he loved her. Really loved her. Really, really, really loved her. She was moody and bad-tempered and she couldn't cook, but he didn't care. Sometimes she sat on the bed and read poetry to him, her long legs crossed and his old shirt-nightie riding up past her knees; her voice rising and falling and the words he couldn't understand flowing all around him. He thought he might faint with the beauty of those moments. He didn't care because she was funny and beautiful and clever - all the strange moods, burnt food and quiet times couldn't stop his lips quivering or the blood rushing in his ears when he looked at her.

If he woke up in the morning and she wasn't lying next to him, he had to get up and find her. She was usually sitting at the back door, her stool dragged to the very edge of the step, blowing her cigarette smoke out into the early air, a cup of steaming extra strong black coffee on the floor beside her. He would rub her shoulders and wonder what she was thinking about. She never told him, no matter how many times he asked - go back to bed, she'd say.

At night he couldn't go to bed unless it was at the same time as her. His eyes could be red-rimmed and drooping, but if she was still up, he was still up. Her early-bird and night-owl ways left him tired and drained from lack of sleep. He didn't care.

His long days at work went by faster when he thought about her. He imagined her in the bath, drying her hair, slipping on her clothes, drinking a coffee, eating an apple, and always thinking about him as she waited for him to come back to her. In his mind's eye she was always at home and waiting, never at work, never looking after her patients or laughing in the canteen with the other nurses, never.

He drove as fast as he dared to get back to her. If she was on a late shift he paced around the house like a caged bear, driven slightly mad by the solitude, unable to settle till he heard her key in the lock. It made her angry sometimes. Space, she shouted at him one day, I need some space, let me breath. He always listened when she explained it to him - how she felt smothered, closed in, overwhelmed, but he didn't understand, couldn't take it in. But why, he asked, I'm not horrible to you, I love you, that's all. Once she had looked up at him with her big green eyes full of fire and tears and said - I've never been loved before. Her voice was so tiny and jagged with sobs it made him want to cry too. So, he fended off her anger, let his narrow shoulders bear the brunt of every bad mood, flare of temper and silent moment. Because he loved her, loved her, loved her. Through the ups and downs, through the squalls and storms, he forgave her everything and loved her more.

She stayed with him because she loved him as much as she dared.

Then the babies came.

They'd been to that old pub down on the Quayside, the tables were old beer barrels; there were beams on the ceiling and hunting scenes on the walls. They didn't like it much but Friday night was live music night. Upstairs in the dark and stifling back room, she jumped and danced and clapped and sang - the condensed beads of other people's breath and heat dropping on her from the ceiling. She loved it. He wasn't much of a dancer, he stood on the edge of everything and watched her. Sometimes she beckoned him to her and pulled him into her arms, her voice in his ear - dance with me Ed, dance with me – her breath soft on his cheek. And they'd dance, thigh to thigh, hip to hip, chest to chest, lip to lip.

There was no dancing tonight. They stayed downstairs, their drinks trembling on the beer barrel table as the bass beat reverberated through the building. She rubbed the sides of her glass, feeling it's coldness against the soft pads of her finger tips. Ed was talking and talking. His Dad was worried about her - it wasn't normal, girls drinking pints, and those tattoos of hers, she's a bit…..well…..you know, son, he'd said. Yes, Ed knew - different, Dad, that's all. Just different.

Connie listened to him prattling on. She shrugged. She didn't care what Ed's Dad thought. She didn't like his Dad, or the way he treated is timid little wife. Upstairs the band was singing something awful and suddenly she'd had quite enough. She tapped his knee - let's go, she said, taking him by surprise and pulling him out of the door into the warm night.

They walked up the Quayside side by side. Her arm around his thin waist and her hand pushed in his pocket, hugging him tight against her and rubbing against his bony hip. The city was buzzing and teaming and alive. Full of life and light and noise. They walked under the bridge. He could hear the kittiwakes, awake and restless at the noise of their feet echoing around the huge arch. There was a ship tied up against the opposite quay - a floating nightclub - the fluorescent lights shone down into the river, glittering and glossy on the black water.

'I'm going to have a baby, Ed.'

She carried on walking, leaving him behind with the words bouncing around his brain. A baby…. Christ.

'C'mon, Ed. Catch up!' She turned to face him, hands on hips. Stunning in the moonlight, the reflections from the river bending and moving over her.

A baby….

A baby… shit.

A baby…. hell.

The baby was beautiful. Fat and pink and happy. A smiling baby with dimples in all the right places. Connie called her Stella. Stella star.

'For God's sake, Ed.' She said that a lot in those days. She was tired, Stella was toddling all over the place and baby number two was on its way. They'd bought a house next to his parents. Money was tight. She was just tired.

Baby number two was not so beautiful. Long, thin and white, with see - through skin and blue veins showing. She cried all the time. He called her Claire.

Baby number three. It was called James.

THE LEAVING, CONSETT, 2000

'Lost my wallet,' he says, 'just fell out of my pocket and disappeared. We looked all over for it.' He wipes his hand across his brow - worried, but not about the wallet. She clashes the pans about and stirs everything a bit harder, gritting her teeth to stop the words spitting out - you stupid man. And here she is with the gas bill not paid. Christ.

'Never mind.' she says, keeping her back to him.

'But Connie ......' Something about the set of her shoulders makes him shut up. God, I'll have to pay for this. She's going to be cross all night and not speak. I'll be in for it for the next two weeks. Not like it's my fault it's lost. It's not like I threw it away. Time to make it better. He snakes his arms around her waist, nuzzles his lips into her hair, 'it'll be alright Connie,' his voice gentle and tender, 'I can borrow a bit more off Dad.' He holds his breath.

She shrugs him away. 'Again.'

'I know, but he'll be alright about it. He'll not mind. Honestly, he won't.' His breath stays caught in his chest. She turns round fast, catches him off guard and pushes him away, almost knocks him over. Bloody hell, she's a strong bugger. He'd liked that about her once upon a time, but not today. That day she'd taken a massive hammer to that old coal bunker in the yard and hadn't stopped till it was bashed to bits - that had been a good day. She'd been flushed and sweaty, rubbing her aching hands down her thighs. Geez, Connie! What's got into you? Glad that wasn't my head! - he'd said. And she'd run at him, jumped at him, wrapped her legs around him, pulled him into her dirty arms and laughed and kissed him till he went weak at the knees and they'd fallen on the ground. Sometimes she scared him with her intensity, her desire.

Released emotions, she said. Bloody crazy, he thought.

'I know he won't mind, but I do. I'm sick of it. If it hadn't been the wallet then it would have been something else. One thing after another it seems to me.' Her voice is quiet, reasonable even, but her eyes are hard and her mouth like a slit. He sighs. He knows all this, he knows and he is sorry, but he can't help it.

'It's just life Connie. It's just the way things are.'

'Is it? Well, I'm sick of it. That's all.' She pushes him away. Hard.

They've all gone out and she is left alone, sitting in the kitchen with a pile of dirty dishes, a dog that needs a walk, clothes to put in the washer, beds to make, and carpets to hoover. She thumps her mug down on the table just break the silence.

Ed isn't a bad man, he's kind, sweet, friendly, and he's a great Dad. The kids always go to him before her. He's never angry, not like her. She loves the kids. She does. She's too hard on them sometimes, too quick to get cross, but when she looks in on them last thing at night she remembers how much she loves them. Then her heart could burst. But they want too much all the time, especially now they're all teenagers - take me here, take me there, pick me up, where's my shoes, she's got my stuff, God I hate you - that was all she heard these days. And not a moment for herself. Always doing things, finding things, fixing things, making ends meet, making the best of everything. And now the bloody lost wallet. It's crap, that's what it was.

Not a moment to herself - that's a laugh, it'll take her 20 minutes to clean up and then she's got another 400 minutes to do … what? Bloody nothing. That's bloody what. Well, today is the day. She is going to do something. Something bloody big. She throws the mug in the sink. It smashes against the tap and she doesn't give a damn.

Lovely. The house is tidy, there's a casserole in the slow cooker, the school clothes are ironed for tomorrow, her bag is packed and the note's on the table. There are 307 minutes till they all get home. They'll be angry and worried and upset, the kids will cry. Well, it can't be helped. There's some money in the bank, Ed's Mam and Dad are just two houses away. She'll be back in a week or two.

She goes upstairs and digs her wooden jewellery box out of the wardrobe. Ed made it for her that first Christmas before the kids were born. A Christmas spent in her freezing and grubby bedsit - a good Christmas, free of parents and children and obligations. It's a pretty box, the not- so- secret drawer is lined with a piece of her old red shawl. The money is jumbled up amongst a few old photos, a tatty map and some scrappy letters. She counts it into piles on the bed. Nine hundred pounds she'd saved and scrimped for - a tenner here, twenty quid there. Money she'd squirrelled away because she knew this day would have to come. She gathers it up, arranges the Queen's head the right way round, and pushes it into her bag. Mustn't forget the brooch. It's too pretty to hide anymore, she pins it to her jumper. Right. It's time to be off.

She catches sight of herself in the mirror and stops. Who is this woman looking back at her? Long hair scraped back in a ponytail, sad and tired eyes, a bit too fat. How had she turned into this woman? Not herself at all. She hadn't been herself since … oh, God knows when. It wouldn't be long till something let go and she exploded in a puff of smoke and star-filled flames, there'd be nothing left but the lingering smell of fireworks and shredded guts hanging off the lampshades. She'd better make her move now, before she gets any nearer to the big bang.

She can't take the car. Ed is bound to call the police and that will be the first thing they'll look for. Shame, but that's the way it will have to be. She hitches her bag further up on her shoulder and sets off up the road, and doesn't even cast a backwards glance at his Mam and Dad's house as she goes past.

Town is full - it's market day. All the old dears are out with their friends, shopping and chatting and wondering where to go for a cuppa and a scone. Their voices flow round her as she pushes her way through them, their snippets of conversations catching her attention.

'Here, Marge, did you hear about Sheila's grandson? Only gone and crashed his dad's car. Drunk, they said. Broke his leg.'

'No? Well, they were too soft on that one, right from when he was little.'

'I know…. little sod he was…..'

None of them had any idea what she was up to. No idea at all. Shame. It would give them something else to gossip about.

She pushes on. Past the stalls of fruit, meat, bread, and cheap slippers. Past her favourite, "Carol's Clothes". That's where she'd bought the posh frock. She'd seen it on her way to pay the gas bill, just hanging there, sparkling in the morning sun. It was those dew drops of light that had caught her eye. She'd rubbed the material, so soft and so fine, between her fingers, held a wisp of cloth up to her face and sniffed it. A trace of cigarette smoke still lingered amongst its folds. It smelled of someone. Someone who wore perfume and red lipstick, someone who went to parties and lost her shoes and didn't care, someone who laughed and flirted and danced and sang and smoked menthol cigarettes and ate
chocolate; someone like her. Bugger. Someone like her? Not anymore. She'd drawn in that other life with every sniff. The bill had not been paid that week.

She stops for a moment to admire the brooches, jostling higgledy-piggledy on their black velvet tray, colours clashing.

'Hello, love.' Big, bustling, red-faced Carol. A woman of substance.

'They're so pretty aren't they?'

'They are, love. No one wears them these days, more's the pity.'

'I do,' she says.

DURHAM RAILWAY STATION, 2000

Such a pretty railway station, very old-fashioned with its white, lacy wrought iron-work on the roof, plenty of hanging baskets and only 2 platforms - one for up and one for down. Shame it was spoilt by the high-street chain café and newsagents. Why couldn't people leave things alone? God, she sounds like Ed's mother. Always harping on, in that little-girl voice of hers, about the good old days and how it was better then. Maybe it was.

A few people are sitting near the coffee shop, guarding their suitcases and staring blankly into the air around them. A couple more flick through the magazines. No-one looks happy. Poor them. She loves travelling. She's stuck with the odd package holiday every now and again, what with Ed and the kids and the dog to put in kennels. Last year they'd managed to save enough to go to Spain and she'd been beside herself with excitement in the airport; she'd dragged the kids into every duty-free shop and looked at every bag, bottle of perfume, case of wine and pair of flip-flops she could see. Stella had been exasperated with her, rolling her eyes and whining about everything; following her around and commenting on everything her mother looked at. Put that down. You can't be serious. That's horrible. God. Honestly. Mother. Really. Connie had wished Stella wasn't there, she didn't want to hear that dismissive tone in her voice making her

feel stupid and silly. Jesus Christ, Stella, she'd said, leave me alone, I'm having some fun. Stella had stalked off tutting and grumbling, but at least she had left Connie alone. In the end she'd bought some fancy designer lip-gloss. Twelve pounds it had cost. She'd really wanted a bottle of proper perfume to replace the couple - of - quid - copy in her suitcase, but she definitely couldn't afford that. She'd sprayed as much of the perfume on herself as she dared and strolled away feeling like a princess. God, Connie, sit over there, you're making me cough with that stink, Ed had said,
flapping at the air in front of him with a newspaper. The kids had laughed.

ATHENS, 1976

The first time she went abroad it had been so different. They'd planned it for weeks. It was that hot summer, that summer of legendary sun, too many ladybirds and too little water. Anita's sister had married a Greek and she'd upped sticks and moved to Athens. Amid the months and months of tears, and the wailing from all the mothers and fathers, a little boy had been born and this new, Greek baby was being brought home to meet English Granny and Grandpa for the first time. So, off they went - six best friends and a key for the sister's apartment.

Connie hadn't been anywhere before, not really. Oh yes, she'd been on day trips to the seaside, she'd even been to Scarborough for a week. But never 'away', not far away, in an aeroplane. Anita told Connie's mother she would look after her, that everything would be fine. Her mother had umm'd and err'd, but Connie had begged - please, please, it's only two weeks, please. Mother eventually gave in - anyway, a couple of weeks without Connie would be a nice break for her.

They left England at some unearthly hour, giggling and acting the goat in the crisp almost-morning. She listened to them cracking jokes, watched them pushing and shoving each other as they walked across the tarmac to the plane steps. They were excited. So was she. But scared, so scared she thought she might cry. She stared up at the navy-blue sky, the edges tinged with peach and pink, and sucked in the sharp air. The world was spread above her. Waiting for her to reach up and touch it. It made her shiver. And feel a bit sick.

The rumbling of the wheels across the tarmac, the lurch into the air, the soaring calm as they shot above the clouds and out into the bright blue, and then the dropping turn as the plane headed out over the North Sea terrified her. She gripped Anita's hand tight. Her head throbbed and her stomach churned. She tried to read, thumbing through the magazine in the pocket of the seat in front of her, she tried to talk, she tried to eat her meal. In the end, all she could do was sleep, only stirring when someone needed to step over her legs on the way to the loo.

A few hours later and they stumbled, bleary-eyed and tired, straight into the Athenian sun and the overpowering smell of Greece - hot tarmac, petrol fumes and the faint aroma of sewage. Everything blindingly white, the buildings, the roads and pavements, even the tree trunks. The incandescence of this blazing, sizzling place was almost agonising and not like anywhere she'd been before. This heat is really, really hot – someone said, and they all laughed.

They bundled themselves into a battered estate car, the taxi sign held on with a rusty bit of wire. The driver squeezed them in, pushing and shoving, encouraging them with hand signals and his smattering of English, to move up, to squash close. He put one of the boys in the boot with the rucksacks. They were sure it must be illegal but they did it

anyway, because it was Greece and it was foreign and it was different. Any tiredness was forgotten, it was all giggling and chattering as they piled in. She sat next to the driver and showed him the bit of paper with the address on. He whistled through his teeth and exuberant moustache - many drachmas, he said.

Driving through the Athens traffic was hair-raising. Tyres squealing, tooting and more tooting, lurching this way and that through the narrow streets and flying too fast along the wide avenues. The driver shouted at this car, screamed at that bus and waved his hands, taking them both off the wheel at every opportunity. They laughed and screeched and enjoyed the rush of wind flying in and sucking their breath away. She hung her head out of the window like a dog, let her lips peel away from her teeth, felt her tongue dry and her cheeks fill with air.

Breathless and bruised they swerved to a halt outside a squat apartment block on a leafy suburban street. Striped awnings hung at every balcony and skinny cats skulked at every doorway, streaking away into the shade as the six of them came up the path.

'I've got the key.' Anita said, jingling it out of her rucksack pocket. She pushed it in the lock. The key didn't budge and the door stayed firmly shut. They all had a go, wiggling and jiggling the key this way and that, but it just wouldn't turn.

'This is no good. What we going to do?' Anita was nearly crying.

'Don't panic. There's a café place just up the road, I saw it as we were coming past. Let's go for a drink and think about it,' Connie patted Anita's arm, 'we'll manage.'

A few old men sat in the bar, fiddling with small strings of beads and sipping coffee from teeny, tiny cups. All was cool and quiet, only the clicking of the beads to break the hush.

'Kalimera. Good Morning.' He was younger than all of his

customers. 'You are English?' He smiled. What on earth were all these kids doing in his café, looking so sad? Tourists never came to this part of his city.

'Oh! Thank goodness. We have come to stay in Louise and Georgos Stathakis flat. They sent us a key but it won't work she is Louise's sister and they are in England and now we can't get in and we don't really know what to do and it's too hot. Much too hot.' The words came out in a rush and she started to giggle at the silliness of the situation.

'Ah. I see. I know them. I am Andreas and we are lucky because my friend is a lock man. He will come and fix. I will telephone and he will come soon.' He waved them to some seats. The clack of the beads had stopped for a few minutes when they trudged in, now it started up again, louder. None of the old men were looking at them but they

whispered to each other. Connie watched them - such big moustaches they had, never mind, time for a cool drink.

None of them knew how long a Greek 'soon' was. And it was a very long time. When the 'lock man' arrived the sun was starting to cool, they had been introduced to everyone in the bar, played with the local cats slithering round their legs meowing for titbits, had lunch, taken turns to have a shower in the flat upstairs, tried a few Greek beers, and learnt to say "hello", "thank you" and "where is the toilet?". Connie asked about the beads that the men caressed and twirled endlessly.

Andreas winked at her and pulled a string of amber beads out of his own pocket. 'See, I have them too. They help us to worry - not to pray.' He laughed. 'Komboloi. The old ones have nothing to do when their wives kick them out in the mornings, so they come here to drink coffee and talk and rattle their beads.' Connie added them to her list of things to buy.

The lock man filed the key down a touch, refused to take any money, and they eventually collapsed into bed, half-drunk on Mythos beer and excitement. She was too hot and sweaty to sleep, she opened the window as wide as she dared and listened to the strange world moving outside and waited for the new Greek morning to come.

It started well. Of course it did. They shuffled along with the crowds of tourists to all the famous places. They stood in queues, sat on hot buses, and looked at everything Andreas told them to look at. After a few days of pushing and shoving and not quite seeing everything, she knew she wasn't enjoying it. There wasn't the sight of the back of

another head, the following of another waving umbrella, or the reading of another plaque that she could stomach. She wanted to sit still and notice the small things, quietly and on her own - that big hairy caterpillar wiggling its way across the road, why was it so big? Would it get to the other side before it cooked? Why are there so many stray cats and dogs? Who fed them all? What happened to them in the winter?

Her favourite times were the evenings spent in the cafe, eating and drinking, asking questions and listening to Andreas translate the old men's tales of Ancient Greece, of battles lost and won. She asked him about the cats. Oh, the council come and put down the poisoned meat and then they are gone. He didn't bat an eye lid as he said it and was surprised when she protested. He was scornful - Pah! You English! Too much money if you can look after pets, he patted her hand to take the sting out of his words.

The first week wasn't even over before the arguments and tears started. Connie didn't like the bickering, it made her unhappy. She didn't want to stay with them and she didn't want to stay in Athens. She wanted to see more, go further. The other's thought she was mad, but Andreas encouraged her - you will be safe, he said, keep away from the foreigners, but the Greeks will be fine, they will look after you. And it is only for a week, you can't go far, or get into much trouble in a week. The ferries from Piraeus will take you anywhere you want to go, maybe Aegina or even Spetses. Anita said she was crazy to listen to Andreas, and anyway, what would her mother do when she found out she'd just gone off on her own?

'Mam won't know. I'll meet you all for the plane home, she won't be any the wiser,' she said, 'unless you tell her.' Connie hugged her tight, trying to make her feel better.

'I'll come with you.'

'No.' Connie shook her head, 'I'll be fine.' It was settled. A whole week and one day to be on her own and do something a little bit wild, a little bit out of the ordinary. And all the time, deep down inside her inexperienced heart, she knew she wasn't coming back for that flight home, knew she was going to walk, run or sail away from all the people and all the places she couldn't bear to go back to.

She had been so young, so full of that youthful bravery and the daring of the not knowing. It didn't enter her head that she might get lost, lose her passport, run out of money, meet horrible people, or get lonely. Not once did she wonder what her mother would think; not once did she imagine the panic at the airport when she didn't turn up.

Ah, but Connie, if it did go wrong, there was that flight to get back for, wasn't there? If you got too frightened, too lonely, too poor, you knew you could run back to the safety of home. Well, that made it easier for you, didn't it? After all, in that young head of yours, you were off on an adventure, but everyone needs a 'just in case' plan, don't they?

Andreas took her to the port in his old orange Beetle, he hugged her and wished her luck - see you in a week, he said, and winked. She pushed her way through the gates and into the crowd. When she turned to wave goodbye he was gone, only the orange car to watch as it threaded its way through the traffic.

Hundreds of people, cars, buses and wagons filled up the hot sunny day with their noise and fumes. Crates swung high above her head and onto the ships waiting at the dockside. Big ships and little ships waiting for their cargos. What to do, what to do? She pulled her bag up onto her shoulder and forced her way towards the ticket booths. Sick of the crush and excited to be off and away, she joined the shortest queue and found herself bound for Crete. Not Aegina or Spetses. Well, what the heck, she thought, not knowing how far away Crete was. And if she was going to Crete, she might as well go to Matala because it was the only place she'd heard of.

She sat upstairs on the highest deck, so hot it was like sitting in a hairdryer, squashed in with a group of Americans. She watched the sun glinting on the waves and the dolphins leaping in the spray, felt the throbbing of the engines vibrating through her entire body, as the ferry took her away across the sea.

She'd never met an American before. They told her that the good times in Matala were over, that the real hippies were gone - there are only thieves, junkies and Joni Mitchell wannabes left now, a girl said, drawling her words out into a whinny of a laugh, showing all her teeth and gums - don't go there, kid, you'll get into trouble. The rest of her group nodded in agreement - Makrigialos, they said, that's the place to go, no one knows it's there yet.

A day and a night on that little ship as it bustled and busied its way over the horizon, leaving a trail of bubbles and foaming water behind it. A day and a night when she could have been lonely and afraid of the unknown, but she wasn't. She drank beer, ate dry cheese sandwiches and snuggled up close to the American boy with the long golden curls, who whispered in her ear like a Siren. No, she said, no. But she let him kiss her on the lips until he almost took her breath away. And then the sun rose again, the new day started and that little ship nosed into the harbour. She waved him goodbye at the bus station and realised she didn't know his name, but she had his map. He had scrawled across the front - Go to bus stop. Find right bus. You are sweet and pretty. I love you already.

The island baked in the sun and she baked on the bus to Irapetra, rucksack between her feet and her head turned to the window. The bus bounced along the country roads, scraped past walls and corners of buildings with only an inch to spare, and zig-zagged too fast up, down and around the hairpin bends. The hillsides were still tinged with green and sprinkled with bright flowers, heads up in the April sunshine.

She got a crick in her neck trying to look at everything. Fields and fields of gnarled old olive trees, forests of pine with white beehives at their feet and far–off mountains capped with snow. More to see here than in Athens, even with all her ancient glories to be admired.

There were stringy old men leading grumpy mules which sneered their lips and jinked on boxy, black hoofs in protest at their heavy loads.

An old pick-up van passed them, the back piled up high with chairs, a tangle of legs, and no sign of any rope to hold them on.

On every hilltop a tiny white church, its rooftop cross stretching straight up into the sharp blueness of the heavens.

Passing through a small village she looked out at a gathering of stout old women sitting on the steps of the church, all dressed in black, with thick tights and head-scarves. As they talked they fanned themselves with handkerchiefs edged in lace. They waved as the bus went by, a quick flurry of white, she waved back.

Bare - chested boys in flip-flops and shorts, long hair flying out behind them, cheering and gesturing as they buzzed past on their scooters.

The countryside flattened out, dried and yellowed; ragged, flapping poly tunnels lined the sides of the ever-widening road. Slower and slower the bus went, caught up in the increased traffic and eventually trundled into dirty, dusty Irapetra. Everyone climbed out and stretched. Families hugged and kissed, friends slapped each other's backs and chattered. Soon there was only Connie left, standing alone on the pavement looking for her next bus. The bus to Makrigialos.

Oh yes, she had been so young then.

BACK HOME, CONSETT, 2000

"Dear Ed, Stella, Claire and James
I love you all very much. Look after each other. There are no
Ithaca's."

That was it. She hasn't even signed it and not a single kiss.
What the hell did it mean? Stella holds the note out and shakes it in
Ed's face, 'Ithaca, Dad. Homer's Odyssey. It's all about the journey.
For Christ's sake.' She sits down on the kitchen chair and looks at
him. Just looks. Her green eyes, like her mother's, full of tears. He
feels uncomfortable, stupid, because he's never heard of Ithaca and
because he doesn't know what to say. She gathers James and Claire
into her arms, kissing their teary, snotty faces. 'Don't cry. She'll be
back soon and we can ask her about all the exciting things she's done
and all the wonderful places she's been. C'mon, let's go, Dad can talk
to these policemen.' She
shepherds the younger ones into the front room. She's a clever girl,
like her Mum.

The police ask a million and one questions. Was she
depressed? Did he think she could harm herself? "Harm herself" what
the hell did that mean? What time did you last see her? What did you
talk about? Is she in debt? Has she been unwell? Any special places

she goes to? Does she have any family members she could have gone to visit? No, no, NO, NO and NO, she never talks about her family, he tells them, only the odd time. He knew there aren't any brothers or sisters, her father had died when she was young and she never mentioned her mother. And no, he didn't ask about them. The policeman wondered why. Well, because if he did, she made it plain that she wouldn't talk about them and that was the end of it. Because that's what she's like secretive and grumpy. These policemen didn't know Connie at all.

They go upstairs to see where her clothes are, see if Ed knows what's missing, what she might be wearing, what she's taken with her. They are nice and all that, but their radios keep crackling and squawking. Tinny little voices, belonging to faceless people in some beige room somewhere, repeat her name over and over again. 'Constance
Parker....... Constance Parker.......... Constance Parker........' It's like the telly. It isn't real at all.

He knows what's missing - jeans, black jumper, a couple of T- shirts and her posh frock - that long black one with scatters of crystals flung all over it and all swirly at the bottom. God knows where she'd got it from - look at this, she'd said, when she brought it home and pulled it out of a crumpled old carrier bag. LOOK! ED! And she'd twirled and whirled around the front room, holding the dress up against her, its arms outstretched like they were ballroom dancing. It was a beautiful dress. She'd never worn it.

He wishes he hadn't laughed. He can't remember why he'd teased her, why he hadn't taken her out that night. She would have looked lovely in it, fresh and new and beautiful. Is that why she's gone off somewhere? To wear her sparkly dress? He wants to cry but he can't, because there's a policemen in their bedroom rifling through his wife's wardrobe, and he's saying something to him. Why that dress, Mr.

Parker? Why would she run off somewhere with that? Does she have a lover, Mr. Parker?

Lover? Ed is embarrassed, he cringes, feels his cheeks flush. Why couldn't that policeman have said "boyfriend"? Lover, bloody hell, what kind of a word is that to use when he was talking about his wife?

Looks like she took something out of this, Mr. Parker, what do you think it could have been? Ed looks the contents of the jewellery box scattered on the bed. He has no idea - oh, wait, the brooch is gone. A brooch Mr. Parker? What sort of brooch? Was it a present Mr. Parker? Ed shakes his head. He doesn't know, she didn't say.

That bloke knew bugger all about his wife, the copper says over cups of coffee and biscuits back at the station. Bugger all. Don't reckon she's a topper though. Just done off for a bit fun somewhere, that one, I'll bet. Grass is greener. He dunks his biscuit with a sigh and a slurp.

THE FIRST ARRIVAL, MAKRIGIALOS, 1977

A crescent of warm sea edged with coarse yellow sand and pebbles, a tumble of white buildings on the shore, a ruined mansion nestling in the bare- cragged hills ringing the huge bay, and that was all there was to Makrigialos. It was getting late. The hills glowed pink in the dropping sun. There was no one about. Doors and windows were all shut tight. What on earth was she doing in this no-where- place with her shoes full of dust and her toes all gritty? This wasn't even a proper road. It wasn't even a proper place, just a clutch of raggle-taggle old houses stretched along a dry dirt track.

It had been such fun on the ferry and on the bus, because she was going somewhere. It was exciting to be travelling through the world. She'd felt brave and grown up, talking to Americans, kissing a boy, and running away into the unknown. How clever of her. Now she'd arrived and she was here. In Crete for goodness sake. How had she got here? Why was she here? What should she do? Where could she eat? Where could she sleep?

She heard a clip - clop in the distance and looked towards the sound. Only a donkey, far away, picking its way up a dry path. A dog barked. She needed the loo and she really wanted a drink of water. She stood in the dust and ever-deepening gloom, rucksack at her feet and tears in her eyes and had no idea what to do next. Maybe she could run after the bus as it jolted its way back to Irapetra. Jump on. Go home. What an idiot she had been.

Surrounded by all those other travellers she'd felt safe, there'd been lots of people to ask what to do and where to go. Now she was on her own. And getting frightened.

The shout was so close it made her jump. People were arguing somewhere. The dog barked again, more ferocious this time. A door opened in the cafe across the track and a man came falling across the threshold. He rolled onto the ground, a skinny, long-nosed black dog hot on his heels and nipping at the seat of his jeans. More shouting. A woman ran out with a tea towel in her hand. She hit him with it again and again as he struggled to stand up, his feet scrabbling for purchase in the dry dirt. He was laughing and trying to protect himself from the slapping cloth and the snapping, snarling dog. Connie had no idea what the woman was shouting, she was almost sure it was "Get out, you
bastard, and don't come back!"

The man managed to scramble to his feet and turned to the woman and put his hands up to the sides of her face. He kissed her hard on the mouth and darted away, laughing at the top of his voice and
calling for the dog to follow him. 'Ela! Kutavi!' C'mon! Puppy! 'Ya'sou. S'aga po,' he shouted from a safer distance - bye. I love you.

'Afiste me isiho!' the woman yelled back, shaking her head - leave me alone. She looked across to Connie, shrugged her shoulders and muttered something. Connie smiled, it was probably "Men! Idiots!" The woman tucked the tea towel into the waistband of her skirt and woman came over to her.

'Kalimera. Pou vriskontai oi filoi sas?' Hello. What are you doing here? Where are your friends? She spoke in Greek but she knew this girl was probably English, American or German.

Connie shook her head, 'Milate anglika?' Andreas had taught her how to say this – do you speak English?

The woman laughed, 'Of course,' she said, 'I speak good English.' She was proud of her English. After all, didn't her brother live in Australia and hadn't he taught her well?

'Come with me,' she said and took the girl into the café and sat her down. It didn't take her long to organise a drink and some food.

'From the well, clean and sweet. Good, yes?' the woman said proudly as Connie gulped down the water put in front of her. Connie nodded. It was delicious. She ate the little cheese and spinach pie, feeling a bit self-conscious under the direct gaze of this woman who watched every mouthful go down.

'Milk from my goats made that cheese.' Again, that proud tone, pleased with herself and her goats, 'I have a few rooms too, since the hippies have started to come. Things will be busy in a month or two. There will be many people on the beach and in the cafe. A few English maybe. You will be needing a place to stay for a few days, come on, I will show you my nicest one.'

The woman led her out of the door, across a small courtyard to an old stone goat shed - there is no key, she said, we have no need of keys here, and she lifted the ancient latch. It was so pretty inside, with its blue and white curtains and flowered bedcovers. The bare walls were painted white, the old flagstone floor polished to a magnificent shine. Under one window was a massive, ancient bathtub and under the other, a white, wooden bed.

'Oh. It's perfect,' Connie said, 'but I only have enough money for a week and then I'll have to get back to Athens.' Even as the words were coming out of her mouth, Connie knew they were already a lie.

'Until then you can stay here, and you must call me Vaso,' the woman said, turning down the bedcovers. She pronounced it with an 'o', like in 'top' or 'pop'. Connie practiced it, but it came out as Vasooo.

'No 'ooo', just an 'o',' Vaso said and laughed.

Later, when the girl was settled and she was cleaning up the café, Vaso wondered if English parents had any common sense at all - fancy allowing such a young girl to wander through Greece like this. She would never let this happen to her children when she had some. And she was a quiet one, this girl. She hadn't told her much - a little about the friends left behind in Athens. Pah! Athens! Horrible place. Even though she had never been off the island. Pah! All that trouble with the students and the Communists! And for what? It would not touch them here in Crete, she knew that much. Anyway, her Grandpa still refused to think he was Greek at all, being born before the Union and all that - Ei mai apo tin Kriti den einai Ellada, he would shout, thumping his closed fist on his heart - I am from Crete not Greece! She would smother him in kisses, 'Papou! Don't! You will drop down dead with this rage inside you.'

She pushed the broom into the cupboard and went off to bed. She tossed and turned for a long time, her mind full of this girl, why she was here and what was going to happen to her. I will not ask her, she thought, she will speak in her own time.

THE RAILWAY STATION, 2000

Connie buys a ticket to London. Of course she does. Just a single. She goes to the little window and peels the notes from her stash like a second-hand car dealer. She wants to lick her thumb and deal them out onto the counter.

The nearest empty seat is next to a young woman with two children. The little one in the pushchair is red in the face and screaming, his big brother is bashing him on top of his head with a fluffy rabbit. Stop it, the mother says in a weary voice, I won't tell you again. But Connie knows she will. It is going to be a long journey for that girl, with those two kids to entertain, and a noisy one for the people in the same carriage, they are already turning to each other and rolling their eyes. Why are people so intolerant of small children? Connie wonders. She hears a loud Tut! Someone is bound to offer some helpful advice soon.

It had happened in a flash on that fraught and tiring day, still etched on her memory. Little Stella standing up on chubby legs, Connie holding tight to the baby reins, had leaned over the back of the seat and dunked her bread into the stranger's soup. Red gloop splashed all over the tablecloth and the man's shirt. He was outraged – really, he said, you need to teach that child some manners. Not letting her stand on the seats would be a good place to start. He had hissed the words at her as he mopped at the spreading stain. She doesn't know how many times she said sorry. Her face was hot. Everyone was looking. She could feel the

judgment of others falling on her like an avalanche. Little Stella was crying and sobbing, scared of the commotion, holding her arms up to her. And Connie had ignored her and plonked her down in the seat, making her cry even harder.

Connie had wanted to rage. Rage at that man and those by-standers who looked blankly at her, or through her, with nothing better to do. They needed to see how tired, how miserable, how drained she was - look at me, I have 3 babies and one pair of hands. I am doing my best. Always doing my best. Trying to get it right.

She wanted to yell and shout until someone came and lay her in a quiet, darkened room. A scream was close to bursting out. If she let one single squeak past her lips Connie knew she would never stop. She would scream until the windows cracked and the glass shards flew like daggers right into their smug, outraged faces and hard, dead hearts. She stuffed Stella's fat, little arms into her coat, dragged her out of the café and pushed the buggy so roughly the pink, baby lips of the other two started to quiver. The on-lookers gazed at her through the plate glass, thanking God for their perfect lives. And they were happy not to be that awful woman with her awful brats.

Ed had told her not to fret, not to care, and teased her for being so angry about it. Kids do stuff, he said, you know that. Don't bother your head about those people, you don't know them, why do you care what they think? He had hugged her, patted her backside and gone back into the garden to finish the rabbit hutch he was building for the new rabbit.

When everyone had gone to bed, she crept down stairs in the pitch - black night, opened the back door and let the cold, damp air flood over her. She found the empty milk bottles, felt them, cool and clean in her hands. She held one to her forehead and rolled its smooth chill across her skin. Then hurled it as far as she could out of the door and onto the path. She smashed them all. She threw them so hard, she felt sure the whole street would wake up. No one stirred. And because she was good and kind and someone might hurt their feet in the morning, she swept up all the mess and chucked the broken glass in the bin with a mighty crash. Still, no one heard. No curtains moved. No lights snapped on. No one came to ask her if she was all right. No one came to get her. No one came to help her.

It was raining now, but not real rain, not those big, fat drops of cleansing rain. Hard, fast, sideways, stinging rain. She walked onto the lawn, let the wet grass and mud squish up between her toes, peeled her nightie off and lay down. The rain pinged onto her skin. Like darts.

'Where've you been?' Ed muttered when she sneaked back into bed.

'Nowhere.' She turned her back to him.

'I don't suppose…?' He stroked her belly, his arm draped over her, heavy and hot, she felt him harden against her.

'No.'

He sighed. She was in one of her moods. Again. Geez.

He didn't really understand, did he, Connie? All that anger bubbling inside you - it wasn't about the soup, the kids or those people watching, was it? You knew that but you didn't know how to explain, what to say, or what he would think if the words came pouring out. So, your fury remained, deflected by his words and stunted by his hug, but still fiery inside you, like larva. Poor

Connie. All those broken bottles and wet, freezing rain helped a bit didn't it? But not for long.

'Dear Mam

I am in Crete. I am OK, so don't worry. I have some money and I will be home soon. Please don't panic. Everything is alright. This is the address and there is a phone here, so I'll ring you soon.

Love

Connie.'

Was that all she needed to put? She couldn't think of anything else to say and maybe she would get home before the letter anyway. The address looked strange - it was difficult to think of that list of little black words as home. She wouldn't ring, not yet. Was it really only a few days since she had got away from her mother and out of that quiet house with its sour atmosphere and lifeless rooms? It felt like forever. She shoved the letter in her bag.

She pulled back the curtains. The sky was clear, the sun already hot, and Vaso was out and about in the courtyard, singing a little song to herself as she hung out the tablecloths. She could even hear the sea.

The first thing to do was have a good bath and wash away the dirt and grime she had accumulated on her travels. She eyed the bath tub apprehensively. If she sat in that thing she was sure she wouldn't be able to see over its rim, it was immense. Years ago, Vaso's brothers had dragged it from the ruins of the big house up on the hill. They used it as a water trough for the donkey and the goats.

Every family in Makrigialos had something from the big house. Standing on a rise above the village, it overlooked them all. It had been a beautiful building once upon a time. The roof had long since fallen in. The peeling, wooden shutters hung askew, the ornate, filigree balconies were just a lacework of rust and rotten metal. Chiseled into the stone arch over the front door was the year it had been built - 1898. In the overgrown gardens, a lonely, red rose bush would flower and the village lovers would pick the scented blooms for their girls. Only the very old ones remembered who it had belonged to. Vaso's Grandpa told the story of the rich people who had lived there many years ago, but when the leprosy came to the island they had gone away. Left everything. There had still been plates and cups in the cupboards and fine linens in the drawers, according to Papou.

When Vaso decided to convert the goat shed for tourists, she told her brothers she wanted that big bath tub for the new bathroom, they had laughed and laughed - rooms to rent! Pah! Who would want to stay here? And who is going to sleep in an old goat shed? Or bathe in an old goat trough? They slapped each other's backs and guffawed, tears
rolling down their cheeks as they writhed around in fits of giggles. And they refused to help. Headstrong and stubborn and with their laughter still ringing in her ears, she hitched the tub up to the poor old donkey and let him haul it down the hill to the café. She scrubbed and scrubbed till the tub gleamed, and there it stood, on its battered curlicued legs, beautiful against the whitewashed walls of her newly decorated goat shed.

Connie turned the huge taps, the water spluttered out for a few seconds, then stopped. She called out to Vaso, 'excuse me? Signomi?' There was a gurgling and a clunking and loud bubbling. The water gushed out like a fountain, it bounced out of the bath and onto the floor, she tried to reach the tap but she couldn't get near.

'Vaso!' she shouted 'Vaso!'

'Goodness me. I thought there was a murder in here!' Vaso said, as she bustled in. She turned the taps off in one brisk movement. 'These taps are old. You must be gentle and turn them little by little. Like this. Give them time or we will have this chaos!' She waved her hand at the watery mess, but she was smiling.

'Come, you will help me clean it up and, when you are washed and dressed, I will make a Cretan breakfast for you.' So, they set to, mopping up the water with the towels and all the while Vaso talked and talked and laughed.

'I'm not sure I can eat this.' Connie poked at the rusk in her dish. Vaso had soaked it in warm milk and honey - it looked like baby food.

'Eat. It is good. Then you will have coffee and we will go out. I will show you the village, you can meet everyone. I have vegetables to buy – you can help. Then you will have a sleep. But first you will eat,' Vaso pinched her arm, 'you are too thin. Eat.'

The coffee was much worse. Poured into a tiny cup, it was as black as black could be. Connie sipped it. Her face screwed up, it was bitter and so hot the cup burned her lip. Her mother didn't approve of coffee for children so Connie's taste was more for tea. Vaso ignored her and nodded in encouragement. She sipped again.

'Ugh, Vaso!' There were sludgy bits at the bottom and it was getting stronger and stronger. Vaso laughed, 'You funny English! You drink Nescafe and think it is good. A green fruit gets ripe slowly – you will get used to it.' She ignored Connie's protests and filled her cup again. She was talking and talking. She was 25 and her boyfriend hadn't asked her to marry yet. He was close to it, but hadn't quite popped the question. Papou was in despair about the situation and begged her to find someone new, just in case he never did. He is an old man, she said, in his day the girls were married at 14 and had their husbands picked out for them. Vaso was not going to allow that. Oh, no. That was not for her, definitely not. But she had known Timos since they were children and had loved him for many years, she said, laughing, so it is almost the same.

'Was that your boyfriend you were hitting with the tea towel yesterday?'

'That was him. Timos. He comes here to annoy me and he brings that ugly dog of his. He would like to stay here with me. At night,' her voice dropped to a whisper, 'but I won't let him, well not every night!' She laughed. Again.

'Kosta and Elena live in Heraklion with Mama, since poor Papa died - there is lots more work there - Mama has a café too, but I did not want to go. I would be sad to leave the village and Papou, so I stay here and look after this one. Papou used to help, but he is too old now. I can manage by myself. I am only really busy in the summer with the hippies and the Germans who come. Thee mou! Oh my God! Papou does not like the Germans. Many people died here during the war. One day he will have a heart attack and fall down dead because of the Germans. He is a stubborn man. I tell him all the time to stop living in the past.

Phillipos lives in Australia with his family, he is the oldest one. I miss him so much, and his beautiful little children, but one day he will come back to Crete. Come back to us forever. They always do.'

Connie thought Vaso was the most beautiful woman she had ever seen, plump, with long, wavy black hair and eyes that danced and twinkled. She was so full of life. She touched Connie as they talked, sometimes stroking her arm, pinching her cheek, patting her shoulder. Connie had never met anyone like this before - her family were reserved and quiet, cool and composed, but in this room, with this woman,
everything was excited, rapid, laughter and sunshine.

Vaso carried on with her tale and started to prepare the meal for later, peeling and chopping onions and throwing them all into a big pot as she chattered. She motioned to Connie to come and help her, gave her a knife and a big bag of potatoes. Peel and slice, she said. The time passed quickly as they two of them stood, side by side, peeling and chopping and talking.

'Ela! C'mon,' Vaso said and gave her a nudge, 'we are done for now and you have been a good girl to eat up all your breakfast. Now, you will meet Papou. He will be waiting for me.'

Connie went after her, almost running to keep up, through the courtyard, past the goat shed and out of a huge, wrought-iron gate. From the big house, Vaso said, giving it a hefty shove with her shoulder. All of a sudden they were on the beach, the sea only a few feet away, its lacy waves lapping leisurely onto the sand.

'Yes.' Vaso said, hearing Connie's surprised intake of breath, 'the sea is right here. The waves come all the way from Africa. It is quiet now, but in the winter it is black and it is wicked! Sometimes there is a stone coming 'Bang!' straight through the shed window and

'Crash!' into the bath.' Today it was blue and gentle. Only a whisper of sound and a shiver of movement.

Papou's house was a few yards away, the back door facing the water's edge and a gnarled old pine tree throwing its shade over the roof. Such a tiny house and stuffed to overflowing with things, every surface covered in frilled cloths, vases, jugs and trinkets. A faded photo had pride of place above the fireplace - a stern-faced young man with a moustache, arm in arm with a plump and pretty girl, her cheeks and lips tinted a delicate pink. She had smiled shyly into the camera on that day, so long ago. Sitting in the middle of it all, on a grand old armchair, was the Grandpa. Vaso ran over to him and kissed him all over his bald head and wrinkled face.

'Why are you sitting here in this stifling air, Papou? It is bad for you. I will get a chair and you can sit outside in the sun.'

'Pah!' he said 'what do I care for sun? I have had a lifetime of sun.' He grumbled almost non- stop as Vaso fixed him up with a seat, a drink, his hat, his stick and settled him down at his front door, facing the dusty road. He could watch the world go by out there, and pass the time of day with all the neighbours. They chatted away in Greek. Connie hung back, feeling embarrassed, not knowing where to put herself, or what to do.

'This is Connie,' Vaso pulled her towards the old man. He looked her up and down.

'Kalimera, ti kanete?' Hello, how are you? He looked grim and was as gnarled as his old pine tree. She felt sure she should curtsey, or shake his hand at least. But when she looked straight into his eyes, she saw that they were friendly under those magnificent eyebrows.

'Kala, efharisto. Esis?' I am fine, thank you. And you?'

He grinned. Vaso scolded him, 'Papou, do not tease her. Leave her alone, she is just a girl.' They carried on chatting to each other. Connie heard her name and wondered what they were saying.

A week went by in a flash. Neither of them mentioned the return to Athens, or going home to England.

Another day opened up, fresh and inviting, but Connie had slept badly. She wanted to stay more than anything in the world. It was so lovely here, so full of life and talking and laughing and sunshine. Besides, there wasn't enough time left to get to Chania or Heraklion; no time or money to find a ferry or a flight and get to Athens. Not now. And she had let an extra day slip past. Vaso would have to be told, and she was scared. What would she do if Vaso said she had to go? She had no money for another ticket. She had no money to pay the rent. And what had her friends thought when she hadn't appeared at the airport yesterday? Had they panicked and gone home without her? Had they shrugged their shoulders, knowing all the time she was never coming back for that plane? Had her mother got her letter? Oh dear. It was all a bit of a mess. She dragged herself out of bed and prepared to face Vaso, steeled herself to ring home.

Vaso listened quietly as Connie sobbed out her tale. The girl was upset, crying and red-eyed and sorry. Sorry she had lied, sorry she wanted to stay, sorry she had no money, sorry, sorry. Stop being sorry, it is done now, Vaso said and mopped the tears away with the corner of her apron. The truth was she didn't mind one bit if this girl wanted to stay. She liked her now she was starting to liven up a bit, and it was nice to have a girl around again; someone to talk to and joke with, apart from her boyfriend and Papou and the old men who came to the cafe. She didn't get much time to see her friends, she missed her brothers and sister, and anyway, Connie would be a big help with the tourists coming soon. Come on, Vaso said, leading her to the telephone, ring your mother. And so it was settled, as quickly as that because Vaso had

decided, and when Vaso decided then it happened.

They made their own routine without even realising. In the mornings when it was quiet and there were no customers, Connie chopped and peeled the vegetables while Vaso went to make sure Papou was up and about. Then they sat and had their breakfast and talked and tidied and talked some more. Vaso told her all the local gossip, explained who was who, kept her right in village matters, praised her when her Greek was understandable, made her laugh when it all went wrong. She asked Connie a million and one questions about England, marvelled at Connie's tales of the traffic and the crowds - they tell me it is like that in Athens, she said, stop, start when you are walking. Pah! I would die from lack of air. Yes, thought Connie, me too. Lunch time could be busy, depending on the weather and the time of year, Vaso told her. Vaso's handmade pies and pastries were always ready and pots of coffee were always on the boil for whichever workman, farmer, friend or

visitor happened to drop in.

'There are no women.' Connie mentioned one day.

'Oh no,' Vaso said, 'they are at home, with the babies and doing all that housework. Sometimes the younger ones come, the ones with no husbands and no babies, but they will stop once they are married.'

Connie raised her eyebrows, 'No 'Women's Lib' in Makrigialos, then,' she said.

Vaso laughed. 'For me, yes. I have to work in the café, because there are no men to do it. And that is ok. Maybe, one day, it will be like that for the other girls, maybe they will be able to think more about themselves and not only about the babies or the husbands.' Connie's eyebrows arched even higher.

'I know, I know, I want the babies and the husband too,' Vaso said, 'but I will have the best of both worlds.' She flicked Connie with the tea towel, 'come on lazybones, we have things to do.'

Fishing days were the busiest days of all. The men pulled their jaunty little boats up onto the beach and left them right outside the café door. The villagers would be waiting with their pots and pans and bowls, ready to carry away any fish they haggled over. There were sarpa and red mullet, sardines, octopus and sometimes the funny looking Garfish. It has green bones, Vaso said, ugh.

Connie couldn't bear to look at the fish, their glistening eyes already dulling. Some of the poor things were still alive, gasping and thrashing in watery panic. The octopus was the most abject of all. Groping for something to hold on to, curling his tentacles around any solid thing he could find, trying to pull himself up and over the side to get back to his sea. Or squeezing himself thinner and thinner and sliding, slowly, surreptitiously along the bottom of the pretty boats. A single tentacle pushed out in front, its tip gently tap-tapping on the boards as he searched for a gap, any little hole to push himself through. But there was never any chance. His defiant squirt of black ink was no deterrent against the rough hands that eventually reached down, fingers burning on his drying skin, and threw him in a bucket.

Connie couldn't look at the octopus then as he writhed himself into knots, his big black eye

staring up at her, his skin already changing colour. She felt his horror, his suffocating powerlessness. It made her feel sick.

When the selling was over, the men would come in, shaking the sand and fish-scales from their clothes; always careful to leave their boots outside to avoid a telling-off from Vaso. Someone would hand Vaso a few of the best fish to cook. The men would sit and smoke and laugh, eat everything put in front of them and drink plenty of wine,

keeping up the constant roar of their rowdy talk. Connie stayed out of the way, trying to be as unobtrusive as the poor octopus. She was

nervous of them, not sure what they might do or say. Vaso could hold her own against the fishermen's barrage of loud and raucous chatter. She wouldn't be able to answer back to them the way Vaso did. So, she washed the dishes and plates and made sure the kitchen stayed ship-shape, while Vaso dished up the food and drinks, and slapped the rough hands away from her.

Yes, they were busy all day on fishing days.

In the afternoons, while the village dozed, Connie swam. Vaso was horrified - thee mou! It is too early for the swimming, you will die with the cold water on you, she warned her, you must wait until August when the sun has taken the badness out of it. Connie just laughed and took no notice; to her English skin the warming sea was just right. When she had finished swimming, she wrung the salty water out of her hair and lay on the sand, slowly turning brown and, when the heat was too much, she sat in the shade of Papou's pine tree. If the sea was no good for swimming, the wind too strong or the currents too fast, she walked up to the big house and nosed through the piles of

stones or poked a long stick into the weeds, but she didn't find much. Just lizards, their
grey-green bodies motionless in the heat, only eyelids and tongues flickering. And ferocious black ants, front legs up and antenna waving at her. Every now and again, she ventured through the ruined rooms and felt the curls of other peoples' memories wrap around her.

Before the evening work started she sat at the family table with Vaso and Papou. Vaso fussed round her - taste this, taste that, she said, you will like this, just eat it. I will fatten you up, make you look like a proper girl, and she ran her hands down her own curvy body, pouting her lips and wriggling her backside like a starlet. Connie ate plenty - except the fish - great plates of stifado, kleftiko or giant beans. She'd never tasted such things. School dinners and her mother's haphazard meals were order of the day at home. Sometimes she had to fend for herself, eating slice after slice of bread and jam, or bowls of cornflakes just to feel full.

No wonder you like this funny little place full of noise and chatter, Connie. At home you can go a whole week with no words coming your way. You think it's your fault that Mam doesn't like talking, don't you? So you keep quiet and stay out of her way in your room, reading and imagining.

People were curious about her, of course they were. Who was this skinny, pale, English Miss who arrived on the bus, looking like a frightened rabbit and carrying only one little bag? And all alone too. Vaso told them all she knew - the girl does not talk much, but I think she is sad and lonely, she said, I can see it in her eyes. I like her. She's a good help to me.

Vaso worries too much, they said, when she was out of earshot, trust her to take in a stray.

One night Vaso asked her to go around the tables and see if anyone needed anything.

'Me? Connie said, 'no, I can't.'

Vaso was scornful. 'Pah! Of course you can.' She pushed her into the room. Connie stood there for a second or two, red with embarrassment, everyone looking at her and Vaso frantically waving her hands at her as encouragement - go, go, she mouthed. But Connie couldn't, she took fright and ran back to the safety of the kitchen and the family table.

Vaso rolled her eyes. 'Goodness me, stop being such a baby, everyone is nice and your Greek is ok. Just wave your hands about if you get stuck.'

The next night, Vaso asked if she would go behind the bar and keep it tidy. Connie thought she might be able to do that, but only if no one spoke to her - of course they will speak to you, Vaso said, they will want a drink so just fetch it. Metaxa, raki, beer. You will understand. Just pour the drink and take the money. But Connie did it in silence, the men pointing at the right bottle and avoiding her eye. When Vaso went to help Papou to bed, Connie was alone in the café and a terrible hush fell over them all.

Everyone watched her, although they tried to pretend they weren't, they kept their eyes down and played with their beads. No one dared speak in case the poor girl thought they were talking about her, or asking her for something. Connie daren't speak in case she made a mistake. They were all embarrassed. The silence was only broken by the clack and snap of beads and string. One night

Connie decided that this wouldn't do. It made everyone

uncomfortable and embarrassed. She felt silly. Vaso was right, she should grow up, stop being a baby - she couldn't hide behind the high, wooden bar for ever pretending to wash glasses and dust bottles of Metaxa. She lifted up the wooden hatch-top and came out with a pad and paper. Old Yanni the shepherd was sitting at the table closest to her.

'Would you like another drink?' she said, 'My name is Connie, forgive me if I make mistakes.' The beads rattled more vigorously. Yanni blushed. Her eyes filled up with tears and she started to turn away, to go back to dusting the bottles. Suddenly, Yanni let out a great guffaw, slapped his huge hand down onto the table top.

'Brava!' he roared. He jumped up and kissed her hand.

'Harika poli.' Pleased to meet you. And they all clapped. Then the talking began.

On Sundays when everyone went to Church, she sat on her bed and wrote to her mother. Without fail there was a letter to take to Irapetra every week. She had no idea how long they took to get to England, she asked the lady in the post office but she just shrugged - no one in Irapetra writes to England, she said, maybe a week, maybe a month. Connie told her mother everything that happened, who everyone was, what she was doing and apologised over and over for not coming home. Letters from her mother were few. They were short and not very sweet. There was always something wrong, some disaster to report, she was lonely, she missed her, she was cruel to stay away for so long, come home, come home, what a bad daughter you are, after everything I've done for you, stay there for all I care.

Vaso shook her head - she is a crazy woman, she said, when Connie showed her one of the letters. She should make up her mind, stay, come back, what does she want? Connie didn't know. She knew her mother was furious, but out here in Crete, so far away and with only the tight little words to look at, Connie didn't feel the guilt piling up on her so intensely. She could fold the letter up and put it to one side, even tear it up if she wanted to, so the words couldn't hurt her.

Another week went by, then another, and another. Soon a month had passed. Every Friday Vaso solemnly handed her a little brown
envelope, apologised that there wasn't much money in it, but in the summer! Much more!

Her spoken Greek got better and better. She went to Irapetra with Vaso to buy some clothes one day and managed to explain that these jeans were too big and she would like them in black please, if possible. The woman had smiled at her and gone to get them. Vaso nudged her - see! You can do it. She still couldn't read it - the written word remained as indecipherable as hieroglyphics.

The Goat Shed had become Connie's place. 'Go to Connie's place and tell her there is a letter here for her,' or 'Go to Connie's place and ask her to come and help me with this,' or 'Go to Connie's and tell her Georgos - the rascal - has come to see her....'

People knew her, waved at her, chatted to her and asked her how she was. They invited her in for cups of coffee, asked her to tell Vaso this and that, invited her along to weddings and christenings and the occasional party when they invited Vaso. She was brown and plump and smiling. No longer silent.

Sometimes, late at night when she was lying in her bed staring at the stars through the window, she could hear Vaso and Timos talking in the courtyard. Vaso would shut the café door and chase Timos away with a kiss and a warning, before she went up the outside stairs to the flat above. He always made to follow her, laughing and cajoling, then went home with the dog scampering at his heels, blowing her kisses until he was out of sight.

'Will you ever let him in Vaso?' she asked one day. Vaso pointed at her wedding finger, 'When the time is right.' They both laughed.

'Poor Timos!'

'Pah! He can love me all he likes, but we will be married first!' Vaso smiled at Connie, 'anyway, he has had a little taste of what will be, and now I will make him wait.'

'Vas!' Connie wasn't really shocked at all. She was jealous. She had no boyfriend to think about, no husband-to-be trying to get into her room at night. She wanted a boyfriend. She'd liked kissing that

American boy on the ferry. She'd liked the feel of his hands on her body. She'd liked it when he'd pushed himself against her and whispered in her ear, it had made feel grown-up. When she went back to her room she scrutinised herself in the wardrobe mirror. No, she wasn't pretty - her eyes were too big, her nose too small, her cheeks too round, too many freckles. On the other hand, her legs were long and her hair was glossy and thick. The problem was she was just too big, too tall, too straight up and down, too broad shouldered and big-footed - just not girly enough. She turned around and around watching her healthy, strong body in the mirror as she moved, feeling the soft swish of her hair against her back. The cool breeze drifted in through the window. She opened the door and stood naked in the moonlight, letting more air waft over her, and imagined the flutter of a million little kisses across her skin. When she went back in and lay on her bed, her head was full of American boys with golden curls.

The Scops owl in Papou's pine tree hooted in the darkness. What had disturbed him as he listened for his mate? He swivelled his tiny head towards the sound but it was only the quiet groan of a gate hinge, and the soft scuffle of a footstep in the sand.

The vegetable man was pouring potatoes from the big scoop into her string bag when they heard the bus come rolling up the road. Hey, he said, some tourists. They both watched, the potatoes forgotten. Foreigners. Half a dozen girls in maxi dresses and straight, long hair hanging from centre partings, struggled down the steps of the bus in their platform shoes. Phew! Thank God, we are off that stinking bus, Connie heard one say. Four stout-shoed women with expensive rucksacks and walking poles, followed them down. Germans, the veg man whispered, nodding towards the four women, they like to walk. Then a couple of families - two tall, thin dads in tight jeans and cheesecloth shirts, two skinny wives in floor-length smocked dresses, and four
children squealing with excitement.

'Where will they all stay?' Connie asked, knowing she was taking up one of Vaso's rooms.

The Veg man shrugged his shoulders, 'Vaso will not like girls, they will be trouble, and the Germans will be happiest in Analipsi, in that new hotel.'

The new hotel, the only hotel, had been finished just in time for summer. Squat, square and painted white with blue shutters, 25 bedrooms, a bar and a swimming pool. How the old men had laughed when the Germans came and bought up the scrub land next to the beach - what will they do there, they said to each other? It's no good for goats and no good for vegetables, too salty. Hahaha, they laughed.

Then the building started. That's a big house they are putting up, they whispered. Vaso told them off - don't be so nosy, she said. But, one day she ran into the café and told anyone who would listen that Yanni had asked old Manos and he had asked Roula who found out from Yiota that it was a ….

hotel! A hotel? Oh, how they had laughed. Who would come here? They had giggled for days.

The travellers looked tired and hot. The girls were grumpy and whined at each other, complaining about the heat and the sun and the dust. Vaso came over from the café. She had room for the two families and the others should walk up the road, turn left a little, follow the hill and they would find the new hotel. Perfect for them. The German women set off at a pace, the straggle of girls followed along behind, discontent and moaning and shuffling their sore feet. Isn't there a taxi? No taxi! Well! We should have stayed in the town - another chimed in - at least there were proper hotels there.

'See,' said the Veg man, 'I told you. They are grumbling, I can hear it in their voices. They will be trouble.'

'I'm sure they'll be fine once they settle in.' Connie said. The Veg man just shook his head and handed Connie a brown paper bag of kumquats. 'For you. From my tree. Don't eat the black bits.'

Every day the bus came and dropped off a few more people. The pace of life changed. The café was busy all day now, full of different people, different voices. Vaso put tables and chairs outside on the beach. Each table was covered with a blue and white checked tablecloth - the colours of Greece, she said, clipping them tightly to the edges to stop the wind whipping them away to Africa. A tiny vase of flowers sat next to the menu, dainty and pretty. She unfurled the stripy awning above the door, made sure the grasshoppers were not still sleeping up there, and pushed all the windows open as wide as she could. The little cafe took on a cheery air, it looked fresh and neat and full of summer.

The beach filled with pale people of all shapes and sizes, the sea came alive with bobbing heads and balls and airbeds. The old men retreated up the hill to the kafenion in the big village although Connie still bumped into them in the fields, or passing the time of day with Papou. They were replaced by the young ones without wives or girlfriends. They loitered in the bar every evening, after their work was done. Half a dozen of them, all cleaned up, hair brushed, best clothes on and enveloped in a miasma of cheap aftershave. The foreign girls were like magnets to them. They were so different to the girls they had grown up with - these girls were bold and free, these girls wanted a little exotic

romance, not marriage and babies. Vaso kept her eyes on all of them and sent the boys home to their mothers if they got too drunk, or leered too much.

Connie liked these almost-men. They were all close in age, not quite adults but more than boys. Once the meals were finished, she sat down amongst them, chatting and laughing and drinking beer; always ready to jump up if Vaso shouted for her to do this or that. Connie admired one or two, even wondered if she could become a girlfriend, but it was pointless. She was under Vaso's watchful eye and was as untouchable as any Greek girl. And her Englishness confused them. Here was a girl they couldn't chase because they were terrified of Vaso, but they could sit with her, talk to her, tease her, throw their arms around her shoulders, kiss her cheek and no one minded. No one got over-excited and had them lined up to visit the Priest, ready to proclaim the marriage bans. She became 'one of the boys' in a way that no Greek girl could. Vaso is tough, they whispered to Connie, trying to keep out of her way, under her radar. No, she said, no, she's not, she just seems that way. They rolled their eyes and shrugged their shoulders - if you say so, they said.

Yanni's grandsons were the boys she liked the best of all. The three brothers, Gregor, Sebastianos and Iakchos. Iakchos was the oldest, still only twenty-one, he was her favourite. Handsome, gentle and quiet, perhaps a little serious. He had a girlfriend somewhere she had never met. She liked him, they got on well. In another time, another world, perhaps she would have loved him - just a little. While his brothers
gambolled around like puppies, drinking too much, always up to some silly nonsense and hunting for girls, he stood back, watched their antics and shook his head.

'Connie,' he said, 'those boys are fools. They try too hard, they imagine they are Theseus saving all of Crete from the Minotaur. They are wooing a girl, not getting ready to slay a beast.'

She laughed. 'Maybe there will be someone to woo me one day,' she said.

Iakchos took her hand and patted it gently. 'Without a doubt, because you are prettiest, funniest, sweetest girl here. Don't worry, a good man will find you one day. Trust me.' And she did.

The village had woken up. There was shouting, laughing, screeching, when the wine and beer flowed there was singing and dancing till the early hours. Connie and Vaso cooked, cleaned, washed laundry, served drinks and meals and complained about never getting a chance to sit down. At night, when the café eventually shut, they rubbed their aching feet with peppermint oil and wondered who would turn up next.

She never wanted to be anywhere else.

'Psst!' Connie was waiting for the bus to Irapetra. She turned around. A man stood there, slightly askew, his hat akimbo and his clothes too big.

'You are very pretty. Will you marry me?' he hissed at her. Connie moved away from him. He stepped in front of her, blocking her way, 'will you? Will you?' he tried to grab her hand, pursing his lips as if to try and kiss it.

'Theo! Enough. I will tell your Papa!' The man shambled off, cursing at Timos.

'Who was that?'

'Oh! It's only Theo. He lives up in the big village. Take no notice of him. Sometimes he is trouble, he is a bit...' Timos twirled his index finger at his temple, not sure how to say it.

'Trelos?' offered Connie. Crazy. Timos laughed, Connie's Greek was really coming along.

'Don't worry he will not hurt you. You must have seen him on his little scooter, the one with the fish painted on it?' Yes, Connie had seen him. 'His mother and father have a kafenion in the big village. His father beat him too many times on his head when he was little. One day, they say he picked up a cat and threw it into a big pan of boiling water. Meeeooouuuww! They sent him to the crazy house after that, but when he came back he was still...' Timos twirled his finger. 'If he bothers you again, tell him you will speak to his father. He is scared of him.'

'I don't like the sound of them.' Connie said

'His mother is ok, she is the goat lady. She keeps a lot of them up on the hills.'

Connie had seen her many times when she had been up at the ruins of the big house. She was small and tough, with a long grey plait reaching almost to the backs of her knees. One day, when Connie had been walking in the old garden, she had seen her leading an old Billy goat up to the sweet grass and it had suddenly started to gallop, pulling her over and dragging her a few yards up the track. Connie had rushed to help. Entaxi. Entaxi - I'm Ok, I'm OK, the goat lady had shouted, picking herself up and hauling the Billy goat back under control. Since then she always waved whenever she saw Connie.

'What's she like, the mother?' Timos twirled the finger and rolled his eyes. Suddenly, he took hold of Connie's hand. It made her jump, she tried to pull away, wondering what on earth he was doing. 'Connie, Listen to me. I must tell Vaso a bad thing and she will be very sad.'

'What?' The ground seemed to tilt a little.

'Yes, she will be sad and I want you to help her. I must tell her soon. You must be there.'

'Tell me what's wrong. I don't like this.' Timos face had changed, his smile had gone and his eyes were teary. 'Timos! Tell me. Are you ill?'

He shook his head. 'No. I need to go away and she will not want me to. I have to be tough and, with her, I cannot. She will cry and beg me to stay and I will want to. But I need to be away from this place and see what is around the next hill.' He gripped her hand tighter, 'You must help me, Connie. I will go mad in this place.'

Connie knew Timos had dreams, knew he wanted to be away from this tiny village - lucky Phillipos to be in Australia, he had said often enough. How lucky to be out in the real world, where people didn't worry about the donkeys' feet or the goats' udders, where no one has to pick wild greens in the spring. How lucky to be in a place where the money is good and there are too many things to buy, and as he spoke his face twisted with the anger pent up inside him. When he watched TV in the bar he wondered out loud when Makrigialos would be like the places he saw. Never, said the old men, never! Thank God! Then they would argue and Timos would start to rage, until Vaso came and soothed him. He will sulk for a few days, she said, and then he will be fine. He will be as if nothing is wrong.

Connie understood his need to fly away. She had tried to explain it to Vaso but she wouldn't listen. He will never leave me, he loves me too much. I know this. I love him too much to let him go, she said.

Today the world will change, Connie thought. And she was worried.

ON THE TRAIN, 2000

The train is not too full. She tries to settle herself - please don't let anyone talk to me, I can't be bothered.

She leans her head on the cool window and looks out at grey sky and black clouds scudding by. The seat prickles the backs of her legs. The armrest pokes into her hip. The man opposite her has his great big feet far too close to hers. She is uncomfortable. Every part of her feels jammed in. Her skin doesn't seem to fit anymore. Her hands have become fat and huge, her wedding ring is too tight on her finger. Her head is big as a balloon. Her heart thumps fit to burst clean out of her chest.

You have felt like this before, Connie. Many times. When Ed comes in from work, when the kids want their tea, when you have to think about the shopping, when nothing changes, when you are on your own, waiting. Waiting for what? When you are wishing. Wishing for what? When you remember. Remember what? Then you shake your head. No point in any of that, you tell yourself. No point at all. Because it won't do any good.

She closes her eyes - I just need some air. I need to feel alive again. That's all. Just some room. Room to breathe. Room to breathe.

The words roll over and over in her head, the rhythm of the train turning them into a little lullaby.

And the train takes you away. Away from your husband, your children and away from your life. Maybe you will breathe again.

Timos stared into her eyes. 'Help me, Connie. Help me tell her. Help me tell her I will come back. That if I stay I will go mad. I will be like Theo. Crazy.' He was close to tears, 'I love her so much, but I will be no good. I will always be wondering, thinking of what could have been. If I stay I will make her sad for a whole lifetime. If I go she will only be sad for a little time. Please Connie.' He wiped the back of his hand under his eyes and rubbed the tears off onto his jeans. She knew this would be the outcome for them if he didn't leave and explore the world for a while, because she felt the same herself. If he didn't try, he would get bitter and angry and take it out on Vaso. He would blame her and they would never be happy. His resentment would spill out every day until eventually Vaso would not be able to console him, or love him enough, to make everything right again. Vaso had to let him go.

'I'll help you,' she whispered. What else could she say? She was his friend after all.

He hugged her and walked away, head down so she could not see him crying, the dog trotting along at his heels, jumping up, trying to entice him to play.

All thoughts of going to Irapetra were shooed out of her head. She couldn't go back into the café, Vaso might have seen them talking and ask her what was going on. Connie wouldn't be able to tell her, it had to come from Timos. She wondered when he was coming back. He said tonight - but what time? She would have to find out. She started after him up the donkey track. The dry dust floated up from the path, the grasshoppers whirred, and the sunshine bounced all around her. The grass was sharp and scratched her legs. She shouted after him but he didn't hear; he was used to hiking up and down from the big village to the sea every day, and he was away and gone, around the bend in a flash. She knew she wasn't going to catch up with him.

She should have turned around, gone straight back to the café and waited for him to come to see Vaso that night. But she didn't. She carried on up the hill, towards the ruins of the big house.

LONDON, 2000

The train comes alive. People pull their jackets on, gather their belongings together and drag their bags from the overhead compartments. She looks around. Everyone is consumed by their own affairs. No one looks her way. The man with the big feet has gone. Time to get ready. Time to get off.

She pushes her way out, down the step and onto the platform. She has always liked the smell in King Cross station. Hot metal, engine oil and an occasional waft of expensive after-shave or perfume as a
gaggle of business types rush past her in their sharp clothes. And then, when she is through the barriers, there is always the smell of coffee and snacks to look forward too. She's hungry, it's been a long time since she left the house. What would be going on at home? They might be
panicking and crying and angry. Ed will be trying his best to look after the children, especially James. She knows it will be Stella who will be dealing with everything. She is so capable. So clever and bright. Claire is the funny one, she'll be making them laugh, keeping them cheered up. Ed's Mam and Dad will be there, stoic and dull. His Mam will be making sure they are all fed and watered and his Dad will be looking

at Ed in a knowing way. It will be a 'told you so' look. A look that says, 'I knew from the start that girl was never right.'

She shakes her head to rattle the thoughts out. No use dwelling on all that. It would be easy to get back on the train and just go straight home. Easy as could be. But she can't. If she goes home now she will fade away and die. She will be rubbed out, like a pencil mark. She wants to feel like a bold slash of the pen again; to feel indelible. Christ. Perhaps it's best to have a cup of coffee and a sit down, and stop thinking too much. She goes into Smiths to buy a magazine to read in the café, so she won't look lonely. She sniffs them. Mmmm lovely. Another thing Ed laughs at - I just like it, she tells him. I like the smell and it makes me happy. Why does it bother you? He never has an answer, he just shrugs his shoulders and rolls his eyes. She wants to kick him when he does that. How dare he?

She sits with her coffee, glances through her magazine and listens to the rumble of trains, the hiss of the coffee machine and the hub-bub of people going about their business. She thinks about where she is going. Because she knows where she's going. She has always known, right from the moment she put that first ten pound note in her wooden jewellery box. She's going to go back to Crete. Back to the sunshine, back to Vaso, back to her blue and white room with the big bath on its wonderful legs. She knew it then and nothing has changed her mind. No matter that all those years have passed by. With every note that went into that box she felt the pull of the sand under her feet as the sea washed in and out, smelled the hot dusty road and heard the dog barking as he scampered around her legs. And when she gets back they'll throw their brown arms around her, kiss her and hug her. Vaso will drag her to the family table and sit her down just to look into her eyes, and then they will all cry. The three brothers will run down to the café from their house in the hills, full of excitement and laughter that she is back to be their friend again. And he will be there. Looking on from a distance, wondering what all the fuss is about. Wondering who this woman is, turned up out of nowhere and wearing a fancy brooch?

Kings Cross was as it always is. Crowded, busy, full of too many people shuffling, striding, standing still, and all in her way. Connie knows London like the back of her hand, but she doesn't like it much. She thought she did once upon a time, when she lived there after Crete. She had been quite the city girl in those days. Always busy, working, going out, drinking, meeting friends, having fun. When she walked to the bus stop in the mornings amongst all the other commuters, she felt important, powerful, brave.

London could make her feel that way. But, every now and again, it made her feel tiny, nothing, lost. A miniscule speck in the great,
moving mass that is a big city.

At night when she tucked herself in to bed in her rooftop room, listening to Martha and the Muffins on her crackly transistor radio. That made her lonely.

When she walked through the park to the pub and when she got there no one had waited for her and they'd all moved on. That made her lonely.

When her friends invited to parties and they showed her off as if she were an exhibit - she's from OOOP North, y'know, they said, proper country girl. Ha ha ha! That made her lonely. She went to a party once and someone gave her some caviar - she sniffed it, poked it and when she spat it out everyone had laughed at her. That made her lonely.

When her boyfriend didn't come to pick her up and she saw him later with Theresa on the back of his motorbike. That made her lonely.

When she sat at the top of the Common, on her own, late at night, looking down on London spread out below her, orange and shimmering and twinkling. That made her lonely.

London wore her out. One morning, she packed her London life into a small suitcase and went home. She didn't tell anyone. The people at work wondered where she had gone. Her things were forgotten on her desk. They rang her doorbell. No reply. The landlady got no rent and found the rooms deserted and empty; just a cup in the sink and a slipper under the bed. Then their lives swung and turned and they forgot.

She went back to her small town, where she knew everyone, where people passed the time of day in the street, where people spoke their minds and didn't pretend to like caviar.

Her mother's house had waited for her. Dark and empty since her mother died. Connie had run away to London after that terrible day, and now she had run away again: home. Because they all come home in the end.

Today she only walked as far as the Taxi rank. There would be no surprise visits to old friends, no nostalgic trips to her favourite haunts, because any good times had been forgotten and replaced by the miserable memories of aloneness and isolation. There was nothing in London for her now.

She leans into a Taxi - can you take me to Gatwick, please? There, the words were out before she could think to stop them. And of course he could. She sits in the back, trying to ignore his chatter about the economy and the weather. I am coming. I am going. What am I doing? There isn't a scrap of sense in any of this.

'Where are you off to, then?' he asks.

'Crete.' She looks through the mirror into his pale blue eyes, almost hidden in a doughy, slab of a face. Not the fierce blue of Ed's, but they are kind and friendly eyes too.

'I've been there,' he says. 'Hot. Not very good beaches where we were. Went to some place where they kept all the lepers.'

'Spinalonga.'

'Yeh, that's it.'

She closes her eyes. She doesn't want to look at him anymore. And when she opens them she wants to see her friends, her bed, her beach; wants to see all her things, exactly as they had been.

MAKRIGIALOS, 1976

Connie ducked under the branches growing too close to the doorway. The trees had arched into a green canopy, replacing the fallen roof. The sunlight struggled to get in. It managed a sliver here and there, an occasional shaft of hot light, teeming with dust fairies floating gently in circles. Up and up. The hum and hush surrounded her. All was cool.

There was a chair beside the fireplace. She didn't think it had been there the last time she came. She sat on it. It creaked and groaned, the rush seat almost worn through and one leg slightly shorter than the others. There were some apple peelings, just tinged with brown, lying on the marble hearth. She pushed them with her toe, wondering who could have been here so recently. She hadn't seen anyone on her way up the hill and she hadn't heard anything.

She should have gone. Gone back down the track to Vaso. But she didn't.

She called out - kaneis ekei? Anyone there? Her question soaked into the walls and the tree roof and was gobbled up, never to reach the open air. No answering voice came back to her. Ah well, whoever had been there must have left or they would have said something. After all, it was Makrigialos, where everyone knew everyone else and everyone was nice and everyone liked her.

She went to the foot of the huge staircase, the treads faded to a soft silver-grey. She knew exactly which stairs were rotten, which ones would not hold her weight – after all, hadn't she been up there a hundred times before? Nothing to hear but the hum of a lost bee and the shuffle of her feet on the stairs. Along the hall and in to the biggest bedroom; this was her favourite part of the house. It was beautiful. The tattered remains of brocade curtains still hung at the windows, the faded wallpaper, crowded with birds and flowers, still clung to the walls; the dusty fragments of handmade rugs lay under her feet. She loved it. A collapsed four poster bed stood in the middle of the room. Sometimes a bird

fluttered in through the broken window, but not today, everything was hushed, dim and languid.

She heard a scuffling noise behind - oh, hello, she said, it's you, I wondered who had been here. And she smiled.

Vaso looked at the clock. Where on earth was Connie? It was after 3, the bus had been an hour ago. She knocked on her door. No reply. She went to check with Papou, but he hadn't seen her all day.

She rang Timos. Timos had seen her in the morning waiting for the bus - Theo had tried to upset her, he said, you know what he's like, but, since then…no, he hadn't seen her. Maybe she had met someone in Irapetra and would come back in a taxi later?

She rang Georgos. They had a soft spot for each other those two, she had seen the way he looked at her and the way Connie blushed when they talked. He hadn't seen her either.

She rang the brothers - no, we haven't seen her since last night, Iakchos said, when we tried to teach her that Greek dance.

She rang everyone she could think of. No one had any idea where Connie was. No one had seen her all day. Not since she was talking to Timos at the bus stop. Well, she thought, I will wait another hour and if she is not back I will have to look for her.

She paced around the café. She was behind in her work, there was much to do, the evening meal to sort out and the bar to restock. She couldn't settle. Something was wrong, she could feel it. Maybe Connie was swimming, maybe she had fallen asleep lying on the sand. Oh, Vaso thought, I hope not, she will be burnt to a crisp. Silly girl.

The gate down to the beach was shut but she went through it anyway, down to Connie's favourite swimming spot. No, not there. She turned around to face the village, looked up towards the hills. Of course, she will be up at the big house. She liked it there. Vaso set off up the road, angry that she had panicked, and angry with Connie for going up there without letting her know. Angry with her for going up there at all. She hated the place.

Connie opened her eyes. Wherever she was it was gloomy and hot and smelled of coffee. Her head ached and her body felt as heavy as lead. She was stiff and sore, she wanted to sit up but she didn't have the strength. Someone was shuffling and moving around her. She felt sick.

'It's Ok. You are Ok. You are fine.' The voice seemed to be coming from a long way away. A face came into view. It was the goat lady, she mopped her head with a cool, wet cloth and kept crooning gently to her. 'You will be fine, you will be OK.'

'Where am I? What happened?' whispered Connie, not really sure if she was even speaking out loud.

'You were at the big house and you fell down and bumped your head. Theo came for me and we carried you here.' The goat lady soothed Connie's forehead with the cloth.

'Oh. I can't remember,' she turned her head to face the goat lady, 'thank you.' And the world went black again.

Vaso pushed her way past the trees and bushes. The branches grabbed at her clothes, pulled at her hair. This place scared her. She came up here when the grass was new and fresh and sweet for the goats, but she never, ever went into the house.

When they were little, her brothers had told terrible tales of the ghosts, monsters and murderers lurking in every room, ready to pounce on the unsuspecting. Especially if they were little girls. She was always too afraid to go in. The boys ran around the house whooping and wailing like ghosts - Vasssooooooo, they screamed, wweee aaarrreee ccooommmiiinnngg for youoooooo. Their little boy voices trembled and shivered around the walls. She would run away with the goats

trotting behind her, their bells clanging loud enough to raise those dead. When Connie heard the stories she just laughed - don't be silly Vaso, she said, it's fine, there are no monsters up there.

She swallowed hard and went in, brushing the leaves and dust out of her eyes and hair. She shouted for Connie, but it came out as a tiny croak.

There was no sign of her in any of the downstairs rooms. Only dirt and decay. Oh God, she would have to go up those rickety old stairs. Her mouth was dry. She tip-toed up the treads, testing each one carefully, just in case there was a soft part. Every single board creaked sending shivers through her whole body. She kept calling and calling for Connie, but the house stayed quiet, apart from the groaning of the stairs and sighing of the trees.

Thank God, the bedroom door was open; she could just see the corner of the bed, she pushed it a little wider. The hinges gave a crack, loud, like a gun going off. She jumped, threw her hands on her heart to try and stop it beating like a drum or flying right out of her chest. Bastarde! Dear God, please let Connie be in here.

Her head was pounding as much as her heart, she was sweating. She looked around the ruined room, almost bursting into tears when she realised Connie wasn't there. God this place! There was no beauty here for her. The room was mouldy and damp, falling down around her ears. Look at those curtains, hanging off in strips and the rugs all tattered and threadbare and Connie's bag just sitting there on the floor amongst all the muck. Connie's bag! She shouted and shouted her name. Still no

answer. She snatched up the bag, ran down the stairs and out through the door with no thought to her safety this time. Never mind the rotten stairs and the broken treads. Never mind the clawing branches and the falling leaves. Never mind her legs scratched and torn by the clinging weeds. She ran and ran, stumbling and tripping over the tussocks of grass, her legs getting too far ahead of her body until she fell, sprawling full length onto the track. She lay still for a moment, her chest heaving. When she sat herself up, rubbing her knees and trying to catch her breath, she caught sight of a man picking his way along the ridge of the hill. A man she didn't recognise. A man with a rucksack and a stick. Would he hear her if she screamed as loudly as she could? He might come and help her look for Connie. But he was too far away. Nothing to do but pick herself up and carry on running, down to the village and straight to Papou's house.

The window was open, it was dark now and much cooler with the evening breeze blowing in. Connie pushed herself up onto her elbows and looked around. She was lying on a single bed with a clean sheet over her, the room as neat as a new pin. There was a mumble of voices in another room and the sounds of people moving about. That's right, she was in the goat lady's house - she had fallen down and bumped her head. She swung her legs over the side of the bed. They were bare. Where were her clothes? Her jeans and T - shirt were gone. There were no clothes on the chair beside the bed. She stood up carefully, her head throbbing, and pulled the sheet around herself. Every part of her was sore and aching, her legs, her arms, her back and her head. She felt
herself start to reel. She sat back down on the edge of the bed incase she keeled over and noticed the cuts and bruises on her legs. What on earth?

'Hello, any one there?' she croaked. The mumble of voices stopped, there was a moment of silence then the door opened.

'Ah. You are awake now. Good. I will get you a cold drink. Sit still.'

'What happened? Where are my clothes?'

'Don't worry. I will get you a drink first,' and the goat lady was gone. She had left the door open. Theo and his father were sitting side by side on a worn-out sofa watching football on the tiny television. Not looking her way, just watching TV and sipping their beer. She needed to get up to shut the door, she didn't want them seeing her with just a sheet wrapped around her naked body. She needed to get back to Vaso's, but she sat as still and quiet as she could so no one would notice her.

'Please get my clothes,' she said when the goat lady came back.

'Drink first, and take these pills for your head. Then we will get you back to the village. There is no phone here so I could not call Vaso. Now you are awake, I will send the boy to the village and they will come to fetch you. You are OK.' She patted her leg. 'You are fine. There was some blood and your clothes were spoiled. I have some fresh things for you. These will do until we get you back home. I put some witch-hazel on your bruises, I hope you don't mind.' She put the clothes on the bed.

'Oh, you are very kind. How did I fall? I can't remember. '

'I don't know. Theo said he was coming up the hill on his scooter, he heard a scream and when he went to see who it was, he found you lying on the floor in the big house. Maybe you fell down the stairs. They are very old.' She shrugged and headed back to the door, 'get dressed, Vaso will come for you soon.'

Connie pulled on the jeans. They were too big. Funny, she thought, I was in the bedroom, I can't remember falling down the stairs. Did I hit my head? Maybe that's what happens when you hit your head? You can't remember anything. She was glad the jeans were so big, they didn't rub against the bruises and scratches on her thighs. She glanced at the door, it was tight shut, she dropped the sheet to pull the T-shirt over her head. My God, her chest was bruised too. What was that mark on her breast? And that one on her shoulder? She went over to the wardrobe and looked at herself in the long mirror. They were strange marks, almost circular, slightly raised, red and bruised. Her head hurt too, not like a normal headache, more like a burning. She pushed the hair at the back of her head out of the way and twisted round to try and see the sore patch. There. A bump. And some hair was missing, a little bald spot she could feel with her fingers. What had she done?

Everyone was out looking for her. Timos said it would be fine, they would find her. But where could she be? People had gathered outside the café; slumped on the wooden chairs waiting for someone to come and tell them something. Vaso was inside with Papou, Connie's bag clutched to her chest and Papou holding her hand almost as tightly. She could still hear shouting. Connie. Connie. Her name was ringing out amongst the pine trees, echoing around the hillsides. Iakchos and his brothers were up there, poking through the juniper bushes with long walking poles and their torch beams arcing across the dark sky. They hadn't found her.

People can't wander that far with a bump on their heads, they just can't, Vaso kept saying over and over again. People don't just disappear without their bags. Unless…unless something has terrible has happened. She must have fallen down and hit her head and wandered off somewhere in a daze. Yes. That must be it. But it was so late now. She told Timos to take the dog up the hill when the others came back, maybe he would find her. I will make some coffee, she said, shaking herself free from Papou's hold, people will need some tonight.

The moon was bright as a pearl; casting her brittle light down on the hillside. The time passed, the voices rang out and all they could do was wait.

A different light appeared over the top of the hill. It weaved and bobbed its way down the track towards the sea. Someone is coming, Vaso said, who is it? She turned and shouted at everyone, rousing them from their tiredness. They lifted up their heads and looked towards the road. The wavering light wound on and on towards them, getting a little closer and a little bigger with every intake of breath they took. The night was suddenly quiet. Everyone was hushed and watching, mesmerised. The gentle 'put put put' of a little engine fell into the space where the shouting and calling had been. It was Theo, the silver fish painted on his scooter swimming in the moonlight. Vaso ran towards him, arms outstretched and screaming at him - is she alright? Is she alright? He climbed off the scooter, Vaso grabbed him, as if to shake the words right out of him. He struggled free.

'She is hurt. You will have to come and get her,' Theo announced. Vaso burst into tears. Iakchos had seen the scooter and run down to the café, his brothers not far behind.

'We will come too,' they said, but Vaso shook her head.

'It would be better if you wait here, we don't know what has happened to her yet. Wait with Yanni. That house. It is a terrible place. So many bad things…' Her voice trailed off.

Iakchos put his arm around Vaso. 'Thank God she is found,' he murmured, 'she will be alright.'

Vaso looked up at him, 'I hope so.' she said, her voice small and tight.

It took them ten minutes to get to Connie. The goat lady showed them in and there she was. Small and pale, in someone else's clothes, her eyes full of tears at the sight of them. Her face laced with blue and black bruises. Her hair matted with dried blood.

'Well, now. What has happened here? Come on, we will get you home, mikri mou - my little one.' Vaso pulled the weeping girl close to her and looked at Timos over the bloodied head. Her eyes betrayed

everything she was thinking and feeling. Timos took the others into the sitting room and, as Vaso soothed and hushed, the talking started. Rapid and staccato, much too fast for Connie to understand.

THE AIRPORT, 2000

She goes to the first desk. No, just package holidays from here madam, the girl says. Her eyebrows are arched like scimitars, her face is too brown and her lips are impossibly and perfectly red. Go to the desks over there - she waves her hand to the right and smiles Connie away. Everyone is pushing and bustling and moving. So much noise, talking and laughing, children squealing. They all seem to know what they were doing. Connie feels hot, alone and stupid surrounded by these hundreds of people in holiday clothes, their trolleys loaded up with suitcases. Her jumper is too thick and her bag is too small. She sees a sign for the ladies' loos. She must sort herself out for a moment. Take a breath and just think.

It is really, really hot in the ladies. She pushes her way into a cubicle. Loo roll on the floor and splashes on the seat. Not to worry. She sits down. What am I doing? What the hell do I think I am doing? All of a sudden she is over taken by the force of it all, overwhelmed by the sadness of it, the silliness of it. Poor kids. Poor Ed. Poor her. And the tears run. Her face screws up into an ugly mess and she cries and cries. Her chest heaves as she tries to stifle the noise of her sobs.

Crying doesn't come easily to you does it? Why don't you ever cry, Connie? What is it you say, 'We all have a most accessible emotion and mine is anger'. Yes, that's it. And my God, you can get really angry. You can raise the roof, never mind your voice. You can shout till you're red in the face and the children run away from you, up to their rooms with their doors shut tight. Even Ed walks away when you are like that. He doesn't fight back, he doesn't try to calm you down and he doesn't even try to ask you what's wrong does he? He just looks at you, shakes his head and walks away. Why does he do that, Connie?

They think it all comes out of the blue, all the rage and the shouting. They think you are over-reacting to some insignificant little event - maybe one of the kids takes too long to find their shoes, maybe Ed has left his rucksack in the middle of the dining room table or his keys in the fruit bowl. Such little things to provoke such a huge amount of anger. But we know better, don't we Connie?

Poor Ed, all the times he's asked you, all the times he's tried to help and you've shoved him away. No wonder he leaves you alone these days. He is a simple man, not complicated like you - he just wants you to be happy and if you're happy, then he's happy. All he wants is to do is go to work and come home to his wife and his kids, have his tea and play with those children of his. He doesn't understand. He used to want to. You must remember all those times he tried to talk to you, all the times he begged you to tell him what was wrong. Oh, well, it's too late now. And today, of all days, you are crying.

Connie pushes the flush - the whoosh of the water will drown out the noise of her sniffing. She doesn't want anyone to notice. No fuss. A group of women come in, giggling and laughing and teasing each other about the things they will get up to in the sunshine. Connie gulps her tears away and listens. They are happy. Happy. She can't remember the last time she felt happy. Right. This has to be done. Then I will know, she says almost out loud, then I will know, then maybe I can be happy, and maybe Ed and the children can be happy. She unpins the green and gold brooch and pulls her jumper off. She tucks the brooch in her bag and shoves the jumper into the sanitary towel bin. Pushes and shoves and rams it right in and snaps the flap shut.

Right. She is ready. She straightens up her shoulders, lifts up her chin and takes a deep breath. She comes out of the cubicle hoping no one can see she has been crying - as if anyone would take any notice of her anyway - she scrutinises herself in the mirror, not liking what she sees at all, and splashes some cold water on her face. What I need is some make-up, some clothes and something done with my hair, she whispers to her reflection, but first, I must buy a ticket.

After a few false starts, more arched scimitar brows and smilingly dismissive waves, she manages to get to the right place.

'Yes, Madam, we can help. Unfortunately, I can't get you onto a direct flight, you'll have to fly to Athens, then take a domestic flight to Crete.' He smiles at her. A real smile this time, from a young, handsome young man with the whitest teeth she has ever seen.

'I could take a ferry couldn't I?'

'You could, but I can't organise that for you.'

'I know. I'll buy the ticket to Athens, please.'

All the lovely shops. All the delicious smells, perfume and

coffee and hot bread. Oh, she likes airports. She buys expensive make up, some even more expensive perfume, a maxi dress, some flip flops and a hat. A big white sun hat, with a floppy brim. That 70's look is all the rage - again. When she comes out of the ladies for the second time everything is altogether different, she is different. Hair brushed, face made up, the right clothes on.

Only two hours till the flight. Two hours to wait.

Two whole hours to spend in W H Smiths, sniffing the books and magazines.

MAKRIGIALOS, 1976

Connie was tucked up tight and safe in her bed. Vaso and Timos were alone in the cafe, everyone had gone home now they knew the girl was safe. Midnight was creeping up on them.

'What happened to her?' Vaso asked. Timos held Vaso's hand, palm up, circling his finger round and round on the soft skin.

He didn't know. He didn't really want to think about it. 'She is back home. Ask her tomorrow,' he glanced up at Vaso's face, her eyes were bleary and red, 'ask her when she wakes up.'

'But, her face, her head. And all those bruises on her legs. She had marks on her chest, Timos. Marks that looked like bites. What happened to her?'

'They aren't bites, Vas, she fell. Theo said he found her at the bottom of the stairs. She must have slipped.'

Vaso snatched her hand away from him. 'No. I saw someone walking away from the big house. A man. And anyway, her bag was in the bedroom.'

'She got frightened by something. She ran away and fell down. That's all.' His voice was calm, gentle.

Vaso stood up. 'I'm going to bed. The café will stay shut today.' Timos hugged her, whispering to her, telling her not to worry - all will be well. He called the dog and left her standing in the café, her big brown eyes brimming with tears and her head full of bad thoughts. She watched him go and went to check on Connie.

She was lying on the bed, just as she had been left. Her eyes were open and she stared at the ceiling. 'Vas, there was someone there. The chair was moved. I saw the apple peel.'

'Shhhh. Time to rest now. I will sit with you until you sleep and I will be here when you wake up. Stop. Close your eyes. Sleep.'

SOMEWHERE OVER THE ADRIATIC, 2000

The view from the window is nothing spectacular. Clouds, a patch of green far, far below, a splash of blue, more clouds.

Her stomach is full of butterflies. Her head feels light. Her hands are shaking.

The murmur of people talking is irritating, her ears pick up the 'tsuh-tsuh' sounds of every 'S' in every word and it's driving her mad. Ed says she's got hearing like a bat - only fixed on the high frequency sounds or crunching and chewing. God forbid a clock ticked too loud.

She shoves the headphones deeper into her ears, turns the radio up and closes her eyes. Not long now. She falls asleep.

The sun had risen again, the sky was still blue and Vaso was still there, thank God, sitting upright on the chair, head tilted back against the wall and eyes shut. She looked so uncomfortable. Connie reached out and touched her hand. It was cold.

'I'm awake.' Her voice was thick and slurred with sleep. She stretched her arms and rolled her head to get the knots out of her neck.

'Oh, Vas, did you sit there all night?'

'I did, and it is fine. How are you?'

Connie didn't know how she was. Her head was still aching, her whole body felt sore and crumpled. As if she had been rolled up tight, like a piece of scrap paper, and kicked into the nearest wastebasket.

'Come on, you can get up, have a wash and I will make us some strong coffee and breakfast. We will not worry about what happened, not right now. We will go to see Papou later and you can lie on his sofa until your headache goes away. We will all look after you.' She smiled and took Connie's hand.

Vaso liked to look after people. Her friends teased her sometimes - what that girl needs is a husband and a clutch of children round her feet, they said. Today, she had Connie to look after. And maybe tomorrow, or next week, she would ask her what happened.

ATHENS, 2000

onnie sits quietly in her seat. She is waiting. There is the usual scramble - people unclicking seatbelts, standing up, stretching, stepping into the aisle and getting in each other's way. She will wait, won't move until there is no queue, until everyone has got off. She forces herself to keep still, feels her breath in and out, listen to her heart beat. She closes her ears to the noise of the other passengers as they leave her behind. She wants to step into that Greek sun alone, breathe in the hot smells without being rushed by the push of people behind her, or hindered by someone in front of her. She wants to step into that other world and be consumed by it. Overtaken by it. And she doesn't want anyone else to be in it with her. It's hers.

The stewardess smiles. Thank you for flying … but Connie isn't listening.

It's hot. The tarmac is melting, the air is shimmering, the sun is blinding. Sweat forms on her lip and forehead.

She lifts her face to the sky. Her pale skin is ready to soak up the sun.

Visitors filled up Papou's little house all day. The brothers brought tiny gifts of sweets, honey from their bees and flowers from their gardens. Iakchos stroked her hair and held her hands. Gregor and Sebastianos perched on the edge of Papou's sofa and didn't know what to say. Her face was so bruised and black, it was hard not to let the shock they felt show in their own faces. They tried to joke with her, make her laugh. They cooed and petted her. The English Miss who appeared from nowhere, has crept into their hearts. They are hurt because she is hurt. But what hurts them more, is that this has been done to her by someone from their village. Someone they know, someone they talk to every day, someone they sit with in the evenings, someone they watch football with, someone who is a husband, a brother, a son.

Someone they love.

Connie lay on the sofa as she was told, accepted the gifts and wondered why all these people had come to see her. Was she ill?

The visitors chatted quietly amongst themselves, sometimes breaking their conversations to fuss over her, or get her a drink. They were speaking too quickly and quietly for her to keep up with their chattering. She caught the odd word. Something about Roula and roses.

Come in. Come in, she's asleep. She was hurt. Fell, they said. Have a biscuit, here, take the plate, I have had too many.

Coffee?

No. That wasn't a fall. Her eyes are black, her hair ripped out. Vaso said she is bitten, bruised.

No. That is a man's work.

They looked at each other. Biscuits and cups stopped half - way to the mouths of these kind people who have lived in this quiet little corner of Crete all their lives. This tiny village by the sea, where nothing happened and nothing changed. These friends and neighbours who knew everything and forgot nothing. It was only an iota, a moment,
before someone said it…

Remember Roula.

There it was said, and only a second had passed.

Yes, poor Roula. Beaten and forced to give in to a man.

That was a long time ago.

Yes, a long time, but how long? They gazed into the distance and remembered, munched their biscuits and slurped their coffee.

It was the summer that my Anna was born.

And she is … how old …six?

She is five. Her name day was December 9th. She is five. They sucked their teeth.

Five? Well, that has flown past quickly.

They think of Anna - pigtails flying in the summer breeze - and they think of Roula and the secrets she keeps inside her broken heart. There was no one in the old rose garden behind the big house when she was found - petals in her hair and bruises on her legs - no one else to be seen. And they remember how they asked and asked her who he was, who did she see? Who, who, who? She wouldn't tell them.

We should have told the girl. We should have told her not to go up there by herself.

But why? No one has thought of Roula's troubles for years. Why bring it up again? Poor Roula.

Yes. But this. Again.

What now?

Who?

Connie rested her head back against the cushions and nodded off to sleep, surrounded by the subdued talking and the stifling heat. The bees buzzed in Papou's pine tree, the waves washed gently on the sand, and Vaso wondered what to do next.

She doesn't have to go to the carousel to collect a suitcase. And she is pleased. Everyone else is crushed, standing on each other's toes, getting in each other's way, they are hot and tired, far too grumpy and tetchy to be civil. But not Connie. She strides away from them, floating on air, separate and free of them. Free of everything. Just her. No. That's not right - just her and Greece. Free to do as they like. For a while at least.

It would be wonderful to get the ferry to Crete - all that sea and fresh air - but it will take hours. First a taxi to Piraeus and then it would have to be the overnight ferry. She could fly. Much quicker, but such a lot of money. She stands still for a moment to think, surrounded by mothers hugging their sons come home to them with wives and children, with tales of money made. Her heart lurches. Her children will be sad. She'll ring them and tell them where she is. It's a good idea, now she is too far away to turn back.

She listens to the ring - ring, ring - ring. The phone is on a special table in the hall with a padded leatherette seat and a cupboard for the phone books. She smiles and thinks of cartoon phones jumping and
jiggling as they call out - ring-ring, ring-ring.

'Hello?' It's Ed - weary and tired.

'Hello, it's me.' She hears him catch his breath.

'For Christ's sake, Connie. Where the hell are you? For Christ's sake.' He starts to cry. 'Jesus, Connie.'

'Ed, listen. I'm alright.' Connie doesn't cry. Her voice is strong and brave. 'I'm in Greece. I know you won't understand it, but I'm all right. Really I am, just let me get on with it.'

'Jesus, Connie, the kids are frantic, the police have been ... what do you mean you're in Greece? What the hell are you doing?' He is pleading now. 'Just get back home. We'll fix it. Whatever is wrong we'll fix it.'

'No. We won't. Only I can fix it. Tell the kids I'm fine. Tell them I just wanted a little holiday. A rest. I have things I need to do here. Things I need to find.'

'Connie.' He is angry now. 'Just bloody come home.'

'No. Not now. Soon. I love you Ed.' She puts the phone down gently. She can hear him pleading until the click cuts him off. She feels sorry that she is putting him through so much pain, but she can't put a stop to her plan. Not for him. Not now.

If she could see him see him, right now, at this very second, would it be enough to send her back home? He is crying, his big hands pushed up to his face, struggling to rub the tears away with his gnarled workman's fingers. Poor Ed. The children are at his mam's house, eating up all their tea, like the good children they are. His is alone. Poor Ed. Totally alone. He is frightened.

She wipes her sweaty hands down her dress, pulls her bag up on her shoulder and pushes through the crowds to the taxi rank.

Her mind is made up. It will be the ferry. She needs time to think. Time to prepare herself for all that is waiting for her, far away over the deep blue sea.

Vaso and Timos sat outside in the shade of the old pine tree with Papou and some of the old men. They talked and talked, speaking fast and very quietly. No good would come of it if Connie were to hear them.

'Look,' Timos said, 'she can't remember anything, she thinks she fell. Isn't it best to leave it that way? She's fine. Just a few bruises. And we don't know that anything else happened to her, do we?' The old men nodded. Sometimes things are better if they are left alone. Vaso rolled her eyes. Timos glanced at her. There was going to be trouble. 'She might never remember, and look at poor Roula. Upset all the time. Won't go out. She is frightened of everything. Sometimes she is crazy in the head. What if Connie is like that?'

The old men nodded more vigorously. Vaso tightened her lips - the words would come spilling out soon enough. She knew it. Timos knew it. The old men knew it and they were prepared. Vaso was like her father, God rest his soul, full of passion and too easily outraged. It killed him in the end. A heart attack the Doctor said, but they knew it was the bad temper that made his blood too thick to flow.

'Vaso. You must try to help her. Tell her she fell. It will make her feel better.' Timos was cajoling her, it made her angry when he spoke to her in this wheedling voice.

She slammed her hands on the table and stood up. She was shaking. Red-faced. 'No. This is wrong. What do you think happened to her? You saw the marks, the bruises everywhere. You think a fall pulled out her hair? There is a man here who has hurt her. A man we know. A man who has done this before. A man who will do this again. For all I know, it could be you. Or you. Or you.'

She pointed at them all in turn, and for the smallest of moments they almost agreed with her. 'She must be told. She must be helped to remember. What if it had been me?' She sat back down and started to cry, letting the tears drip onto the table, the stain spreading, bigger and bigger, into the cloth.

'But it wasn't you,' Timos carried on, not looking at Vaso, 'and Connie will go home after summer. It will be forgotten by Christmas.'

Vaso knew she had lost. Knew that the next time it happened - in two years, five years or ten years - they would sit here again and remember the little English Miss who came out of nowhere. Oh! - they would say, such a skinny thing she was when she came here. Vaso fattened her up. How long ago was that? Hmmmmm? They would think of this moment and feel ashamed.

'So? She fell? Vaso?'

'You know she saw the apple peel in the fireplace, don't you?' Vaso said. 'You do know this? She knows someone was there? She is not stupid.'

Timos ran his hands through his hair. He wanted Vaso to be quiet. 'I know. Look, if we keep telling her she fell, then she will believe it. She doesn't know anything about Roula. Tell her something frightened her, maybe it was a man, maybe it was a bird, maybe it was a branch. I don't know. Just tell her she got scared, she ran and fell down the stairs. Anyway, why did she go up to the bedroom if she thought someone was in there? Why didn't she come back straight away if she thought someone was there? Why did she wander around up there all the time? On her own?'

The tears had stopped now and it was words that came pouring out of Vaso. Fierce. She roared them out. Timos reeled under their force.

'This is wrong. Are you all stupid? You think this is her fault because she went up there? Is it her fault someone hurt her like this? Is it? Of course it is, according to you men. And someone will tell her about the last time. Of course they will. Then she will remember. You think Roula doesn't remember? You think Roula is the way she is because she has forgotten? No. It is because she remembers. Just because no one talks about it, doesn't mean it didn't happen. She remembers and it makes her sick.'

The old men nodded so hard their heads could fall off. That made sense.

'But the girl will go home. She will remember at home. Someone will help her at home. For God's sake Vaso, we aren't her family, we don't need to help her. It will only bring trouble.' Timos said,

keeping his voice soft and gentle. Vaso stared at him, not believing she was hearing those words out of his mouth. Her Timos grown foolish and cruel before her eyes.

'Go away, Timos,' she hissed. 'Go away. You are an idiot. I don't want to look at you.'

He tried to ease her anger, tried to tell her it was for the best. She wouldn't listen. Papou hesitated for a moment after Timos had gone, banging the front door behind him, and put his arms around her, 'I am sorry, Vaso. I am sorry for your friend.'

'Timos is wrong, Papou.'

'I know, Vaso.' She patted his arm.

Meanwhile, Connie slept and her bruises began to heal. The cuts and scratches started to mend themselves.

SEA OF CRETE, 2000

'It has been hot today. Yes?' Connie looks up from her book. 'Hotter than Clacton-on –Sea?' His accent is German, she thinks.

'Yes, definitely, although I've never been there.' She lets the book drop onto her lap and looks at him over the top of her sunglasses. He is tall and nut-brown, hair grey, but still handsome.

'Ahh. Me neither, but I have heard of it, I worked in London a long time ago.' He laughs and sits himself down next to her. The breeze is strong. The gulls are wheeling close to the ferry, watching for any scraps the passengers might throw out to them. One catches a crust in mid-flight and the others scream in protest. The biggest one must be flying at the same speed as the ferry, it looks almost motionless, effortlessly slicing through the afternoon air, wings outstretched and head straining forwards, a beady eye fixed on her. She could touch it if she wanted to. She sits and waits for him to speak.

'They say we will see dolphins here. Do you think we will?'

'No.'

'Oh. Why?'

'Not that lucky.' She shifts her weight in her seat, feeling shy and clumsy, out of her depth. Why is this handsome man talking to her? Why has this man sat down next to her to make polite conversation? What does he want? She feels all wrong. Wrong size, wrong shape, wrong hair - just wrong all over. Like a puzzle put back together in a haphazard way, left on the shelf and forgotten for much too long. He needs to go away.

The sun is beginning to dip its rosy edge into the darkening sea. It might get chilly soon - maybe she'll have to go inside. She didn't pay for a bunk so she'll have to sit up all night, listening to people sniffing and snoring and shuffling backwards and forwards to the loo. She doesn't mind. It feels right. The noises of life around her will remind her she is alive. In another place, another life and another time it would drive her mad.

She picks her book up again, hoping this man will get the hint. She looks at the words but isn't reading. He is too big next to her. Taking up too much of her air. Too much. She can smell his suntan lotion. She wishes he would move, go away and sit next to someone else. Someone who wants to spend time talking to him, flirting with him, accepting a drink from him. Someone who will make him feel good about himself. Make him feel he is still the young man he once was. Make him feel he still has the charm and wit he had when he was 30. Someone who will help him fill up the cracks and creases of his middle age. This is what he will want - not her, run-down and worn out.

She looks out to sea, catches the gull's eye and wonders if the gull has a girlfriend somewhere. A little dowdy, plump-breasted girl-gull with a clutch of gull-toddlers squawking at her heels, waiting for Daddy to come home with a beak full of silvery dinner. The gull's yellow eye is blank. Maybe he would eat his chicks. Peck the living daylights out of them and leave them bleeding on the sea-glass and pebbles. She shoos the picture out of her head.

A teenaged boy runs over to the man, speaking in German, she makes out the word 'Papa'. Their conversation is short and animated.

The man stands up, 'I must go, my son tells me he has seen a dolphin at the front of the boat. Two in fact. So, we are lucky after all.' He nods his head at her and walks away, holding the boy's hand tightly as they sway between the chairs. He looks back, waving, beckoning to her, 'come and look too,' he mouths. Connie shakes her head - no, she doesn't want to. He turns back to the boy and she is forgotten.

It's much cooler now and she goes below deck. There is hot coffee in the bar, snacks under plastic cloches and blankets piled up on the end of a bench - for the passengers, the barman says, for the cold nights, please help yourself. She wraps one round her shoulders. It smells dusty but she can suffer it for the sake of a little extra comfort. Perhaps throwing the black jumper away had been a mistake. She props herself up against the back of the seat, eyes shut and her bag between her feet.

The ferry is crossing the Sea of Crete now. Santorini is out there, just a few kilometres away across the dark sea. Beautiful Santorini with its volcano and brown, sun-blessed bodies dozing in their cotton sheets. Not spoiled yet by the massive cruise liners and the nine thousand
tourists who will spill onto the jetty and climb that hill astride donkeys with broken knees. Not yet - maybe in five years the biggest ships will start to come.

Connie will be in Crete soon. The ferry will bump up against Sitia in an hour or two.

Connie had loved Sitia in those olden days. Far away from

everywhere, it was one of her favourite places. A straggling clutch of flat-roofed houses - blue and pink and white - falling down the steep hill sides to the coast. It was a relief to come upon the first few buildings after the heat of that high road on the seared, dry, buzzing plateau - the promise of cool drinks and shade not too far away. And then, winding down to the sea, making sure not to hit the sharp corners of the buildings with the wing mirrors, watching out for the mopeds appearing from
nowhere. The road, narrow, narrow, narrow until suddenly there it was - the bright blue sea and the bobbing boats.

The harbour area was wide and lined with palms and flowers. A place to watch the world go by, maybe to watch the Sunday 'volta'. Connie loved the 'volta' and begged Vaso to shut the café and take her on most Sunday evenings. Vas snorted - it is just an old thing, she said, no-one really cares anymore. But they went anyway.

Sunday evenings, as the sun lost his strength, all the neighbours - friends and foe - out in their finery to walk and talk and look at each other.

Young men - all scrubbed clean and hair neat - watching the girls in their best clothes strolling by.

The girls, surrounded by their little sisters and baby brothers, mothers and grandmothers and aunties.

The boys – eyes wide open and watching - nudging and shoving each other.

The girls - eyes cast down but peeping up through black lashes – wondering if their favourite boy is looking. The mothers hissing at them to hold up their heads, but not be too bold.

A place to watch the old men playing cards - duels and old battles re-enacted with diamonds and hearts.

A place to watch the old ladies - plump and rosy-hot - fanning themselves with their lace handkerchiefs and giggling at the silliness of their men.

A place she had come to with Vasou many times. Across the barren, dry hills, the car straining up the steep winding road where no one else seemed to be. Once they had got out and stood on the plateau above the town, the sky intense blue, not a cloud, and the noise of the grasshoppers almost deafening, too loud to talk over. Connie had felt ill that day, sick. The old car's engine fumes made it worse. Vasou rubbed her back as she vomited into the dusty grass.

The throbbing of this boat's old engines and the constant rolling in the sea swell is making you feel a bit sick tonight too. You won't get much sleep. Or is it your nerves? Your excitement is gut wrenching, twisting your innards into coils and knots. Everything you have done is whirling and reeling. Almost too much to think about - unbelievable. Is it only 24 hours since you were washing dishes and making beds, with only the dog to talk to?

And now?

Now, you are in an adventure.

Now, you are in a new story all of your own. There is no one else who knows this story. No one knows the ending. There is only the now. And the now flows in your head and heart, as hot as molten gold.

There is only you.

Only. You.

Only.

If only.

She shivers, pulls the blanket closer around her and tip-toes amongst the sleeping people, climbs up the stairway and out onto the highest deck. People are packed in tight up here too. Some asleep, some only dozing with half an eye open to the world, some sit alone and stare out to sea. Two men are slapping cards on a table with excited and

delighted whispers - money is changing hands. They laugh with each other. An old man sits beside them, smoking a cigarette and fiddling with his beads but he watches what is going on. He claps when his son wins a hand - bravo, bravo. She would like to ask them where they are going and who they are going to, but her Greek is rusty. She hasn't really tried to speak it. Not yet. Funny that she understands such a lot. It will take a while to get her Greek tongue awake again.

'Hello.' It is the German.

'Oh. Hello.'

'My boy is sleeping. I thought I would get some air.'

Connie errs and ums, trying to sound noncommittal, wanting to seem uninterested.

'Where are you going? After Sitia?' he asks, leaning on the rail. He is too tall and she pictures him tumbling forward and falling down into the sea. Waving and screaming and gulping for air as he is hurled up and down and around in the wash of the boat. His eyes fixed on hers, begging for a hand to pull him out. For goodness sake, stop that, she says to herself.

'Makrigialos. It's on the south coast. To see friends. And you?' she says, not looking at him. He hesitates for only the briefest of moments ... 'I am going to Aghios Nikolaos. My wife was Cretan and I am taking my son to see where he is from,' he looks sad for a moment, 'she died when he was just two. Cancer. We live in Athens now, with my second wife, she is Greek too. My son wanted us to make this trip together. It was all his idea.'

'Oh.' Connie can't think of anything to say. She feels mean and stupid that she'd thought badly of this nice man.

We all need to know where we come from, we all need to know who made us, who formed us and who left us behind. We all need to know.

'By the way, the dolphins were beautiful. Very.'

'I wish I had come with you to see them.'

'Yes, I think you would have liked them.' He touches a hand to her shoulder, 'I hope you have a good time with your friends, you look like you need cheering up.'

Words come rushing out of her because he is a kind stranger and she can't stop. The words crawl over themselves to get out into the open. She tells him everything. Almost everything. The dawn light creeps up on them and, when the ferry turns towards the smudge on the horizon that is Crete, she is still talking.

He shakes her hand when they find a quiet space on the dock. He asks her if she wants a lift to Makrigialos in his hire car, he says he doesn't mind. She declines. He thanks her for sharing her story with him, he feels honoured and hopes she finds what she is looking for and becomes happy again. He is a good man, a decent man and she will never see him again. She watches him walk away, his arm draped across his son's shoulders, he glances back at her and smiles. She waves. Thank you, she shouts to him before he disappears in the crowd.

C onnie was quiet and subdued for days and days after they said she fell. She didn't tell anyone about the other painful and sore places she had, the ones that couldn't be seen but that she could feel. She stayed in her room most of the time, only coming out in the afternoons to go for her swim. The water washed the bruises, cuts and grazes - inside and out - and the salt healed them. She couldn't stop feeling the patch on the back of her head, the soreness felt nice and the feel of the stubbly hairs made the tips of her fingers tingle.

She struggled to get to sleep. She tossed and turned in the heat, wishing and wishing she was asleep, but her thoughts weaved and wandered as she tried to make sense of what on earth had happened. All she remembered was climbing the stairs then waking up later in the Goat Lady's house. Every now and again there was a flash of something else - curtains, jeans, her bag on the floor, an apple. Vaso just shrugged when she tried to ask her what had happened - you must have fallen down, she said, I told you it was dangerous up there, and she went back to washing the pots and pans, or changed the subject.

Today Connie was lying under the old pine tree. She had dozed off in its shade when the sun was hot, and now she had woken up with a jolt. The beach was quiet, the sun was starting to cool and the waves were creeping closer to her feet. It was getting late, she must have been there for hours. She picked up her towel and wrapped it round her shoulders, her hand catching on that sore part of her chest. She peeled down the top of her swimming costume to look at the marks. One was red, hot and itchy - maybe she needed some cream or something. But first she must go home, get dressed. She had promised Papou.

Papou had been to see her every morning for an hour or so. She would hear the squeak of the gate, a little tap - tap on her door and a wheezy cough to announce he was coming in. He sat beside her at the little table, drinking coffee with her and reading the newspaper. If something interested him he would read it out to her, showing her the Greek letters and the words they made. They talked a little about this and that, what was going on in the village, what her friends were up to. Sometimes they just sat, quiet and companionable. This morning he had ignored the paper and fussed around her, complaining about her staying indoors too much, patting her hand from time to time to show her he wasn't angry.

'You must get up, get dressed, go out,' he said, 'and not just to swim. Brush your hair and put on your best dress. Show everyone you are well and happy. They are all worried about you.'

'I know, Papou. Tomorrow. I will go out tomorrow.'

'It is always tomorrow, tomorrow, tomorrow.' Papou grumbled. 'Vaso could do with your help, the café is busy. She needs you.'

Connie shut her eyes. She knew. The summer was nearly over.

'Papou, what will I do when the winter comes? Will I have to go home? Timos said I will have to go home when the tourists are gone.' Timos had come to her door yesterday morning, upset yet still able to tell her that she must leave, still able to deliver words that cut like a knife - after all, Vaso was not her mother was she? She must go back to her family. They were not her family were they?

'I don't want to go home Papou. I want to stay here with you and Vaso and everyone. I want to stay here.' She started to cry.

Her sobbing cracked his heart. So, Timos had told her to go had he? He was an idiot. Maybe it was the right thing. Maybe she should go home, forget everything. Maybe there was no place for her after summer was gone, but that boy was not the one to say it. That boy was proving to be harsher than he had ever thought possible, and he'd been so fond of him too. Now he couldn't bear to look at him. Even Vaso wouldn't speak to him. Her eyes were red from weeping and her throat was sore from shouting. There was big trouble between them. Timos had telephoned Phillipos last night and told him he wanted to come to Australia - not next year, but right now. Oh, Vaso was so angry.

Everything was changing. Last night Yanni said there were bulldozers at Analipsi, tearing up the salty ground next to the German Hotel. Bulldozers! And this time they knew it would be another hotel. Bigger and better than the German's. What would happen next year when it was opened? More people would come. Papou was worried for the village - there will be trouble, he said to his friends in the café. They sipped their Metaxa and nodded, thinking of the old days when there were only goats and sheep eating up the grass on the hillsides. Someone said it would be good to have these tourists, good to have their money.

Pah! Papou said, they will bring their money and their trouble. Look at Matala - drugs and sex and thieving. That's different, that is the hippies not families, the young ones said. You are a stubborn old man, stuck in your ways. We will have families and swimming pools full of children. Isn't Yiota already selling plastic arm bands, flip-flops, hats and beach balls?

Pah! Papou was not convinced. Pah!

The old men sipped and pondered. Maybe it was good, maybe it was bad. But it was certainly changing. We must make sure there is no trouble they agreed amongst themselves. We must tell our children not to sell the land, our land, to any Tom, Dick or Harry who turns up. We will have a meeting. Yes. Soon. In the church hall. Yes. That is a good idea.

Papou pushed the thoughts to one side and took tight hold of Connie's hand.

'You will stay as long as you like, little one.' There, it was said. Never mind Timos and his stupidity. 'You will stay with us forever if you want to.' The poor little English Miss. She will have trouble too, no doubt, after this terrible thing. And who best to help her than Vaso and Papou.

'Papou. I will go for my swim and then I will come to the café. Tonight. I will. I promise.'

He cupped her chin in his hands and smiled right down deep into her eyes - expyno koritsi, he whispered to her. Clever girl.

Now it was time for her to keep her promise to Papou. She washed and dressed and slipped her prettiest dress on over the bruises and marks.

Vaso was finishing the evening meal preparations when she went into the café. 'Oh. You are here. Good. You can help me.' She looked angry. Connie felt her eyes brimming again.

'I am going to go and see the doctor first. Look.'

'Bastarde,' Vaso muttered. 'Come with me.' She led her into the pantry and rummaged around furiously, knocking bottles and jars this way and that, until she found what she wanted. The iodine stung and made Connie catch her breath. Vaso dabbed it on roughly, taking no notice of Connie's wincing and protests - shush, this will fix it for now, she said, in between expletives Connie didn't quite understand. When she was finished, she flung her arms round Connie and hugged her, still muttering and cursing in Greek all the time.

'I am sorry I am so horrible. I am happy to see you here again.'

'Have I done something wrong Vas?' Connie said.

'No. You haven't. It is the world that is bad. Not you. Come on. Have something to eat. I will take you to Irapetra to see the doctor in one hour, and then we will have a busy night tonight and keep our lips up.'

'Chins, Vas. Keep our chins up.'

SITIA, 2000

The man at the ticket kiosk tells her it is two hours till the bus to Makrigialos. Good. She will have time to have a look around. The old fortress is still there to watch over her. The amphitheatre of white and blue and yellow houses stretches all around her and up to the edge of the high plateau. The harbour area is much smarter than she remembered. What a difference. The new pavement is the smoothest, whitest marble and slippery under her feet. It is beautiful, but it will be treacherous in the rain. The palms are bigger, the stray cats are gone and even more pots are overflowing with bright geraniums.

She sits on a bench a few feet from the harbour wall watching the water slop gently against the stones. It's still early. Behind her the bars, cafes and shops are just beginning to open up. Everyone is getting ready for the new day ahead. Beer and food is being delivered, the road cleaners are sweeping, women are watering the flowers and everyone is busy. There is whistling and shouting, bursts of laughter and the clanging of barrels, scooters zip up and down, people call out greetings to each other. Somewhere a man shouts for his wife - what, she shouts back, I'm busy, do it yourself. Connie waits in the early sun and watches and listens. She soaks up the fresh morning in this half –

remembered world, lets it seep into her and thanks God she is here.

Your children might love it here too, you know. You'll have to bring them one day. Show them everything you loved in the olden days. If they ever forgive you when you get back home.

Out in the harbour there are boats of all colours, shapes and sizes now - not just the old fishing boats anymore. Way out beyond the harbour entrance, a white yacht glitters in the sunshine. It wouldn't have been out of place in Monte Carlo. Three people climb down the ladder and jump into a speedboat. She watches it zoom and bounce over the waves, the noise of the engine getting louder and louder. It pulls up right next to her, a young man jumps off and threads the rope through a metal ring. He is laughing and telling his friends to hurry up. They are
handsome and rich - their sunglasses are Ray-Ban, their linen trousers are Armani and their T-shirts are Dolce Gabbana. They wish her a good morning and walk away, chattering and relaxed. On their holidays –
self-assured and confident with not a care in the world. Lord, oh Lord, how things have changed. She looks down at her dress, made suddenly conscious of its crumpled grubbiness, and she has only washed her face once in the last day and night. Time to buy some fresh clothes and find somewhere for a scrub up.

The nearest shop is all plate glass, spotlights and air conditioning. Skinny, contorted mannequins in ludicrous skimpy outfits, pose in the windows. The girls inside are elegant and perfect. Connie walks in and straight out again, not even giving them time to speak to her.

Nothing she can afford in that one. Most of the shops on the harbour front are the same. Designer clothes and real fur coats. Connie is amazed. Fur? In Crete? No one wears real fur these days. She will have to ask about that when she gets to Makrigialos.

Further back from the harbour, in the winding maze of alleys, she knows where she is, she remembers these streets. Here, in the cooler, shady lanes, she feels more at home and she might be able to afford something here. She walks into the first clothes shop - well, not just clothes but linen, bedding, curtains, shoes, perfume, make-up, trinkets, pots and pans. Everything a woman could want. The girl greets her. Oh dear, it is time to speak some Greek.

'Tha ithela na agora'so pantelonia and ....and.....a dress....parakalo.'

'I understand, trousers and a dress. Of course. Maybe a shirt also?' The girl looks her up and down and smiles, 'these will be your size, here, on these rails.'

'Your English is wonderful.' Connie says, not sure if she is pleased by this, she wants to speak as much Greek as she can, now she is here.

'Thank you. And you have the accent of Crete but you are English? Yes?'

'Yes, I am, but I learnt my Greek here, in Makrigialos. I haven't spoken it for many years.' She picks out a pair of pale blue cotton
trousers, a white floaty top, a long, loose dress swarming with swirls and whirls of greens and blues, some new underwear and a pair of gold leather flip-flops.

'Ah, Makrigialos. They have the countryman's accent over there. The Greek will come back even if you are only here for a week.

You'll see.' The girl takes the clothes and starts to ring the prices into the till.

'Posa kostizi?' ventures Connie with a little embarrassed laugh.

'Very good. 65 Euro, parakalo.'

Connie is pleased with herself for using her rusty Greek and they chat a little longer. She asks if there is bathroom she can use to change her clothes and perhaps have a quick splash of water on her dusty face. 'Ame!' the girl says using the slang word back to her – sure. Connie is thrilled. It makes her smile for the first time in a dog's age.

When she gets back to the bus stop she is fresh and clean in her new clothes; ready to meet them all again.

It hasn't entered your head that they might not be there has it? You haven't allowed yourself a moment to think that. You haven't given a single thought to what you will do if they are gone, moved away, or dead. Of course they will be there, because you wish it, because you want it so much. They will be watching for you to jump down from that clattery old bus, run across the dusty road where the donkey's clip-clop and the skinny black dogs bark. Fingers crossed.

AT THE DOCTOR, IRAPETRA, 1976

Vaso parked the car and they made their way to the doctor's house. When the tarmac was laid for the new drive-way, the workmen had let it flow down the slope and out into the main street. No one cared. No one was bothered. People just stepped over the lump or parked their cars askew on this new hillock.

Connie stopped and looked down at it, 'Why has no one fixed this?' she asked.

'It doesn't matter,' Vaso shrugged.

'In England it would matter, someone would complain and make sure it was put right.'

'Well,' said Vaso, 'good job we are in Crete then. We only have to worry about the sunshine and the blue sky.' She stepped over the lump, 'Come on, I phoned while you were having something to eat, the nurse said if I pay she will let the doctor see you. I will pay.'

A queue of people waited on the veranda, some with bandages, some with sticks, and some with glum, spotty children perched on their knees. A thin, tired-looking man, wearing round wire-rimmed glasses, groaned slightly and leaned his head back on the wall, grumbling about his pain. He pressed an old wool sock to his ear - a spider has crawled in there and it's eating into my brain, he said to everyone. The man sitting next to him edged away, surreptitiously sliding his bottom up the wooden bench - after all, some people look alright but, inside, they are crazy people. Nonsense, the nurse said, you have too much wax in there, it's only earache, that's all. She motioned Connie and Vaso towards the doctor's door - he is waiting for you, go straight in, she said.

The doctor spoke to her slowly in Greek. 'You will need some antibiotics for this,' he peered up at her. 'How did this happen?'

'I don't know. I think I fell and when I woke up I had all the cuts and bruises and these two marks.' The Doctor looked at Vaso and spoke rapidly to her, turning away from Connie. 'Look, I can understand what you are saying if you don't talk so fast. What are you talking about?' Connie said.

He didn't answer, went to his cupboard and got out a small tube with a stick in, took a swab from the oozing part of the mark, sealed it up and put it in a tray. 'I will send this for tests,' he said, speaking directly to Connie again. 'And you must put this cream on every day for
infection. Let me see the other marks you have.'

She showed him her legs, the bruises were faded to a dirty
yellow, but still visible. An arc of four on the outside of each thigh, one on the inside. Five on both of her upper arms, her back and shoulders still black and blue.

He peered at them and felt the bump on the back of her head, he let out a small sigh. 'Tell me again, what happened? And when?' He didn't look at her face, just kept examining the marks.

Connie remembered all she could - about a week ago, she was going up the stairs, going into the room and then, nothing. No, wait, she thought there was someone there, the apple peel in the hearth. But she didn't see or hear anyone. No. She did. 'Vas, There was a man there. I saw his jeans out of the corner of my eye. He was behind me.'

The Doctor pulled his stool up in front of her so he could look straight into her eyes and took hold of her hand. He glanced at Vaso. Vaso nodded her head, just a little, almost imperceptibly. Connie started to panic. She was sure Vaso was crying, and why was the doctor was speaking so kindly and softly? What was happening? Was she dying? Her brain went numb, her mind blank and somewhere in a little corner, deep down where only the most awful thoughts and fears and dreams lived, a box opened up. A tiny lid lifted, just a crack, but enough to let another horrible thing slide right in.

'This is a bite. And I think it is a human bite. In fact, I know a human has done this. It is easy to tell by the shape. Only you know why this is here. I think this bump might be because you have hit your head, or you have fallen. These bruises are fingermarks, and these on your back are where you might have been pushed onto a hard or bumpy floor. Or fallen.' Connie felt faint. 'I am going to send you to the hospital and they will examine you properly. I'm afraid they will examine you all over and do some tests. Just in case.'

What did he mean? A bite? She tried to digest what he had just said. She had not understood properly? Tests? Just in case? Just in case of what? The tiny lid opened a little more and she let the doctor's words pour into the dark depths of that hidden away, deep down, almost
impossible to reach box. So deep, they might never come out again.

They were both looking at her, waiting for her to speak, but she couldn't make her lips work. They were clamped shut, as tight as steel traps. His words were tender as he spoke them, harsh words made as gentle as possible. 'I think you might have been raped.'

All she could hear was the man outside crying about his earache.

NEARLY THERE, MAKRIGIALOS, 2000

The bus rolls smoothly towards Makrigialos. The road is new and wide - no longer that rutted old donkey track widened by a million hoofs, a million feet and a million wheels. Still the winding climb up to the scorched plain, churches still standing on their lofty pinnacles, grasshoppers still scraping their loud music to each other, and the heat still shimmering.

She watches the empty landscape go by. Greece is a funny place - such a wide, new road and not a car on it but this huge, air-conditioned, plush coach and its few occupants. The radio is on, the plinky-plonk bouzoukis accompany a well-known American rock song. Connie likes the way the Greeks do that - just add some bouzouki and make it their own.

There are only three other people on the bus. They don't seem to know each other and sit apart, quiet and morose. The atmosphere makes her feel sad when she should be overjoyed. She wants to hear chatting and laughing and the sharing of stories. Her journey is nearly done. It won't be long till she's there, and this will all be over. She will find her answers. The pieces will slot into place, the tumblers of the lock that has held her heart tight shut will suddenly fall. Makrigialos is the key.

Her head is hot and her mouth is dry. Her throat is full of dust, her nose tickles with the smell of the hot fabric seats. She wishes she had bought a bottle of water in that nice girl's shop - ena boukala nerò, parakalo, she could have said. Mmmmm, she remembered that anyway. She rests her head against the cool window and stares down at the grass verge rushing by. The bouzoukis play on and she starts to doze off.

The bus turns a sharp corner and slows to a crawl. She opens her eyes. The sides of the road have fallen away into a deep ravine. She knows this place - surely there is a narrow bridge right here. She has hurtled round this corner and over this bridge many times with Vaso, her eyes shut and holding on tight. The bus takes extra care to manoeuvre around the bend and over the deep gorge. She sits up. No one else moves. An old man, leading a donkey along the road towards them, waves his hand. The load of rushes topple to one side as the donkey skitters about, frightened by the bus coming close to him. Still using donkeys, then. This makes her happy.

A church comes into view, the steps wide and white, perfect for sitting on the evenings and watching the world go by. My God, it is the big village. Already? They have got here so quickly. The bus winds along the main street, just wide enough for these modern coaches with their giant-eye wing mirrors sticking out on stalks.

Past the school. Children all inside, sitting quietly, learning their lessons.

Past the square. Oh, there it is. She had forgotten that. A black and red torpedo, dragged up from the beach during the war and placed there in honour of everyone who died. Or as a reminder never to fight again.

Past the bakery, full of chattering women. Oh, a priest is there too, buying his daily bread, twirling his beard as he talks, the sun glinting on his cross.

And there is the Goat Lady's kafenion. The shutters are closed and look dirty in the sunlight. A stack of green plastic garden chairs and a couple of tables stand outside. It's still too early for the old men. It will be busy later. The door is ajar and, as the bus slows for the next corner she tries to peer inside, but it's too gloomy and she only sees a cat licking his paws on the doorstep.

Past a house she knows, a door she remembers, a tree grown so big. There are cars parked everywhere, squeezed into ludicrously tiny spaces along the sides of the road - once upon a time there had been none.

She cranes her neck this way and that to see everything. Then the village is gone and the bus is winding down the hill. The bends come sharp and close together. There, in the distance a glimpse of the sea and a clutch of buildings stretching along the bay. The others on the bus are starting to shift and shuffle. She is sitting to attention now, ramrod straight in her seat, holding her breath. The plucking of the bouzoukis is loud in her ears. Oh, it is Makrigialos down there, nestling up tight against the blue, blue sea. Not grown too big, but not the tumble of whitewashed cottages so easily conjured up in her memory anymore. Not the few tiny houses with their back doors on the beach and their fronts on the dirt track - hotels and cafés, shops and apartments fill up every space along the edge of the wide bay. The goats and the donkeys are gone, the paths cut by their feet are gone. There are villas in the foothills, with huge wrought iron gates, their spikes painted gold. There are drives made of marble blocks - no tarmac flowing out onto this new road. There are smooth lawns, flower beds and calm, azure swimming pools.

Closer and closer the bus comes.

And there it is. The big house. The big house is still there. It is still there. And it is different.

The nurse told them to sit in the waiting room and wait for the tube of cream and a letter for the hospital. Vaso held Connie's hand and cursed quietly in Greek. The man with the earache complained about the hot oil the nurse had poured in his ear. He gripped his woollen sock tightly and would not give it up, no matter how many times the nurse told him to leave go. Connie wished they would all shut up. Connie didn't speak, her mouth was still firmly glued shut, her head was aching and her skin was crawling with something. She started to scratch her leg where the bruises were. Perhaps I've got mites, or fleas or something, she thought, maybe I'll have to ask the doctor later. The man with the earache lost his will to fight anymore and left, the nurse held his sock between finger and thumb and threw it in the bin. A fly buzzed in the window. Poor thing, Connie thought, he'll never get out doing that, he needs to fly out of the door, poor thing just bumping his head against the glass. Vaso took the letter from the nurse and thrust the cream into Connie's hand –it made her jump. Vaso's voice was harsh and angry - the appointment is for tomorrow, we will go home now, she said, dragging Connie to her feet and pulling her out of the door. The sun was gone and the café would need to open soon if any money was to be made tonight.

Connie let herself be pulled along, the doctor's words trying to filter into her consciousness. He had been so gentle and calm. Yes, she understood his words, she understood what he thought had happened, but she couldn't take it in. It couldn't be true. He had said her memory would come back sooner or later - after all, what had happened was a big shock, and there was the bump on her head. But, he had said as he held her hand in his, it was likely she would have some amnesia caused by this dreadful and terrible event. It would be normal under the

circumstances. He had told her everything would be alright. But it wasn't alright. If this thing had happened to her, then it was wrong, all wrong. She curled her hand into a fist and dug her fingernails into the palm as hard as she could. She couldn't remember. She felt the pain in her soft skin radiate to the tips of her fingers. She must have fallen.

Vaso was still cursing in Greek, her voice getting louder and louder and her face pointed skyward, as if God could hear her. Stop being so dramatic, Connie said, her own voice tiny against Vaso's rage. She didn't want to listen to Vaso, she didn't want to hear anything she was saying. Vaso was too angry. Connie didn't feel angry, she felt tired. Just tired.

Connie huddled down in the seat, her arms hugging around her body so tightly Vaso thought she might snap in two. She watched Connie out of the corner of her eye as they set off back to Makrigialos. She was still, quiet and ashen-faced, eyes like saucers, staring at nothing.

'Connie……'

'No Vas, not yet. Don't talk to me – '

'But Connie you must talk. You must try and remember. We must know who has done this thing to you.'

Connie sighed. 'For God's sake Vas, I heard a noise, I started to turn around and I glimpsed the jeans. That's all. Nothing else.'

'Good girl. Good.' Vaso patted her leg, 'you remember something. The rest will come.'

'But what if I do remember? What if I remember, what happened? What if I remember? I don't want to remember anything, Vas. I don't.' She hugged herself even tighter. Her whole body was trembling.

'Oh, little one. I know it is horrible. It will be better if you can remember and then you will fix, you will not be driven mad with it. Look at Roula ...' Vaso caught her breath, and her mouth snapped shut. She hadn't meant to say that. No. She had. She wanted Connie to know. Wanted her to know that she could end up like Roula, a half-crazy, shadow-woman crippled with fear and self-hatred and blame and

sorrow, unable to live a life that was good and full. It was that simple for Vaso. The only way to avoid destruction is to stand up and face it. Like she did. Face everything head on and fight - hard. If she could help Connie to be like her, then she would.

'If you talk, you will get over it,' she said.

Connie turned round towards her, face like thunder. 'Get over what, Vas? Get over what? A man nearly killing me. A man pushing me on the floor and … and … doing that to me, I can't even say it, Vas - a man doing what he liked to me when I was half-dead.' It was Connie who was shouting now. Screaming in Vaso's face, spit flying. 'A grown man. Vaso. How will I get over that? And I've never … never … never …'

Vaso stopped the car, took Connie in her arms and they cried and cried, oblivious to the tooting and tooting of the cars trying to squeeze past. She pushed the sodden strands of hair off Connie's face and wiped her brow with the sleeve of her cardigan.

'Come on. Let's get back,' she said, 'I will keep the café shut, we will sit together under Papou's pine tree and watch the stars and the sea twinkling in the moonlight. We will not talk. We will not think. Papou will bring us some English tea, we will just sit and watch the world go to sleep and we will see what tomorrow brings.'

So they did. Papou brought them shawls and drinks and sweet treats. The moon beamed down, the sea shushed against the sand and a lonely little Scops owl hooted forlornly in the tree. He would be flying away soon, off to Africa for his winter holiday. In the spring maybe they would hear his melancholy voice again, and look forward to another summer. They sat and watched and listened to the world turning. And all the while Connie dug her fingernails into the palm of her hand.

'Den thelo na xero. I don't want to know. I don't want to know.' Vaso was shouting at Timos. 'You must do as you please. But I will not watch you go. I will not. I will not wait for you. No. I won't. I will get on with my life and you will be dead to me.'

She wasn't even crying. Connie watched them through the goat shed window, she could hear every word. Timos was pleading, begging, almost on his knees. The dog was barking and barking, running in circles around them, enjoying this new shouting game. Vaso stood like a warrior, hands on hips, sturdy and strong, bending forward every now and again to scream right in his face.

'You are dead to me. Go away. Go to Australia. I will not be here for you when you come back.'

'But Vasou, I love you, I love you. I have to go. I will come back.' Timos grabbed her arms and shook her, 'Listen to me.'

'No. I won't. You don't have to go. There is everything here. Things are moving on, in a few years this place will be busy and full of tourists and we will make more money … and … and …' She ran out of steam, wriggled her arms free of his hold and raised her hand. Connie shut her eyes. The slap was so hard Connie heard the crack from her room. The dog barked and barked some more, jumped and growled and tugged at the leg of his master's jeans - come on, let me play, let me play. Vaso stormed back into the café and left Timos standing there, the excitable dog running this way and that all around him.

Should she go over and talk to him? Timos had been her friend until this thing had happened. Poor Timos. She had understood his frustration, felt his need to get away from his too-tight life as keenly as she had felt her own longing to escape. But he was in everyone's bad books now, and he had been so horrible to her. Even Papou was angry with him. Papou thought he was being stupid and cruel - and what about Vaso, Papou had said, he will make her wait for him, for how long? Until he decides to come back? If he comes back? And then what?

Connie had hugged him tight to make him feel better - but Papou, she said, he will come back, Vaso says they always do. Papou had scowled and wouldn't talk about him anymore.

Yes. She would go and talk to Timos. As she opened the door she heard him mutter something to the dog, she saw him lift his foot and, before she could do a thing to stop it, he kicked the dog in its ribs. Such a hard kick that it sent the poor dog tumbling and yelping into the courtyard wall. It lay there, stunned and shivering against the stones. Timos balled his fists as if to punch it. Poor thing.

'Timos. No. Stop it!' she screamed and ran towards the whimpering dog. Timos' head swivelled as if it were on a stick, like a puppet's, in her direction. He was furious. He didn't care he had been seen kicking the dog, he didn't care that Connie was there.

'This is your fault, little English girl. Your fault. All she worries about is you.' He spat on the ground, inches from her bare feet, grabbed hold of the dog's collar so hard she thought he might choke it, and dragged it to its feet.

She stopped in her tracks, suddenly afraid of him and turned and ran back into the goat shed. This was Timos - nice, friendly Timos with the floppy hair and the soft smile. God. How could he be so cruel? She couldn't believe it. Only that morning Vaso had told her Timos was
going to Australia to stay with her brother. They had been preparing the vegetables, the pots and pans were filled with water ready to boil, the trays of spinach and cheese pies were ready for the oven, the lamb was already roasting. Vaso's voice was clipped and quiet. 'He will go in a few days. Phillipos has a job for him. So. That's that.'

'Oh,' Connie had said, 'he wanted to tell you the night I … the night … the other night. But he didn't have time because of what happened. I was supposed to be here to help, if you were really upset.'

Vaso had slammed her knife down on the table. 'I see. So, he told you first.' Connie had looked up from the potatoes, surprised at

Vaso's tone of voice. 'Well, not really, you knew he wanted to go, Vas, he has mentioned it often enough. He told me because he wanted me to be there when he told you. That's all.'

'You are right, never mind,' Vaso had said, giving her a quick hug and they had carried on making the evening meal. But Vaso had been quiet for a long time and now, only a few hours later, there was all this shouting and the poor, poor dog. Connie collected her swimming things - maybe it would be best to avoid the café for a few hours until Vaso had calmed down. Yes, that was a good idea.

She wished she knew how to help her friend, help her feel better. She had never been in love with anyone, never known what it was like to care for someone so deeply it hurt in your heart when you looked at them. That's what Vaso said it was like. Georgos used to come and see her before ... before ... but he hadn't been for ages and ages. The last time she had seen him had been at Papou's house when she was resting, he had brought her cakes from his mother's bakery. He hadn't been back. She thought he liked her. He teased her and asked her to go for walks with him. She blushed when he looked at her, her face getting hot right up to the roots of her hair. When she talked to him her lips shook and her words came out too fast. You are sweet English miss, he had said, so walk with me, I will hold your hand and pick you flowers. Vaso had laughed and told her to go. She said he was nice, then she had pursed her lips, too old for you perhaps, but not to worry, his mother would keep him in check. But Connie didn't go with him, and now it was too late.

'Connie. Connie.' Vaso was shouting for her. Then she remembered. There would be no swimming today. She had to go to the hospital this afternoon. Oh, she didn't want to go, she didn't want to know anything more. All the split-second glimpses and sounds from that afternoon flew round her head, every minute of every day. And all night. She tried to push them out, tried hard to sleep, but they swirled in head. It was as if she had a whirlpool in there, all the fragments rushing in circles, round and down and up and round again. She wanted to catch them as they went rushing past, wanted to pluck them out from the foaming water. But they passed by too quickly and she couldn't quite reach them. Not all of them. She had a few fragments in her collection. She needed to get the last few, most important pieces but the pain of the red - raw mark on the palm of her hand stopped her reaching out to grab those pieces flowing close enough to catch. Maybe, she would she fall in and disappear into the dark rush of the freezing whirl, before those pieces could be caught.

'I'm coming.' She grabbed her bag and ran over to the café.

Today will change your world forever, sweet little Connie. You don't know it yet. But today will be the beginning of something big.

And as they climbed in to Vaso's old van, the villagers were gathering in the church hall. Papou sat at the front, eyeing everyone who came in and shuffling his papers. Despite the warmth in the hall he had put on his best shirt and his Sunday jacket. He looked his most terrifying. God forbid anyone did not turn up. This might be the most important meeting the village had ever had.

He coughed ostentatiously. Gradually the chatting stopped, the men shushed their wives, the wives shushed them back, and the young ones gathered up their children and sat them on their knees. The room fell silent - nothing to be heard but the squeak of the fans turning slowly above them. The crowd all stared at him. Anticipating. Eager to hear what he had to say.

He had heard of places in the north, Papou said, being overtaken by rich people from Athens buying up bits of land and throwing up great big hotels. Pushing all the farmers and villagers out. Look at

Rethymnon, such a beautiful little city, full of ancient buildings, our history steeped into its very stones, and now it is surrounded by more and more new hotels. They are stretching far along the beach. This would not happen here. He would make sure of that. Maybe it could never happen in Makrigialos, there is no airport and no big road and the mountains will always separate us from that busy Northern coast, but still, we must make sure.

The audience whispered amongst themselves - yes, yes, they said, we have been over there, such a shame. We have seen for ourselves, mile after mile of hotels along that beautiful coastline.

Papou glared at them and waited until the room was quiet again.

He had spoken to his daughter in Heraklion - oh yes, she said, people coming all the time. The airport is overrun with people. The hotels are full, and more and more are being built. People come here for the sun. Lots of them. They complain about the all the building work going on everywhere, but they still come. They don't eat the food, the money confuses them, but they still come. We are busy, busy all the time. I make the chips for them. Greek chips. They like them.

So, there it was. The proof that things were changing.

They all listened and nodded their heads.

Do not sell anything to a stranger, not even a poor, scrubby field only as big as a stamp. Nothing. Even you young ones. The land will all be yours one day, you must keep it for your children and your children's children.

Of course, the young ones whispered to each other.

A bee buzzed lazily, close to a fan. Perilously close. Then it was gone. See that bee, said Papou, if we give in to the lies they will tell us and take their money, we will be like that bee. Enjoying life one moment and then Pouff! Gone!

They all looked up at the fan with the smatterings of bee bones and the remains of legs and wings visible on the blades. No one uttered a word.

No, we must be like the mantis. Always ready with our arms up to fend them off, always ready for a fight. When a mantis lands on the table or on the bed, what do we do? Do we shout and run away?

They shook their heads.

No, we don't, and why? Because here is a daughter of Heracles come to visit us, a daughter of the strongest and bravest man in Ancient Greece. We will be like her.

They all nodded. The old man was right. They would never allow this to happen here because they were warriors, fighters - brave and tough. They could stick up for themselves. Yes.

Good, it is decided. We will all sign this contract and it is settled. The Priest is going to keep it safe for us. When it is done, we will have some wine to celebrate this day.

Was that it? Was it over? The chattering started and they passed the papers from hand to hand, from family to family, each signature written with precision and care.

Papou walked over to Timos. He had crept in late, head down, eyes to the floor, but Papou had spotted him standing by the door on his own. Papou put a hand out to him. He would shake his hand, after all Timos will go to Australia no matter what, he might as well leave as a friend.

Timos pushed the old man's hand away. 'You are an old fool. You have destroyed the lives of all these people in one minute. Think of the money they have all lost because of you.'

'You are wrong Timos. We will build the hotels and the cafes ourselves. We will get the money from the tourists forever. Not just for one summer. They will come. They come now.'

'How will you build your hotels, eh? You think the few people who turn up in summer will give you enough money? This village doesn't have a pot to piss in. And when everyone is angry with you, they will tear up this piece of paper and sell their fields to anyone. You'll see, old man. You'll see.' Timos turned on his heel and shoved his way through the door, letting it clash shut in Papou's face.

'That boy is an idiot.' Yanni said. 'Who would have thought it? Come on, it's time for wine. Forget about him. He might come back from Australia with pockets full of money, but he is so stupid he will probably come back with nothing.'

The two old men walked out into the evening.

'Do you think he is right, Yanni?' Papou said. Yanni stopped and looked at his friend. 'Are you as stupid as him? No, he's wrong. What does he know about the money we have? He's from the big village. They are crazy up there. And they'll be jealous. No tourists will ever go up there. What would they do? Milk a goat?' They started to laugh.

'Yes, we will put on an excursion to a milking shed.' Yanni slapped him on the back.

They were still laughing and joking when they walked into the café - two old friends together with mischief in their heads and secrets up their sleeves. The laughter died on their lips in an instant. Vaso and the English Miss were sitting at the family table, both crying. Connie was tearing a flower into a million tiny pieces. Vaso ushered Papou into the pantry and shut the door,

Connie wouldn't be able to hear them whispering to each other in there, they mustn't upset her anymore.

'They took her away and examined her. The doctor brought her back and told me to tell her, because his English was too poor. They said she's been raped. Papou, I said this, didn't I? I told you. You were all wrong. I will tell the whole village, everyone will know. I will make sure this man is caught. This time, Papou. Five years ago he got away, but not this time. She's only a child herself. No boyfriend, Papou. Ever. No one has touched her. Until now. Like this. Papou we have to make this man pay for what he has done.' Papou rubbed a hand across his eyes. 'But that's not all. She must go back to the hospital in six weeks for a test. And then we have to wait another week to see if she's going to have a baby. A baby, Papou. Dear God.' Vaso pushed her hands through her hair, her face screwed up, her anger was thick in the air between them. 'And then what? This is a disaster for her. I hate this man, whoever he is. I would like to kill him with my bare hands.'

Papou could think of nothing to say. Nothing. He sighed. What to do? He didn't know. Vaso was furious, and she had good right to be. Of course, they mustn't let this man get away with this. Of course, they should do something, but what? And how?

'Papou, I think I know who to talk to. Roula knows who did this to her. I just know she does, I feel it in my bones. I am going to ask her.'

Papou sighed, he thought Vaso would say this. Poor Roula, no one cared about her, not now she was half-crazy. She had become a laughing stock, wandering around the village with her stockings trailing down over her shoes, getting thinner and thinner until she was just a splinter of a woman. Poor Roula. She wasn't much older than Vaso, but she may as well have been a hundred years older they looked so

different. That brute of a father had a lot to answer for. And her mother, poor woman, God rest her soul. He still felt guilty when he bumped into Roula at Church, or in the street. The whole village had talked about nothing for months and months, but Roula wouldn't tell them anything. So they forgot and left her alone.

When they went back into the café, Connie was still sitting at the table. Yanni had taken the remains of the flower from her and was holding her hands in his.

Vaso spoke softly to her, 'Come with me, Connie. I will help you get ready for bed.'

The girl tried to stand but her legs buckled under her, she slid to the floor and started to howl. Great sobs racked her body and she shook like the poor dog kicked against the wall. Yanni picked her up and

carried her to her room, put her down on the bed so gently she might have been made of the finest porcelain. And all the while Connie's sobs echoed around the village. People lifted up their heads and wondered what on earth was making that terrible noise.

Vaso lay beside her all night, let Connie rest her head on her chest and stroked her hair until Connie calmed down and eventually slept. Vaso pulled the cover up over them and wondered what to do next.

Yanni and Papou drank Metaxa in the café until everything was quiet. They were shocked and angry. And sad. This young girl had come amongst them with nothing but friendship and goodness in her heart, but look what had been given to her - anguish and bruises and pain. They didn't know what to do. Perhaps she will be all right, they said, maybe Vaso will know how to help her. We are men, old men, we are no good at things like this.

CONNIE'S PLACE, 2000

Goodness, not only a new road but a real bus stop too, with plexi-glass windows, red plastic seats and graffiti. Connie is the only person to get off the bus. The others must be going to Irapetra. The driver sticks the hazard lights on, jumps down from his seat and runs into the nearest café for a slurp of coffee and a quick chat with his favourite waitress.

Well, what to do now? First, she must get her bearings. She is sure the bus stop isn't where it used to be. Oh. No, it isn't. She has got off at the wrong place. She looks around, shielding her eyes from the sun with her hand. This is Analipsi. Of course it is. Makrigialos is further down the road. The two villages have grown together, almost become one place, there are no fields between them now. And, see, the little harbour is down there. The crescent of beach stretches out below her, the tiny houses crowding up to the sand, just that small step away from the waves. Oh, and some new buildings too, pushed in amongst the old, bigger and whiter than the others, brightly coloured towels flapping on the balconies. She squints against the sparkling light, searches for Papou's house and the pine tree at his door. But it's too far and her eyes have grown a little weaker over the years.

She'll walk, leave the bus to continue its journey without her. Down the hill, turn to the right and then the left, follow the road and she'll come upon the house in time. It is near the harbour end. In her mind's eye she remembers the harbour as it used to be - battered and crumbling and falling away into the sea, a few scruffy fishing boats tied up against the slimy, green stones. It isn't like that now. Even from this far away, she can see chairs and tables set out along the front, all the umbrellas up. A multitude of pretty boats bobbing up and down on the calm water inside the harbour's sheltering arms.

It's so hot now the sun has risen high in the sky. She had forgotten just how hot Crete could be. Silly her. On the other side of the road she can walk next to the sea, feel the salty sea air ruffling her hair and cooling her neck. She runs across the road and there, right in front of her is The Sun Resort. Christ. It is the German Hotel. It is. She knows it is. Not 25 rooms and a tiny, square pool anymore. There are flag poles and sliding glass doors and taxis at the portico dropping people off - people with big hats and expensive suitcases, no bus from the airport for these holiday makers. She wants to go in but it will have to wait. She has more important things to do.

The memories are jumbled, aren't they? You are confused by this reality in front of your eyes. You were so sure absolutely nothing would have changed. Silly of you to imagine that. It's impossible for things to stay the same. Things change, places change, people change. Look at you, so different now you hardly recognise yourself. Lives change. Lives that could have been one way, turn into something far, far removed from all the wishes and hopes, and no one even notices. Until. Until one day. Until one day when something breaks. For God's sake, Connie. This is huge. This is enormous. You are too far from home to stop it. Do you think you want to turn around, to run? Do you wonder what you'll do if no one is there? If they are all gone? Will they even recognise you? Always supposing you find them. Do you wonder what you will do if they don't want you? Oh, God. You are scared. And you keep on walking because there is nothing else to do. Because it is far too late to run. Because you have always run. From everything. It has to be different now.

She forces herself to put one foot in front of the other. It won't take much for her to panic and turn around, run back to the bus, jump on and go back to Sitia, or get another bus to Heraklion and fly home. It's too late, far too late. If she did that, then all this would have been for nothing. A waste of time. She has already wasted more than 20 years.

Another footstep, another slap of the flip-flops.

What on earth is she doing plodding down this road, in this ridiculous heat, with the blue sea to her left and the bare hills to her right? She should be at home, going to the supermarket, making the beds, preparing the dinner. Not here, in Crete, wearing a big, white hat in the sunshine. The enormity of what she's doing makes her head spin - leaving her poor children, her husband and running off like this - it's madness. It's not as if she's only nipped into town to do a bit of shopping and not told anyone. They wouldn't have worried about that. She often went off by herself for a few hours - I'll be back in a bit, she'd say. Ed had stopped asking where she went and what she was doing. It was pointless. She never told him. He gave up worrying about it. And what did she do in those hours? Perhaps a wander around the park, a little

shopping, maybe a coffee somewhere or a walk with the dog. It was her time. A moment or two scratched out of her day to re charge her batteries, time to sit and think about all sorts of things and not be interrupted by people talking to her, distracting her with everything they wanted.

This is altogether different. And what if they are all gone, all her friends?

The sore patch on her palm had come back recently. She opens her hand and looks at it - red-raw skin, right in the middle where she had raked her nails, over and over again, into the flesh. She hadn't even realise she was doing it until Ed noticed it a few months ago, she couldn't quite remember when it had started again. Strange that since she got the ferry to Crete it had stopped. She pushes her sunglasses further up her nose to keep out the glare from the sparkling waves, and walks on, her mind a-whirl, but her feet taking her closer and closer to Makrigialos.

It's a longer walk than she recalls. Her white shoulders are burning, some grit from the pavement is lodged between her toes, the breeze from the sea blows her dress around and threatens to carry her hat away. If anyone noticed her she could be any tourist out for a lunch time stroll, nothing in her head but the lure of Greek salad and a glass of wine.

She could be heading down to the shop to buy an English newspaper to read in a cafe, nursing a coffee while her husband and children have a swim.

She could be heading to the gift shop to buy a fridge magnet shaped like Crete, or some other useless trinkets for her friends and sweets for her work-mates.

She could be going to the cash machine to get more money for her big Greek night out, maybe wishing for too much Ouzo and a quick kiss with one of the handsome waiters behind the kitchen door.

Or she could be a wistful, middle-aged woman looking for lost friends, lost loves, lost lives. She could be that person.

The bottom of the hill levels out into sun- smoothed, shiny tarmac and another new pavement. A hotchpotch of marble crazy paving - high here, low there, watch your step and be careful, another high bit. It makes Connie shudder slightly. It looks like raw meat.

There are fancy shops selling paintings and elegant little statues of deer and horses and pieces of olive wood carved into bowls and
goblets, another shop full of things for the beach, another full of knock-off sunglasses and fake perfume.

The shoe shop is still there, full of dainty leather shoes sitting on their boxes in the window - a riot of pinks and greens and blues. It hadn't changed much, the shoes had always been pretty. She had gone in with Vaso one day.

'Oh look, Vas, these are lovely.' Such beautiful shoes she had wanted so badly.

'Useless,' Vaso said as she turned them over in her hands, 'pretty. But no good.'

'I want them.' Vaso had tutted and handed the shoe back to her, her eyebrows raised. Connie took the sandals to the assistant, explained that she took a size 8 in England. The girl looked blank, rummaged under the desk, pulled out the measuring machine and strapped her foot in - 42 she said. As the girl lifted up the curtain to go into the stock room and Connie saw boxes and boxes of shoes piled up high, taller than the shop assistant, even taller than her. The girl was gone for ages and came back with only two boxes - these are all we have in a 42, the girl said. She opened the first one and took out an ugly pair of brown, leather sandals - the sort the priests and the old ladies wore, usually with socks. In the second box, a pair of black slippers. Connie laughed - no, you're

joking, that's all in my size? The girl stared at her - you must try the men's section, she said, her face blank. Vaso spoke to her harshly in Greek which Connie didn't quite catch.

Perhaps buying shoes for big feet in England had been just as difficult in those days. Can you remember all those ugly, brown shoes your mother made you wear? Good for the feet, she always said. How many times did she remind you about the size of those feet of yours? Eights, she said, eights! Boy's shoes for you. And you looked down at your feet and wondered if they were really, could possibly be, the biggest feet in the world, wondered if you could chop your toes off, like the ugly sisters in the real Cinderella story. You hated all those shoes. As soon as you had your own money what did you do? Only went out and bought the prettiest shoes you could. A size too small. And now your toes and feet are ruined by years of wearing shoes too tight, too pointy and too high. Silly Connie. Ed laughed at you, didn't he? Got the wrong shoes on again, Connie love, he'd chuckle, as you struggled along

behind him in your unsuitable shoes. Oh, but Ed, they're so pretty, you'd say, ignoring his laughing, and the pain.

No time to go in the shoe shop today.

There's a handmade rug shop. That's new. Hadn't this been nothing but a half-ruined old farm house - room for animals at the bottom and the family at the top? A young man sits at a big wooden loom in the window. She watches for a little while. He pushes the foot-bars up and down, throws the shuttle backwards and forwards, clashes the damper on the shimmering threads. Each pass of the shuttle adds another line to the pattern. It's quite mesmerising, beautiful to see. She glances up at the name above his door, perhaps she knows this man's family. But, no, she doesn't.

And here is a pretty shop full of clothes and hats and jewellry. Tiger's eye, turquoise and coral necklaces and bracelets hanging on a stand in the wide doorway, silver and gold sandals in shining rows beside them, gossamer light scarves in every hue entwined amongst straw hats and bags. A bewildering dazzle of summer colour. Inside the shop it is dark and cool; a woman is standing at her till, glasses perched at the end of her nose, peering down at something with such intent

Connie doesn't want to disturb her and she walks on.

Yiota looks up. Was that a customer coming in? Oh, she's gone. Ah well, perhaps she will come back, she looks back down to her

notepad.

The road is narrowing, the buildings crowding together.They are all painted white and the woodwork is the brightest blue. Surely one of these must be Papou's house. One of these must be the café. There are hand written signs - "Room to rent" or "Sorry. Full." There are china name plaques - "Maria's Apartments", "Brouklis Taverna". Some names so familiar it sets her beating faster and faster.

She's walking slowly, looking all around and taking everything in; people bump into her as they squeeze past on the narrow pavement - "Sorry" they say, or "entschuldigung", or "scusa" and then someone says "signomi". A Greek woman. A woman who might know her but not recognise her. It is all she can do to stop herself grabbing the woman's arm and shouting out loud - egó eímai - it's me, here I am. And then the woman is gone without a backward glance.

She is nearly at the harbour now and still nothing is quite as she wants it. These places don't look right at all, she doesn't recognise any of these buildings - they are not the stubby, square and squat little houses she remembers. These are 3 storeys high and much too new. The outside stone staircases are gone, the small windows are gone, the tiny doorways she had to stoop to get under are gone, there are no old people sitting outside. Some of these places have no doors at all, just wide open spaces to walk through, their modern glass shutters folded back against the walls - she can see straight through to the beach and sea out the back. But she must be here. It must be one of these. It has to be. She can't decide. Nothing is certain. What to do next? She will go around to the beach and look for the tree. It will be there, they never cut down the best trees.

The next left turn and she is on the sand. She is cheered up by the sight of the sea - and it's so close, thank goodness. No one has built a promenade over the golden sand, or a shiny marble pavement here. There are verandas and wooden decking overflowing with pots and pots of bougainvillea and geraniums, all busy with people having drinks and food. But there's no sign of her courtyard, her goat shed or the wrought iron gate down to her patch of sand.

The beach is full of tourists toasting themselves to golden brown in the early afternoon sun. The sea is full of screaming and shouting and splashing and laughing. It is all beach balls and airbeds and kids with blow up armbands running in and out of the gentle water. The waves lapping onto the shore are so inviting - she can't resist. Connie slips off her shoes and walks down to the wet - line, lets the sand squidge up between her bare toes, lets the tiny rippling waves wash over her lumpy, misshapen feet. It feels delightful. It has been too long. Far too long.

Connie had always loved water, always loved swimming. Her mother's insistence on swimming lessons from an early age must have paid off. Standing on the harbour wall and staring down at the oil-slicked and murky water might have made her head spin and her stomach turn, but not standing here, ankle-deep, in this blue and cleansing water.

The sea swirls gently around her feet, stirring up the sand, pulling her feet deeper and deeper into its coolness until she feels like she might topple over. Oh. It's so lovely. There is nothing to do but stand there, taking it all in, soaking up all the sights and sounds and smells. It has been so many years, months, weeks, days, hours, minutes, since this cool water has played over her toes. So long. Her eyes are brimming with all those unshed tears. All the tears she wiped away on her sleeves and never let fall beyond the rim of her specs, are threatening to break free. All those salty tears could be an ocean of their own. Enough now. Her nails dig into the palm of her hand. Enough now. Stop.

She turns her back to the water and walks back onto the dry, hot sand. A middle-aged woman, the colour of mahogany, unties a big blow up ring from the trunk of the huge pine tree. Connie stares. The woman throws the rope coil against the ancient tree's gnarled trunk, slides the ring over her scrawny body and heads off for her swim. Connie's legs feel weak. This is Papou's tree. It is, it has to be. There had never been a tree so big on the beach, she has sat under those branches, nestled amongst those huge roots so many times it is like a good friend.

Not time for crying now. Time for joy.

The tree is festooned with bunting, a horde of sea-side things lie around its trunk - air beds, buckets and spades - a family sit in its shade, mother, father and baby. The child is lying on a towel, asleep in the cool green shade of those comforting branches. Connie wants to run over and ask if she can sit down beside them, maybe pat the tree. The father gets up and goes into the café, up the wooden steps, past the pots of flowers with their vibrant blooms cascading down the handrails.

Is this where Papou's house once stood? It must be, because here is the tree.

She realises now - everything she remembers must have been knocked down and replaced. That must be the answer. And that pretty block of apartments must be where the café had been. Absolutely. Her breath is a sucked away, her head is dizzy and her legs are turned to jelly. She sits down on the sand with a bump, the contents of her bag scattering around her feet. The man is coming back with drinks, he sees her fall.

'Oh my goodness, are you alright?' he says, his voice full of concern, 'would you like a drink?' His wife runs over and starts to pick up Connie's things. The posh frock is sprawled on the sand.

'Oh, dear, your lovely dress,' the woman and shakes it free of grit. The sparkles catch the sun and cast rainbows over all of them.

'I'm fine, sorry,' Connie says, 'just too hot, I only got here today and I walked from Analipsi.' The man holds out the cool lemonade for her. 'Please, drink this.' Connie gulps it down, it's been hours since she had something to drink or eat, no wonder she felt faint.

'Thank you. I must go now, I have to find somewhere to stay.'

They help her up and the woman points to the apartments. 'We are staying just there, very clean, and friendly people, you could do much worse. Reasonable price too.'

Connie looks over. She sees the sign above the doorway,

"Connie's   Place   –   rooms   available"

MAKRIGIALOS, 1976

It seemed that everything carried on as normal over the next few weeks. Connie did her chores, she swam; she sat at the family table and tried to eat, and complained about her aching feet. Visitors came and went. Iakchos and his brothers came to see her most nights, chatting and laughing at the bar as she poured drinks and tidied up. Sometimes she caught Iakchos looking at her with a strange expression on his face. One night he took hold of her hand, she pulled it away.

'Stop it,' she said, 'stop teasing me.'

He frowned at her, 'I am not teasing you. I am thinking that you might want someone to talk to. Remember, I am your friend.'

'I know.' She turned back to the bottles and when she looked around again, he was gone.

How could she tell Iakchos she didn't feel real, that she felt as if she were in a film, watching herself getting on with things? How could she tell Vaso she was afraid to stop doing the things she did every day? Afraid to stop incase her head filled up with the other things - the bad things. She didn't want them creeping in there to keep her awake and make her feel sad. Or angry. Or sick. How could she explain to people when she couldn't make head nor tail of it herself, when she didn't have the understanding or the vocabulary? She refused to speak about it,

refused to do anything other than work and swim. No matter how hard people tried to talk to her about it, how many times they held her hand, or looked concerned, she just shook her head and turned away. And dug her fingernails into her palm and scratched the sore place over and over again. It worried them. It made Vaso swear and curse under her breath. Vaso sometimes started to shout for no real reason - the water was too hot, the plates were too cold, the potato man is an idiot, and the bus is late. Oh, she could shout about anything these days. Connie didn't like Vaso's outbursts, Papou said to leave her alone to get on with it and not to be worried - it is Vaso, it is how she copes, he said and shrugged.

Timos never came anymore. Not since the dog incident. Connie heard from Yanni that Timos was going to Australia in only three weeks and he would be gone for a whole year. Papou said he would be glad if he never came back. Vaso never mentioned it. She just kept on shouting at everyone. But not at Connie. Never at Connie.

The autumn was just around the corner. Tourists were leaving and not many jumped down off the bus now. Yanni had come back from the kafenion in the big village and taken up his regular seat in the café a couple of evenings a week, Papou joined him to play cards and dominos. Only one of Vaso's rooms had visitors and they were going home in a week. The days were still warm, but in the evenings the women came out with shawls over their shoulders or knotted around the straps of their bags. The local girls had started to wear cardigans, even during the day. Soon the awnings would get wound back in, all the outdoor furniture would be put away, and there would be no more pretty flowers on the tables. The village was gradually settling back to normal.

Was it only six months since she clambered off that bus? Papou and Vaso had promised her she could stay - of course she could, she was their friend, almost family. There wasn't anything, or anyone, she wanted to go back to England for. Her mother wrote every now and again, begging her to come back in one sentence, then telling her to stay away in another. Connie didn't care. She would stay here. She must. Makrigialos was everything. That was what she told herself when her mind wasn't whirling and wearing itself out with … with the … with the other thing.

Behind the day-to-day, that other thing drove her like a time bomb's clock. That thing she couldn't say, wouldn't talk about; that thing she was pushing away and trying to ignore just ticked and ticked and ticked. The huge relief at being able to stay in Makrigialos didn't even stop the ticking. It kept on ticking. It was loudest during the night, threatening to overwhelm her as she tried to fall asleep. She tuned her ears to the lonely little Scops owl, hooting his peculiar hoot. She longed to hear an answering call for him. A mate somewhere close by who was listening out for him too. A mate to answer him back and be his forever. One night the hooting was gone. She listened and listened. Nothing. She kneeled up on her pillows and leaned out of the window, ears straining to catch even the slightest peep. Nothing. Only a motorbike roaring up to the big village, the breeze stirring the leaves of the tree outside the gate, the scrape of sea against sand, someone laughing in the café. All normal. But no owl. Poor bird, flying all the way to Africa to spend the winter by himself.

Winter. It was coming, and how would she get to sleep now.

The next visit to the hospital came and went without incident. No crying or tears. Just the taking of a pee sample and a few more questions. Connie still wouldn't talk. Another week would have to pass by and then she would have to talk about it. Then she would have to talk to everyone about it. Vaso couldn't stand Connie's silence, couldn't bear to let things go on like this any longer.

'I need to speak to you, we will be going back to the hospital in 2 days. I have left you alone with this, but now we must talk.'

Connie ignored her and carried on cleaning behind the bar.

'Connie,' she came up behind her and put her hand on her arm, 'come on, let's sit and have coffee and, if it helps, only I will talk.'

She pulled her by the hand like a child to the family table and pushed her down onto a chair. Connie didn't look up, she sat in a slump, head down, shoulders drooping and eyes shut. 'I know. I know you don't want to. I know you are ignoring all of this, but it isn't good for you. It isn't. Look at you. You are worn out - big black rings round your eyes. You think I don't see this? You think I don't watch you pushing your food around your plate? You think I don't see you fading away a little every day? Talk to me. Trust me.'

'I do trust you, Vas. I am more worried about having to go home for the winter, and never coming back, than thinking about this… this thing.'

'But you know you are not going home if you don't want to. How many times have I told you this? Papou has told you this too, time and time again. I think you are worrying about that instead of the other things. You don't want to think about them. It is normal.' Her voice was soothing and calm. Irritating.

'I can't talk about it.'

'You can, Connie. You just don't want to. Your mind is stopping you.'

'Oh, you are a psycho-analyst now?'

'Don't be angry with me, Connie. Be angry with that man. I will help you be angry. I am good at being angry.' She tried to laugh a little. Poor Vaso, she had her own problems, what with Timos leaving and everything, but she was brave and tough.

Connie didn't feel brave. Or tough. She felt like she was clinging on to a big wall by her fingertips, waiting for the sliding to start, and then she would slip, down and down. Unable to save herself. Down into a pit of nothing. Only the sound of her fingernails protesting screech as her requiem.

Vaso brought some coffee and cake for her. The smell made Connie want to retch. 'Connie, listen to me. I understand you don't want to remember what happened. I do. But we will go to the hospital again in a couple of days and what will we do if they tell you …'

'Please, don't say it Vas. Please don't.'

'… what if they tell you are carrying this man's baby?' Vaso wrapped her hand tight round Connie's.

'Oh Vas, I can't. I just can't do this. I can't. Really. The whole thing makes me feel sick to my stomach.' The room started to swirl around her.

'So, I will tell you. They might let you get rid of it, under the circumstances or because you are English. They might. Or they might not. Either way, there is a terrible decision to be made. And that will be up to you.' Vaso didn't take her eyes off Connie and she saw her cringe, her skin blanching to a nasty sallow grey. Poor little thing. This was terrible. Vaso had tried talking to her friends about this dreadful situation, but no one was very helpful. No one wanted to discuss it. They all thought it was awful, of course, and they were sorry. Vaso had

decided that they just wanted to forget all about it - just like Roula. Poor Roula, half-dead amongst the rose petals. But no child left inside her.

Vaso had always got on well with Roula when they were younger - wanted to be a little like her too, if the truth be known. Roula had always been a wild one but she suffered for her independence. Her father had beaten her many times after catching her drinking and flirting with the village boys. Vas knew he had beaten her when this terrible thing happened. Told her it was her fault, a punishment for flaunting herself around the village with her skirts too short and tops too tight. Her fault! Pah! The man was an idiot. The old ones always say this. How dare they? No one did anything helpful when this happened to Roula. Oh yes, they all gossiped about it - serves her right, they said, for taunting the boy until he couldn't control himself. That was why they never bothered to find out who it was, because it was her fault. And only now, when she was crazy-sad with it, they felt sorry for her. Poor Roula, if that thing hadn't happened, she'd be married with plenty of children by now, but she ruined herself, they said. How cruel they are, thought Vaso, how cruel to say this now, when it is too late to help her.

She had spoken to Roula just the other day. She hadn't told Connie. It was the day the linen man came with his big van full of clothes, sheets, tablecloths and fancy goods. He had shouted his list of wares from the open window as he drove slowly into the village and a line of women were already waiting at the corner next to the café when he stopped and threw open his doors. The women poured over the goods, comparing this to that, feeling the quality between their fingers and bracing themselves to haggle him down to a good price. It was a warm day but rain was coming; the sky out to sea was black with clouds rolling closer and closer, they would burst on the mountain tops soon. Vaso was looking at the tablecloths when she spotted Roula coming

towards her - small and skinny, black hair piled up on her head, cardigan pulled tight across her chest. They were almost the same age but Roula looked lined and drawn, always tired and red-eyed.

'Hello, Vaso, how is the English girl?' Even her voice sounded tired. She had been such fun when they were younger. 'I heard straight away, you know. They broke their necks to come and tell me. The same ones that blamed me. But they don't blame the little English Virgin. No. they don't blame her.' She didn't look at Vaso, she kept her eyes down and concentrated on the quality of the fabric and whispered the words out.

'Don't be like that, Roula. It's me you're talking to. I told you to fight them all. I sat with you and held your hands and tried to make you stand up to them. You didn't. It was your choice. And it is not your fault this has happened again.' Vaso put her hand on her arm. A gesture of what? Pity, Friendship? A little anger? Roula shook it away.

'That is what they say isn't it? They say if I had told, then the English one would have been saved from it.'

Some people did say that. And it was cruel. Poor Roula had suffered enough without the blame for this thing falling on her shoulders. Vaso was sick of hearing it. Only a week ago, she had banged two bottles of beer down on a table with such force that one broke, spilling the foaming beer all over that loud-mouth from the big village - I'll not have this talk in here, she had told him, you are stupid to say that and if I hear it again, you will not come back. He had laughed in her face and, before he knew it, she'd grabbed him by the scruff of his neck and pulled him off the chair. She'd screamed and screamed at him and tried to drag him through the door. Connie came running out of the kitchen to see what all the noise was about. Yanni grabbed Vaso. Papou grabbed the man. Vaso broke free and squared up to him, even though he was twice her size, still shouting and cursing and her hands balled into tight, hard fists. He put his hand out to fend her off and Papou pushed him away and out into the street. Vaso sat down on the nearest chair puffing and panting. There was silence. No one knew what to do. Then she burst out laughing - Ha, she said, wiping her hands together in a big gesture, he won't come back. See, this is what you will get if you talk those terrible words in front of me. She pointed at them all. They giggled. Only a tiny bit. They were a scared of her and knew what she said was true.

'Roula, do you want to fight now? Do you want to try, it might help Connie?' She had been thinking about this for ages. If it was the same person maybe it would help them both. It was that simple for Vaso. Get them both together to talk about what had happened to them and they would help each other. Easy.

'Vaso. You are not as clever as you think you are.' Roula dropped the socks back onto the shelf and picked up a nightdress. Vaso stared at her, riveted by the quiet voice. 'You think I don't know who it was? Of course I do.' She took the nightie to the van man, paid and walked away. Vaso stood open-mouthed for split-second, then chased after her. She tried to make her stop but Roula carried on walking, head down, thin shoulders hunched, and speaking fast and quietly out of the corner of her tight lips. Like a spy. Did she think they would drag her away and stand her in front of a firing squad? Roula spat the name out as if it was burning in her mouth like poison and scurried away without looking back. Oh. She must tell Connie she knew who it was. Maybe it was the same one? When should she tell her? Soon.

The coffee remained untouched as Vaso talked. She didn't give Connie any time to get up and walk away, shaking her head and waving her hands to ward people off. But it was useless. Connie kept her head bowed and thought of all the countries she knew that started with the letter A, then B, then C. Vaso might as well have been have been
speaking Chinese. There was no getting through to her. Again.

'Connie. One day you will need me and I will be here. Until then I might as well be quiet, but we will be at the hospital the day after tomorrow, you will have to speak to someone then.'

Connie looked up, 'No, I won't. I can't,' she muttered. 'Can you do it for me? Can you tell me what to do? Maybe everything will be all right if you tell me what to do.' A tear rolled off her cheek and dripped onto her arm. Vaso thought her heart would break.

'No. Connie. I can't. I can't tell you what to do. You have to decide. You have to think about it.' Another tear splattered down. Vaso didn't know who it belonged to. It might have been one of hers.

'Please, Vas. Please, tell me what to do. I want you to. What would you do?'

Vaso knew what she would do. She would hunt that man down like a dog and she then would kill him. No, she wouldn't go to prison, not for someone like him. She would make sure he went to prison. No, maybe that wouldn't happen here, in this village, in this time - people would think she deserved it too. Like Roula. They would want it hushed up, swept under the carpet. They would tell her to forget about it. Maybe they would tell her it wasn't all that bad. Oh, he would be shunned. Then he would creep back into their homes and lives as if nothing had

happened, but with a couple of black eyes and bruised ribs he couldn't explain away, while the village boys shook the dust off their clothes and the wiped the blood off their knuckles. Maybe he would see her, pass her in the street and smirk at her, knowing she was powerless to do

anything to him. Knowing he was a man and she was only a girl and he was the one who had won. Because men always won. Pah. It is wrong. All wrong. Better to kill him – quietly and with no fuss.

'It doesn't matter what I would do, Connie. I know bottling this up will only bring you harm. I know that much.'

'How do you know? Why can't I just forget about it?'

'Maybe if everything is all right at the hospital. If there is no baby, perhaps you can forget about it.' Even as she said it, Vaso didn't believe it. 'But it is too much for you to forget. You must make a plan and believe me, if I could do all this for you I would.'

Do what? Vaso thought. There was nothing she could do. It was going to be forgotten about and only Connie would remember what had happened. And she could only help Connie if she made her talk about it. Bullied her. That's what Roula had said when it happened to her - you are a bully, Vaso, a bully who only wants to help me so you have something else to think about, so you don't have to think about your dead father and your family living God knows where. Only an old man, and a boyfriend who can't wait to get away from you for company. Ha! Help me? No, Vaso, it is something to think about other than your own life, only to help you. Vaso had been upset. She was a nasty piece of work that Roula. It wasn't true. Was it?

'I will help you all I can, but you must help yourself a little bit. You must.'

Connie sighed. She knew Vaso was right. Of course she did but she didn't think she had enough strength to do anything. She felt so ill and sick all the time. She just wanted to lie on her bed and stare at the ceiling. Wanted to lie there and let everything go on around her. Let them look after her and pet her and make her feel better. She wanted to fly away like the little Scops Owl - stand on the windowsill and fling herself in the air and soar away into the dark, far above everything, leave the earth behind, disappear into the velvet sky and never touch the ground again. Or be like the fish - lie back into the warm sea, let it fold over her head and pull her deeper and deeper into its quiet, still blue.

'I don't want to talk about it until we go to the hospital. Please.'

Vaso nodded, 'I saw Roula, you know. I asked her if she wanted to come and see you. I thought you might be able to help each other. She told me who it was who left her in the rose garden....'

Connie stood up and shook her head. 'No Vas. That's enough. I never want to talk to Roula. What does it matter who did what? To her or me. It won't make any difference. It still happened and if there's … if there's … something else, we'll find out soon enough and then I'll have to decide. Speaking to Roula won't help.'

Vaso gave in. Connie left her sitting at the table, the untouched coffee and cake in front of her, and headed back into the kitchen to carry on with her jobs.

That girl is in shock, Vas thought, as she sipped the hot coffee and ate the cake. But, what to do? What to do? The more she thought about Connie, the less she thought about Timos. Roula was almost right. But Vaso was not a bully. She was tired, and sad and worried and all the things she didn't like to be. All the things she ran away from. But not a bully. She hoped.

Poor Connie. You don't know what these feelings are, you can't put a name to them. You just feel what you feel and think what you think. You can't question what is happening inside your head, because you are young and you don't have the vocabulary for these things yet. Unless you are going mad. You can't tell Vaso these thoughts of yours, maybe she will think you are crazy. Vaso - so black or white, so right or wrong. So, what do you do? You try to carry on with all these things spinning and spinning like plates on sticks. And you will get weaker and weaker and one day the plates will fall and you might fall with them. There is another path you can take - you can just drop the plates, pick up the shattered pieces and make them into some armour-plating for yourself. Glue them on your tender skin like a shell.

THE MEETING, MAKRIGIALOS, 2000

The man and his wife hand her over her bag - they are cheerful and hope to bump into her later at the bar, they say. Connie can barely manage a nod of thanks she is so transfixed by the sign with her name on it. There it is, as bold as brass, Connie's Place. As she stands and stares a gust of wind pulls at her hat and bowls it along the sand towards the sea - oh, she gasps, and turns to chase it. A tall, skinny young man puts his hand down and scoops it up. He waves it at her.

'Your hat.' He smiles as he hands it back.

'Efharisto, thank you, you're very kind. I shouldn't have worn it really. Too windy. But I'm on holiday and everyone needs a holiday hat.' He is a black silhouette against the sun. 'You're welcome. Enjoy your holiday.'

She watches him walk away and up the steps into Connie's Place. As he pushes the door open, she hears a woman's voice shouting to him in Greek. 'Where've you been? I have been waiting ages and ages for you to get here and finish this. All this needs to be painted
before Papa can put the new pictures up.'

'I know. I'm here now aren't I? Stop shouting.' The invisible woman laughs. Then the door swings shut and the glimpse of life in 'Connie's Place' is gone.

Connie looks back at the apartments and then at the café. What to do? Go in there and book a room? Or go in there and order lunch? She is quite hungry. She shoves the wayward hat into her bag. She doesn't know what to do. What if it is the wrong thing? Should she go away? What should she do? She stands there, staring at the sign.

Connie's Place. There is only one Connie's Place. And this is it. The people she is looking for might be somewhere inside - if they haven't all gone away, sold everything to strangers and moved into a big villa on the hillside. The world around her has faded away as she wonders what to do - there are no kids squealing, no smells of hot doughnuts and coffee, no blue skies and no waves lapping. There is nothing but her name on the wall and the sound of the blood swishing in her ears.

The door swings open and a woman comes out - small, plump and pretty, dark hair showing a little grey. The world comes back to Connie in a rush. It is out of her hands now, because this is Vaso. Unmistakable. The moment has arrived. No amount of preparation for this. Connie doesn't hesitate. Doesn't flinch from it. Doesn't think about it. Just does it.

'Vas? It's me. Connie.' Her voice is a little too loud and it stops the woman in her tracks. The woman looks at her, a frown pushes at her brows, her eyes shoot open wide, her mouth turns into an 'O', her bag falls out of her hand and bounces down the steps to Connie's feet. Her hand flies up to her heart.

'O thee mou,' she says. 'Bastarde.' Vaso shuts her eyes. Connie waits.

'Connie? You are still there? I can't believe it. Am I dreaming?' She opens her eyes again.

'It's me.'

'Kero ehume na ta pume. Long-time no see, Connie.' Vaso is not smiling, her voice sounds hard and her face is white.

Oh God, is she angry? Ah well, it's done now. Time to accept what's coming, and if it's bad you'll just have to go home again.

'I know. I am so sorry.' There was nothing else to say.

'For God's sake, Connie. What are you thinking? Are you crazy? For God's sake. Sweet Jesu Christ.' Vaso comes down the last of the steps and puts her hands up onto Connie's shoulders, looks right into her eyes and kisses her. One cheek, then the other, then again. 'Mou eleipses. I've missed you. It has been a long time.' she whispers. And Connie, her arms still by her sides, rests her cheek against the woman's. The years fall away and in that space, for that second, all Connie can hear is the sighing of their breath and the beating of their hearts.

Vaso pushes her away. 'Bastarde. I thought I was going to die. Well, you had better come in. You have come a long way - you will be staying for a while. You will need a room. I have one. Come on. I am still angry with you so don't think that this is all I have to say. I have plenty to say to you. You have taken too long. Why did you take so long? Why have you come now? No. Don't tell me. Do you have any idea how many tears I've cried waiting for you to come back? Another few letters would have done. I have a good mind to send you away. If Papou was here to see this he would be kissing you all over, but not me. I have not forgiven you. Oh no, I have not. Absolutely not.' She takes Connie's hand and leads her into the cool interior of the apartments. Such a pretty little place - with her name written above the door.

So, the wait is over. All of a sudden the time has passed. The 'now' you have longed for is here. Let yourself be swept up in this new now, Connie. Pay no heed to the next month, week, day, hour or minute. There's no shouting or crying. Everything is calm and understated because this is life, not a film or a TV series. These moments are your life and neither you nor Vaso can possibly know what to do.

Connie lets Vaso pull her along, sit her at the new family table, bring her coffee, drag a chair close to hers, lets Vaso keep talking and talking. Because that's what Vaso wants to do. She can't leave a moment's gap in the chattering for fear that it fills up with the left-over recrimination, sadness or anger. Not a split second to let the hurt spill out into the now. They both know that will have to come, because during the passing of the time they have turned into grown-ups and things will have to be discussed. That's what adults do isn't it? And there are all the others to include. All the people to make things up to, to make things right for. It can wait. For this now, and in this moment, it is greetings, little kisses and gentle hugs.

It's all Connie can do to keep up with Vaso's tales of this done, that done, who is alive, who has died, all the young ones grown up and married with a million children - honestly, Connie you have no idea how much everything has changed since you left, Vaso says, no idea at all.

Vaso tells her about Papou - he never got over you leaving, you know, she says, tears in her eyes. He was so worried about you. So worried. Connie nods - I know, I wrote to him a few times, I tried to make him believe I was all right. Vaso hugs her - enough, no tears, no sadness today, because I am so happy you are here, and I wish the old ones were still here to see you again.

Connie tells her about Ed and her own children at home in England. They talk in Greek and English about the weather, the new apartments, the old pine tree and the new road - all the ordinary things. Connie feels the buried, invisible words trying to crawl to the surface. There would be nothing ordinary left to talk about soon, and then there would be everything to say. Vaso stands up. Does she feel them too? Come on, I'll take you to your room, she says, have a rest, and we'll chat again later.

This is a good idea. The time is coming for the big things.

Don't be scared Connie, isn't this why you've come all this way? Isn't this why you've left your husband and children at home? So you can put things right. So you can find out what's been happening in the world outside yourself and those things you've kept in her head for so long? You'll need a rest, you'll need to be ready for the real talking to start.

The room is pretty - pale blue and white bedcovers, a big flowery armchair in the corner and the photo of young Papou with his rosy-cheeked bride hanging on the wall. Outside on the terrace a table and chairs painted the colour of the sea and sky, pots of flowers and steps leading straight onto the beach. She tells Vaso how lovely it is. Better than your old goat shed, Vaso says, and laughs.

Poor Connie, you want it to be the old goat shed don't you? You want things to be just as they were. You are pining for the days before anything went wrong, before everything got messy and difficult. You want to feel what it was like when you first got here. Feel how you were in those days - young and excited by a world you had never come across before. A world of happy, smiling people who loved each other and looked after each other. A world where you felt truly free, really happy, for a while - until the sadness came rushing in and pulled you back. All these years you have been hiding your sadness behind smiles and tall tales, hiding all the truths that you are so afraid of. The truths you have spent a whole lifetime too frightened to let anyone else find. And all the time Vaso has been happy that everything is not like the old days.

Vaso fusses around her, curses a little more, kisses her again - rest, she says, there'll be time for everything else you need to do tomorrow, and then she is gone, blowing a kiss as she closes the door.

Connie takes her sweaty clothes off. She has a shower and lies on top of the bed letting the warm breeze dry her. The curtains billow in and out of the open patio doors, catching on the armchair. It crosses her mind that this might be Papou's old chair. She can hear the world enjoying itself outside. Lying in this cool room she could be an alien arrived from a desolate, lonely planet and thrown into a world of light and noise. Lying on this bed, the sea full of happy people only a few feet away, she is overcome by tears. She's sorry she has come back, she doesn't feel any better yet.

But that's silly. Of course you don't, because everything is still to happen.

She pulls the sheet over herself, wipes her eyes and falls asleep; the sounds of that other planet fade away.

Vaso goes to the dining room and finds her son and her husband. They are working hard together to get the paint work refreshed and those new pictures hung.

'Come here, sit down. I have something important to tell you.

CONSETT, 2000

E d is alone in the quiet house. The kids have gone to his Mam and Dad's for tea. He wants to cry. She put the phone down on him. Put the bloody phone down when he was trying to talk to her. Christ. What a bloody mess. What the hell is she playing at? What should he do? What the hell is going on? Where the hell is she?

She's in Crete, Ed. She's in Crete looking for something, someone. Maybe she's finding someone, something? Something she has lost or misplaced or forgotten about for far too long.

What the bloody hell? He stands in the middle of the room. A room that only yesterday was so commonplace and so ordinary, has become the most peculiar place in the world. He waits, maybe he'll have an idea? He sighs, not looking at anything, not noticing anything - his entire head might as well be full of wool and barbed wire. Christ. He doesn't know whether to be angry or sad. For God's sake! This is stupid. What about the kids? They're frightened to death. What if she kills herself? Hang on a minute. Why would she? She's not depressed. No, just bloody nuts. He raps his knuckles on his head - come on, Ed, pull yourself together. It's time for action. Right. Think, Ed, think. He gets his coat and gives the front door an extra big slam as he goes out.

The kids are sitting round the table, puffy - eyed and pale, poking their food round their plates, not interested. The telly blares in the
corner. They look up at him when he comes in. His heart could break for them - poor buggers, it's only been a day. They've had to talk to policemen, they've had to listen to their dad screaming and shouting, grandma crying and grandad just being mean. Time to put a stop to all this. He knows exactly what to do.

'She's always been a bit of a one,' his Dad was saying, as Ed pulls up a chair at the table, 'weird and trouble. Oh yes, she hid it well, but I could always see through her. Trouble from the start -' Stella tells him to shut up. '- and you're just like her. Full of fancy ideas, above your station you are, my girl.'

Ed is furious. 'Shut up, Dad, everyone's upset enough without you shoving your twopenn'orth in, stop.'

'You've always been too soft. Big girl's blouse as far as I'm concerned. You should have put your foot down from the start. Put her in her place.'

'Like you do with Grandma.' Stella muttered, not quite under her breath. The two younger ones snigger - Grandad terrifies everyone except Stella and Mam.

'I'm warning you, Dad. Shut up, right now. Come on, kids, get your stuff. We're going home. No use sitting around here moping. I've spoken to your mother,' the kids' faces break into smiles, 'yes, she rang, and she's in Crete. Somewhere she went when she was young, before she met me and we had you lot. She says she wanted to go there to see if we would like it. And she says we will, so we are going to catch up with her.' The lie comes easily. Come on Ed. Keep going. Keeping thinking. The mouths drop open. Ed's Dad starts to bluster.

'No Dad. Shushh. That's what she said. And that's what we're going to do. She knows she's gone about this in the wrong way, she knows everyone is upset and cross with her. But, y'know what, blaming her won't change it. So let's just get on with it, shall we. Let's just go and find her.'

'But I hate the heat, Ed,' his Dad says.

'It doesn't matter. You and Mam aren't coming. This is about me, Connie and the kids. And you can keep out of it. Both of you.' The kids look at each other, Ed is hardly ever angry in front of them, except for yesterday.

His mother starts to snivel, 'I've always liked her, Ed,' she says in her tiny mouse voice.

'No, you haven't, Mam. You've done nothing but tell her off, tell how she could be a better cook, better cleaner, better mam, better wife, dress better, lose weight, put on weight. You've never done anything but criticise her. And I just let you. I just let you grind my girl down. Let you try to turn her in to you. Well. That's it. It's finished. It's over and we -' he pulls the kids towards him, '- we can fix it.'

He's right, of course. He has just stood by whilst his Connie, his girl, has been rubbed away. Time to swipe that pen across a new page. Ed. Good man.

Stella hugs him. He's always been so soft and gentle. There were times she wanted to tell Mam off for treating him badly. She could sulk a lot, Mam could. Sometimes for days. Dad hated it but he never knew what to do. What's the matter with her, Dad, she'd ask, and he'd shrug his shoulders - I don't know, love, she gets like this sometimes, it's the way she is, he'd say, and give her a quick kiss, don't worry. But she did worry. All the time. Mam was so up and down - full of life and laughing one day, silent and grim the next. There were two Mams, happy mam and sad mam - it was so confusing. Happy Mam sometimes stayed for months and months. That was great. They had the best times - trips out, picnics at the seaside, walks in the woods with the dog panting behind them as they hunted for mini-beasts, and searched for pretty leaves to make pictures. And the times they all piled on the big bed and Mam made up stories for them. Then it would end. Mam would wake up one day and stop talking. She would sit at the back door, smoking and

drinking black coffee and forget to make their packed lunches or iron their clothes. It was like she was in a daze. Stella hated it. After a couple of days of that, Mam would start shouting at them all - she was horrible then - shouting and screaming about something insignificant that the week before she wouldn't have given a hoot about. They would look at each other, roll their eyes and keep out of her way. Dad always had a plan, things they could do, when Mam was like that. He took time off work, he had lists and rotas for housework, cooking and walking the dog. He soaked up all their anxiety, protected them from her worst moods and tried to find out what was wrong. Stella could hear them talking at night when she was supposed to be asleep. Mam always angry and arguing and poor Dad trying to keep calm, trying to cajole some sense out of her. Ed never let the kids see him upset or angry with her, they never saw him at his worst, drinking beer and crying in the kitchen, while his wife lay upstairs like Sleeping Beauty. If only a kiss could make her better.

Stella remembered the time Mam went to bed for three days and refused to get up, didn't get washed and didn't eat, didn't seem to move at all. Stella had peeped in at her and saw her lying motionless and fully clothed on the bed, staring at the ceiling. Dad got the Doctor but he just gave her some tablets she wouldn't take. Claire was crying and begging Dad to make Mam get up - she was scared she was dying. James had built a camp down the bottom of the garden, he said he was going to sleep in there till Mam was better. Dad said that was fine, as long as he came in for his tea and brushed his teeth before bed. That time had been the worst. Dad had called them all into the kitchen, pulled them into one of his tightest hugs and said - look I know you're scared, but Mam gets tired, she worries about things, when she's had a rest and a little think, she'll be fine. He promised. And she was. Stella had heard her whistling in the shower a couple of days later. Mam liked whistling, she could whistle like an old man with lots of vibrato and trills, it made them laugh. "A whistling woman and a crowing hen, neither are fit for God nor men" Mam used to say. It was something her mother had said to her, probably to make the whistling stop. And she was back to normal. Until the next time.

Had she always been like that, from the very beginning? Of course, she had. What had Ed first loved about her? Her wildness, her readiness to do things, her fearlessness, that ability she had to take anything on. He had thought of her as brave and tough in those early days. It was only later, when he knew her better, that he realised it was all an act. A cover up. A game she played to keep herself crumbling into a pile of dust. A game that always wore her out until she did start to

disintegrate. These days, he recognised her starting to fall apart before she did and he coped with it all. The silent Connie wasn't too bad, but the angry, harsh Connie was awful. He struggled to understand that Connie. It was as if she were trying to rebuild herself as a tougher person. His soft and gentle nature rubbed up against her abrasiveness when she was like that and seemed to make her worse, more angry. It made him sad that his gorgeous girl could envelope herself in such a hard and horrible skin. He wanted to slough it away and reveal all her shine underneath - all that fantastic, glorious shine. He told himself that she couldn't help it. He tried to talk to her about it, but she wouldn't - leave it, Ed, was all she would say. It didn't last long, a week, maybe ten days, and then she would come back to them - kind and loving and full of remorse.

As the years passed and disintegration occasionally turned into total collapse, he thought she might be suffering from an unknown mental illness. His Mam said Connie had an 'artistic temperament', whatever the hell that meant. His Dad thought she was mad - artistic temperament, my eye, bloody bonkers, Ed, he said, tell her to pull herself together. Ed had just sighed, neither of them had a clue. But, the good times were so good they forgot how bad the bad times could be. Until she stopped whistling.

What had happened to make her this way? Was it being married to him? Good old Ed, quiet, reliable, and dull. The man who can fix lots of things, washing machines, cars, broken toys. The man who can plaster a wall, build a shed and dig a garden. The man who can keep going to his boring job, day after day, without complaining. The man who can get the kids ready for school, make the tea, put the washer on, but can't sweep her off her feet, can't show her how much he cherishes and needs her. The man who can make things and fix things, but can't fix her.

Did you say, 'fix her' Ed? Fix her? She would be furious if she heard you say that.

And what did he really know about her? Only what she'd told him. The bits of her life she offered to share were few and far between. After a drink or two the odd little thing would slip out, a little snippet would be offered. Those moments were to be treasured, when they did come, even though they made him feel so sad for her. And angry at the adults in her life, who didn't have a clue what the hell they were doing.

A mother whose first child had died and whose husband left, leaving her alone with her grief and a spare toddler. A mother who couldn't love another child again - just in case. A mother who pushed the little girl away, who couldn't hug her or kiss her. A mother who was lonely and longed for a man to take her on and wondered if Connie's presence put them off.

A father who took his grief into another family and spoiled that one too, with his drinking and his anger. A father who never came to see his surviving, warm, flesh and blood daughter because she looked too much like the dead child. Parents who died too early, before she could get to know them and forgive them.

Ed knew about Crete. But he was sure it wasn't the whole story. He thought Connie told tall tales about this and that. Lies, really. Lies to make herself feel better. She only talked about all the good things, the times when everything was an adventure and fun and exciting. All stories she liked to tell when the beer was flowing and there were people to entertain.

Then there was that box upstairs, the one he'd made for her. It had a few creased photos in and some tatty airmail letters - the spidery writing definitely Greek. Every now and again he would catch her rifling through it, looking at the photos or reading a letter, but she would put them away and slam the lid down if he came too close. Show me, Connie, he'd asked once, and she had laughed and said no. Just old times, Ed, nothing important. One day he waited until she had gone out, crept upstairs and took the box down from the top of the wardrobe. His heart racing, he opened it up and looked at everything inside. He felt like a thief stealing her life - half an eye out the window, half an ear on the traffic.

The photos were small and tinged a greeny-brown. He picked up the first one, on the back she had written "Makrigialos, Crete. June 1976". So, she was only just seventeen. He flipped it over and his heart lurched. There she was, a Connie he had never known, so young and carefree, long hair flowing, skinny hip bones jutting through her maxi-dress, one hand shading her eyes, laughing at something he knew nothing about.

In another she was sitting at a blue table, outside in the sunshine, surrounded by flowers, a big floppy hat hiding some of her face, and a man standing behind her with his hands on her shoulders. A handsome young man. That moment caught forever. A moment when he did not exist for her. He checked the back, "Iakchos and me 1977" was scrawled across it and little heart drawn in the corner. Obviously a boyfriend.

He picked up the next one - two people standing side by side, a small woman glowering at the camera and an old man staring straight into the lens. Ed could imagine them telling her to hurry up and take the bloody photo. "Vaso and Papou" written on the back in her loopy, childish handwriting and underneath, in a much neater hand, someone had written something in Greek.

The last photo was the same woman holding a tiny baby, just a date on the back, March 1977. There were a few trinkets too, a brooch, more letters he couldn't read and a tiny square of blue cloth.

He turned the things over and over in his hands, trying to make sense of them, trying to understand, wanting to know so much. The air-mail letters, so thin and flimsy, were crammed with words he couldn't make head nor tail of. One postcard of Makrigialos, Crete had been sent to her mother's address and had five words written on the back "Pou eisai? Where are you?"

What did it all mean? Who were these people? And why wouldn't she talk about them? He couldn't ask her. She would know he had been snooping and she'd be really angry. He always thought she would tell him in time. But she never did.

When they get back to the house, Ed says - right, I'm not quite sure what to do, kids, but I've got a plan. Hurray, they shout, a Dad - Plan. A Dad - Plan made them feel safe, meant something was getting done and everything was going to turn out all right in the end. He sends Stella upstairs for the jewellery box - all the clues they need will be in there. Easy Peasey Lemon Squeezy he says to Claire and tickles her
under the chin. They crowd round the kitchen table, holding their breath as Ed opens the box, he makes a screeching noise like a rusty hinge - stop it Dad, Stella says, this is serious, but she is laughing. Ed

passes the photos around to the children; they can't believe these scraps of photos are of their mother.

'Dad, look, she's really young, and her hair! It's so long and it's blonde!'

'We were all young once, love. I never knew she ever had blonde hair either. She likes a secret does your Mam. Have you seen the date?'

'She's only a bit older than me. Isn't she pretty? Did she look like that when you met her, Dad?'

'No, Stella, she most definitely did not. She had jet black spiky hair and safety pins through her nose. But she was still just as pretty.' They laugh. Stella wonders how on earth her mother could have ever been as young as her; Claire and James giggle at the old-fashioned clothes. And Ed? He is remembering the night he met her, standing there in front of him in that hot nightclub, tall and beautiful, with no shoes on. Looking straight into the very depths of him with those green eyes.

They love her so much.

While Connie is waiting in Piraeus for the ferry to take her to Crete, her husband nips down to the Shopping Mall and books a fortnights holiday to Makrigialos. Lovely, very quiet, the travel agent says, perfect for young ones. He presses a few buttons on his computer - and look at that, I can get you a late deal. It's a very early flight though. Let's see if I can get you that holiday. More buttons tap and it's done. It cost an arm and a leg, it would clean out the bank account, and Ed doesn't care.

While Connie is talking to the German man about dolphins and his dead wife, Ed and the kids are packing. Not that they have much to take, never mind, they can buy stuff there. Now they know their mother is all right and dad has a plan, they chatter and laugh and push and shove. Stella admires the pictures of the hotel - The Sun Hotel. It looks quite posh, they'd definitely never been to a place like that before. It's even got a spa. And entertainment on a night time. And it's full board. They usually go self-catering. This is going to be lovely. She forgets to worry about her mother, and forgets to be angry.

Good old Ed, getting things under control and sorting things out. Of course he can do it. He's made a plan.

At the hospital the news had been the worst it could be - no, they said, we cannot get rid of this for you. You must go home to England to sort that out. You have only eight more weeks to decide.

On the way home they didn't talk, there was no crying, no shouting, not this time. Connie sat stony-faced and still and stared through the car window, Vaso kept her eyes on the road. When they got back, Connie went straight to her room without speaking to anyone and stayed there. Vaso sat at the table and told Papou everything - we must leave her alone, he said, she must decide what to do for herself.

The days came and went. Connie sat in her room and thought and thought and thought, about nothing at all and everything. Vaso and Papou came to see her with food and drinks, begged her to get washed, get dressed and urged her to come out. But she wouldn't. Connie said she would decide in six weeks and until then she would stay in her room. Her friends and neighbours came to see her, knocked on her door and shouted to her through the window. She sent them away. The only person who could get through the door was Iakchos - no, he said to Vaso, she told me nothing, she didn't answer my questions, she cried and then she held my hand and went to sleep.

People popped into the café and asked about her, Vaso didn't know what to say to them. She is fine. Just tired. But she told Papou she thought the madness had taken her. Maybe she was a little bit right.

On the day Timos left for Australia he came to see Vaso. She was too tired to be angry with him anymore, she cried and clung to him, begged him not to go. She loved him. She knew she did. He promised to come back, he loved her too and he couldn't remember why he had been so angry. He was sorry he'd wanted Connie to go home, he was sorry he'd thought he could tell Vaso what to think and do. He was just jealous because Vaso worried so much about Connie, and had been so angry with him. Vaso looked up at him through all the tears - hadn't Papou already told her this? You were being ridiculous, stupid man, she said. He knew, he knew - you can look after Connie when I am away, he said, and it'll stop you worrying about me all the time.

When he'd gone and she had dried her eyes, she rang Phillipos in Australia - please don't keep him there, she begged, please send him home to me. Phillipos promised. One year and that was all - one year to get the itches out of his feet and to make some money.

Timos had left his skinny, black dog with Vaso. The poor thing followed her around all day, its long thin tail tucked between its back legs, and its big brown eyes watching the door. It was pitiful to see. It ran to the windows every time it heard a footstep - was it Timos coming round the corner? Poor dog, pining for its master. It drove Vaso mad with its moping about, not to mention the black hairs all over everything. The last straw was the teeth marks in a table leg. She knocked on

Connie's door and went straight in without waiting for an answer, giving Connie no chance to tell her to go away or to leave her alone. She was lying on the bed, staring at the ceiling.

'Look, this dog is driving me crazy with its barking and crying, it's always under my feet and it leaves hairs all over the place. You must look after it for a while. You will be company for each other.' She dragged the dog in. It jumped up beside Connie and thumped its tail on the bed.

'See, it's happy already.'

'What's its name?'

'I have no idea. Timos just called it Puppy.' Connie ran her hand over the smooth, black head and tickled its ears. As soft as velvet. 'Oh, well, I suppose you can stay with me, Puppy.' The dog lay down beside her, thumped his tail on the bed and shut his eyes.

'Good, that's settled then. It's your dog now.'

Now Connie had to open her door every day, had to let the fresh air in and the dog out. The food Timos left for him would soon get eaten up, she would have to go out and buy more meat and biscuit. And he had to be played with. He brought her an old tatty ball over and over again. If she ignored him, he pushed his long nose under her hand and she couldn't help but give in. She threw it out of the door for him time and time again and as it bounced along the sand he jumped and leapt and barked until he found it. He was happy. At night she shoved him off the bed and onto the floor, but after a minute or two she could feel him cautiously put one paw up, and then another. He would climb on, as gently as could be, and nestle himself next to her, pushing his nose against her hand until she lifted it up and stroked his soft, silky head. And there he stayed.

After three days she opened her door and came outside herself. The sun was shining, she was clean and tidy - washed, dressed, hair brushed. The dog ran out behind her and scampered around her feet. Come on, she said to him, we have things to do.

She walked over to Papou's house, tapped on the door and went in. He looked up from his paper.

'Come, sit. I will make you some English tea.' Papou was surprised, but he said no more for fear she took fright and ran away back to her room forever.

'Lovely,' she said and settled into her favourite chair - the biggest, floweriest one. It cheered her up just to look at it. The dog lay down at her feet, his eyes, the colour of amber and caramel, fixed on her, attentive to every little move she made.

All was quiet, except for Papou rattling the cups and filling the teapot. Neither of them spoke. They both felt the importance that the next few minutes could have - the consequence of the next few words might shape the world for all of them. He poured the tea.

'Papou, I have made up my mind. I'm going to let this baby come and I'm going to stay here. First I will tell you who it was. I have remembered everything. Once I tell you, it will never be mentioned again. We will ignore it and that will make me happy. We aren't going to tell anyone, not even Vaso, and we'll carry on as if everything is normal. This baby can't help what has brought it into the world, any more than I can help what happened.' She talked quickly and quietly, wanting to get all the words out before she changed her mind. 'This man will get his come-uppance one day but no good will come of us saying anything. No one will care. So we'll forget about him. We'll be happy for this new life to come into the world, and maybe things like this won't happen by the time it grows up.'

There. It was said. She was finished. She sipped her tea, her hands rested on her belly and her eyes were bright and shiny. Not with soft tears, but with hard glints of diamond and flint. Papou stared at her, and took a great big gulp of his tea. He swallowed it down and cleared his throat, 'if that is what you want, then that is what we will do. Have you told Vaso about this?'

'No, not yet. We'll go in a minute after I tell you who it was. I'm going to write it down and then I'm going to burn it.'

If Papou thought this was an odd thing to do, it didn't register in his face. He reached into his bureau, found an old envelope and a pencil and watched Connie write the name. She pressed the pencil down so hard he thought it might break.

His eyes opened up wide under his beetling brows. Not him? No. Not that one? He seemed a nice fellow. His mother looked after him well. He started to speak...

'No. Papou. It is over.' She took the paper from him, went into the kitchen and set fire to it over the stone sink. The black crumbles of paper curled and floated into the washing up water and that was that. It was gone.

'Come on Papou. Get ready, put your hat on. Let's go and see Vaso.'

CONNIE'S PLACE, 2000

Connie sleeps for hours in Vaso's best room, when she wakes up it is dark and quiet. She peers at her watch in the gloom. 9.00 'o' clock. People will be getting ready to go out for their evening meals and holiday cocktails. She could just turn over and go back to sleep, start afresh tomorrow. All the melancholy and loneliness haven't been driven away by her nap - she shouldn't have left home, shouldn't have left Ed and the kids. She feels cast adrift.

It isn't like the olden days, is it Connie? And that's what you want. Well, it's time to stop and let the past catch up. It's no good lying here under this sheet, in this room, heartsick and sorry and frightened of what might happen if you go downstairs. Come on. Get up. No good lying here worrying about the mess you think you've made.

She swings her legs out of the bed and feels the cold tiles on the soles of her feet. Like an electric shock. There is a little tap on the door.

'Connie? Are you awake?' She wants to say No she isn't, and go back to sleep. Instead, she pulls the sheet round her and opens the door.

'Ahh. You have been sleeping. Good. Get dressed, come down. I have a surprise for you.' Vaso is smiling and looking pleased with herself.

'Oh Vaso. I don't know if I'm up to this. Maybe, it will be too much.'

'Oh, don't be silly. Everyone is so excited you are here. I've been on the phone all afternoon. So many people want to see you.'

It is true. Vaso has rung everyone she can think of. Everyone. They are all shocked and surprised, and as curious as they had been all those years ago when she first turned up.

Connie? No? Not Connie?

English Connie?

What? Connie has turned up and is here? In Makrigialos?

What's that you say? Sleeping in your Best Room? No!

Goodness me! What will happen now Vaso?

Where has she been?

Oh My!

Connie gives in. Vaso is still as forceful as ever. It's creeping up to them, the time they will need to talk about the important things. It could be tonight.

'OK. Give me 20 minutes to get ready.' She tries to smile.

'I know it will be strange for you, for all of us.' Vasou gives her a quick hug and kisses her cheek. 'It will be fine. I promise. You'll see.'

If only Connie felt so sure. If only Connie had Vaso's faith.

She puts on the last of her clean clothes, fluffs up her hair and swipes a bit of lipstick across her lips - best I can do, she says to herself in the mirror. It only takes 10 minutes. Oh God. Her stomach is churning, again, she's too tired to go to see all these people. What is Vaso thinking ringing everyone? It's too soon for a welcoming party, much too soon.

She sits at the table on the balcony and wishes she had never given up smoking. She could waste another few minutes if she could have a fag. Her ears prick up at a strange, haunting noise away in the distance. Almost forgotten and yet so familiar. She turns her head towards the sound. A Scops owl, high up on the ridge, somewhere near the big house. His hooting sends a shiver through her. She never thought she would hear that again, and yet, here they are, together again. A little owl searching for a mate.

And Connie? What are you searching for?

Another call comes, further away, a different note this time, higher-pitched, more drawn out. A female. They begin a duet. A song of love for the little owls. A song that will last forever. Lucky them. She listens for a while but their plaintive calls make her feel even more alone.

Time to go downstairs and face everyone.

She rummages in her bag and finds the brooch. It is there. She hesitates, decides not to wear it and drops it back in.

The dining room is full of people - all happy, chatting and

excited. They're pleased she has come back. Yanni and Papou are long gone and Vaso is sorry they are not here, they would have been delighted that Connie has come back. Timos is sitting at a table with Phillipos and his wife and their grown-up children. Kosta and Helena, back from Heraklion years ago, sit together, surrounded by their families. Vaso had been right, they all come home eventually. Their mother, ancient and gnarled as the old pine tree, sits with the Priest and Roula. Poor Roula is as skinny and tight-lipped as ever. And, over at the bar, Iakchos, Gregor and Sebastianos sit and wait for her. They can't believe she is back. Iakchos thought she was lost to them forever. He pestered and pestered Vaso for information after she left. It was no use. The time flew by and eventually he realised she was gone for good. She might as well have been dead. Connie had been a real friend to him, as close to him as his brothers were, she had been special, a girl unlike any he had ever known. Her sensitivity and gentleness had touched him right down deep in his core. He had felt her sadness in his heart and tried and tried to help her, but she wasn't ready. Maybe if she hadn't gone, if only she had stayed a little longer, he could have helped her feel better. He had missed her so much, missed her big, open smile and her hard, tight hugs. He never forgot her, he just grew accustomed to her not being there. And now she has come back. It is a miracle. She is back.

Children and grandchildren run everywhere, squealing with the delight because they are having a party. There is a buffet and a cake, wine and beer, and some Metaxa for later when the children have been sent off to bed. No one has any idea of the struggle Connie is having. They imagine she's happy because they are all happy she's come back to them. No. They have no idea at all.

There great burble and hub-hub of talking gets louder and louder as Connie gets closer. She wants to run away. She turns towards the outside door, pushes her way out into the cool night air and sits down on the steps. Just for a moment, she thinks, I'll get some fresh air before I face them all. The sky is pitch black, the stars are twinkling, the owls are hooting and she can't catch her breath. Her chest is heaving with her

pounding heart. Panic. That's what it is, pure and unadulterated panic. At least the sea is calm. She looks out at it, the tiny ripples and foam glisten in the moonlight. The young man who rescued her hat is walking towards her. He smiles as he comes nearer.

'Shall I sit here for a minute with you? If you want me to, of course.' He speaks in English, perfect English.

She nods. 'I am scared to go in. I've made such a mess of things. I don't think I should have come back.' She says it quietly, sure he won't have any idea what she is talking about and won't care, but she can't stop the words coming out. Another kind stranger to talk to.

'I can imagine. It must be very hard for you.' He smiles at her. 'You know, Mama has always told me about you. From before I could even talk she has told me everything. You are not a secret to me.' He is looks at her, his green, green eyes searching deep into hers.

'Nothing has been hidden from me. I am Stephanos.'

HOLIDAY TIME, CONSETT, 2000

It's still dark, only 3 a.m but the morning has come - get up, get up, it's Holiday Time, Stella shouts as loudly as she can. She runs into their rooms, bounces on the beds, laughing and ripping back their duvets. They grumble and groan but she can't contain herself - come on, come on, it's time to go and get Mam, get up, time to find her and tell her how much we miss her.

Breakfast is rushed, getting washed is rushed, getting dressed is rushed. They push and shove each other, shout at each other, and check their bags a hundred and one times. "Passports, Money, Tickets, Passports, Money, Tickets" is the Mantra of the morning. And then, all of a sudden they are ready, with ages and ages still to wait until the taxi comes.

'Dad, why don't we take the things out of Mam's box,' Stella asks, 'the photos and stuff? She'll be with those people and they might like to see all the old pictures.'

Ed isn't sure. 'Oh, I don't know. She might be cross we went in the box. You know what she's like.'

Stella, almost too wise for her seventeen years, shakes her head and tuts dismissively. 'Well, it's about time she got over it. Stopped keeping secrets and thinking about herself all the time, then isn't it? She needs to grow up. Honestly.'

Ed grins. Perhaps Stella is right. 'Alright then, let's take them. Everyone loves to see old photos of themselves.'

The taxi toots at the door. The sun is rising, their new day is up and running.

CONNIE'S PLACE, 2000

Connie has no idea what to do. She is struck dumb. The boy is sitting so still and quiet beside her, looking at her with his big green eyes. Is he waiting for her to say something? She stands up - I'm sorry. I can't. I can't do this. I don't know what to say to you. I need to go. I shouldn't have come, she says and marches towards the sea, back straight, shoulders high, head up. She doesn't turn around. He watches her. He has no idea what she is doing but it is probably best to leave her alone, after all this has been a shock for her, she would not have been prepared for their first meeting to be like this.

The night is beginning to wake up. There is the buzz of talking and laughing coming from the dining room and he can hear people around the village shouting to one and other, car horns tooting, music from the bar up the road. The evening is coming alive as she walks in the sea. She paddles her toes in and out of the water, then stands still and stares up into the black sky. He watches and waits. He has no idea what to do either. Her voice comes floating to him on the breeze.

'You must hate me for what I did. Leaving you and running away.' She still doesn't turn around to look at him. Mama said she would feel like this. Mama had waved her finger in his face and told him he should be honest with her, tell her what he thinks, it would be for the best.

He gets up and walks across the sand to her. 'Yes, I have hated you sometimes. But I don't hate you now.' He holds his hand out to her, she ignores it and carries on paddling in the waves, her trousers are wet up to her thighs. 'Come out of the water and let's go in. Everyone is waiting to see you again. We are all very glad you are here. I am glad you are here.'

The moon is shining so brightly, its light is clean and clear. She looks at him, studies his face as he waits just an arm's length away. She can see herself in him, see her youth in this tall, thin boy, with his wide green eyes, his almost pretty features and his nearly blond hair.

'Oh, God. I'm wet. I'll have to get changed,' she says, as if she has only just realised.

'I will tell Mama and she will talk some more to the others. She likes to talk. No one will mind. Come on. Come out of the sea. The hardest bit is over now.'

Why is everyone so much cleverer than her at this? Why does everyone else know exactly what to do and say? Why is everyone else so able to make sense of everything that is happening?

She let herself be led out of the sea and back to the steps. 'Tell Vaso I won't be long. Thank you for being so kind. Thank you.'

It is she who is shy now, because she can't think what to say or how to act, what to do, and he is so calm. This boy is her son. Her flesh and blood. It's not like this on TV when long lost parents and children meet. They run into each other's arms and it's all hugging and kissing and crying, they smother each other in their long-lost love. Instead of kisses, she is smothered with too many years of hiding, all those years of not speaking the truth, never unleashing how she feels, covering it all up. Now, it might be much too difficult. How is it possible that he doesn't hate her? After all that time she kept writing letters and

promising to come back. And all that time she put him out of her mind, boxed him up in a separate part of her heart and memory and forgot about him.

But you didn't forget, did you? You remembered when you were on your own and then you only gave the memories a few seconds of your time. A flash of a tiny boy's face, his green eyes, his rosy lips searching for you. His chubby fingers holding your hair, tight as tight, as it falls onto his face. Lying on his blue blanket, legs kicking as you blow

raspberries on his round tummy. Oh God. It was unbearable. Eventually you shut the memories away. They were blown out of your mind's eye by the grief and guilt and self-loathing that tore you to shreds, and you closed the lid of the magic memory – eating box.

'Did you know who I was when you picked up my hat?'

'No, not at all. Then you came in. I heard you and Mama talking and I guessed who you must be. I have imagined what it would be like, when you came back. Mama has always said you would. She says

everyone comes home eventually. She came to talk to me when you were having a rest.'

'Who is your father?' she asks. Scared that he will know the answer.

He brushes the question aside, 'I know the story. I know all of your story. I told you, Mama has kept no secrets from me. Timos is my father and Vaso is my mother. And you are my English mother. I know what happened to you. I do not need to know anymore. Mama said you couldn't remember.'

So, still a secret to be told. Or still a secret to be buried forever? We shall see.

She leaves him at the bottom of the staircase, without thinking she stretches her palm up to his cheek and he smiles, his green eyes, her eyes, shining in the light. A little tear there perhaps?

Upstairs in her room she rests her forehead against the bathroom mirror, lets the cool glass numb her skin. Her mind is too busy running away with itself. How Vaso must have despaired when the letters stopped, and her own letters came back marked 'Not Known at This Address'. How worried she must have been when she couldn't find

Connie anymore, couldn't ask her when she was coming home to her baby boy. And how angry she must have been as the weeks and months and then years went by. How honest and brave of her to tell this green-eyed boy, who couldn't remember his English mother leaving him, all about her. To tell him who he was, and is, and who he will be, always and forever. And how difficult it must have been as the boy grew up and questioned and wondered and longed to fill in the gaps with only a few tattered letters and old photos to give him his answers. And Vaso had done all this despite the worry, sadness and the anger.

How easy it would have been to keep it all a secret, keep the boy for herself and pretend.

There's the difference, Connie. No secrets. You have kept all the secrets and Vaso has kept none. Those secrets have made the cadence of your life pulse and swing and flow with uncertainty, pain and utter sadness. Oh, you tried hard to make the tempo of life smooth and

regular, but it's always been wrong. It's never worked. It's the secrets that have done this. The secrets have destroyed the normal rhythm of the life you could have had. And all the time you've kept the secrets you've suffered, and Ed and the children have suffered. It can't have been easy for them living with you with no idea what was going on behind all your moods and whims. Flighty and excitable, full of joy or full of blackness. Poor them. They knew no different because the secrets were too deep inside. For better or worse.

She can't think about the last few minutes anymore - she opens the lid of her box, pops the minutes in and slams it shut. Plenty of time later for all that. It's time to go to the party. Her party. She must get these wet trousers off and get ready. She's light headed, faint. She sits on the loo, her head between her knees, and lets the blood flow back up to her brain. God. Her fingers tingle where they've touched the grown-up skin of her baby son.

There isn't much left in her bag to wear, everything is grubby and now her trousers are soaking wet. The dress she bought in Sitia isn't quite right for this occasion. There is the black dress, her posh frock, squashed in the bottom of her bag. She will wear it. She shakes the creases out, it's so soft and so light - a beautiful drape of silk, almost alive with shimmer. Is it too fancy? She sits down on the bed. She used to say nothing could ever be too fancy and there is no such thing as Sunday best. Once upon a time, she would have worn a dress like this to go shopping, and now she is worrying if it is too exotic to wear to meet her oldest friends. And her son.

She starts to laugh. Louder and louder and harder and harder until her ribs and face ache, and she no longer knows if she is laughing or crying or laughing some more.

Connie bloomed through the winter. Once the sickness left her. The café was quiet and the village settled deeper into its winter routine. The wind blew, the pine trees bent and groaned, the grass died, and the goats went away from the hill sides. They trotted back up to the big village to spend the cold days in the sheds and barns. The sea grew dark and sometimes raged against the beach, scouring away the golden sand and casting the pebbles far up onto the road and into the doorways.

Vaso fussed around her, making sure she was fit and well, feeding her up and telling her not to do too much, not to lift this and that, to rest and enjoy - when the baby comes you'll have no time to rest, she said. Papou wondered if she should move into one of the rooms above the café to be nearer Vaso, but Connie refused. She was happy where she was and stayed in her beautiful shed. It was warm and cosy enough for her, and this baby. All was well.

One bright, cold day Yanni and his grandsons appeared at her door. 'Come into the café we have brought you a present,' he said, shyly.

She followed them - Yanni blushing right up past his ears and Iakchos holding her hand and laughing. In the middle of the floor was a big wooden cot, a collection of sheets and soft, woollen baby blankets in shades of green and lemon.

'I hope you don't mind,' Yanni said. She hugged them all in turn, her eyes awash with tears - thank you, thank you, she whispered, unable to express the depths of her gratitude and feelings for their kindness. And they glowed with pride because they had made her happy.

Vaso and Connie spent the afternoon rearranging the furniture, trying to get the cot into the best place in her room. Connie decided to put it close to the bed, then she could reach out and touch the baby without getting up.

'Look, if I take this side down the baby will be right beside me,' she said to Vaso.

Vaso pursed her lips. 'You will smother it. It should be swaddled up tight and lie away from you, so it is safe.'

Connie laughed - that went out with the Ark. Although she didn't really know if it had but there would be no swaddling up tight, not for this little one. This baby would be close to her all the time. She was determined to love this baby as no baby had been loved before. It was a special baby. A baby sent from another realm. Her mind had been made up the day she burnt the paper. She would never question her love for this child-to-be, she wanted it, and she would love it, no matter what. Absolutely. It would be snuggled and cuddled and soothed as no baby had ever been – ever - in the history of babies. She would never let her mind drift back to the moments of its conception. Never allow herself to think of those days in the late summer at all. It would be a new start for all of them.

That's what she told herself. Over and over again.

Secrets upon secrets.

Christmas was coming. Money was tight. She had saved her tips from the work in the summer but it wasn't much. Vaso told her that was how all the villagers managed through the winter - everyone saved up as much as they could and hoped it lasted until the spring came again. Her mother had sent her some money in a letter that made no reference to the baby at all, even though Connie had told her. But her savings wouldn't last forever. Vaso refused to let her worry, told her to stop paying rent for her room and anyway, she said, didn't she have a job when the days warmed up again? The baby will be here, it can sleep while we work. How do you think people have managed all these years? And so she settled into a time of waiting, waiting for the baby and their new life to begin. The days passed quickly and gently, nothing much happened, she relaxed and bloomed and grew. Winter howled down from the mountains but that was all right, she was safe in her goat shed and spring would be here soon and everything would be fresh and new.

The wind was strong and bitter cold on this morning. She'd taken the dog out for his walk along the beach and felt the winter right down into her bones. The dog didn't care about the cold and the wind. He ran and jumped and bounded in and out of the sea, galloping back to her every time she whistled for him, waiting for her to throw something for him. He was a good dog. A happy dog. Vaso had been right, he was good company. When she got back she towelled him dry and left him asleep on his bed, all four legs stuck up in the air and his head lolling over the side, tongue out. Silly dog.

Vaso looked up from the newspaper as Connie pushed open the door. She always read the paper before she took it over to Papou and he always complained that the pages weren't straight.

'I'm going to go into Irapetra this morning to look for some Christmas presents. Do you want to come with me?'

'Well, I think I will. Don't you go buying anything for me. Or Papou. We have everything we need. Save your money.'

'Oh Vas, don't be silly, of course I will buy you something.'

Vaso frowned at her, then smiled her biggest smile. Connie seemed much happier and she was pleased. As they braved the wind to get the van, a car came gliding along the road past them. A car unlike anything they had seen in Makrigialos before - too big, too black, too shiny. Vasou raised her eyebrows at Connie - I wonder who that is, she said. They watched the car drive slowly through the village, up the hill to Analipsi, off into the distance and out of sight. Hmmmmm, Vaso mused. Papou was waving frantically at them from his front door.

'Vaso, come here, quickly,' he was shouting, 'it has started. The invasion.'

'Thee mou. Invasion.' Vaso whispered to Connie. 'What on earth is he on about?'

'Vaso, they are here, people from the city. I don't know if it is Chania, Heraklion, or Athens, but they are here. Yiota told me on the telephone. She says they are parked beside the new hotel being built up in Analipsi. Three men in suits. Suits Vaso! Suits! There will be trouble.' He shuffled up the road towards them, still in his slippers and all his shirt buttons undone.

Strangers. They all knew what that meant. They had heard of this happening up and down the Northern coast. Men turning up in remote seaside villages - Elounda, Malia, Stalis - with briefcases full of money, coaxing people to sell their land. It was everything Papou had warned them about - they will come when the winter is at its deepest, he had said, when people don't have much money and think these men will solve all their problems. And here they were in Makrigialos – today.

Papou hitched up his trousers and tried to tuck his flapping shirt in - what will we do? Neither Vaso nor Connie could answer his Question, but standing in the middle of road, in this biting wind, wasn't the answer. They took him back home and sat him down with a coffee. No one was going to Irapetra today. Vaso had an idea - the Priest had the signed papers from the meeting perhaps they should get them and visit everyone to remind them not to give in, she said, just in case. Papou nodded - yes, it was a good idea. His hands shook as he held his coffee cup, either from cold or panic, they couldn't tell.

'Connie, will you go up to the Priest's house and get the papers? Oh. And tell him to come back here to talk to Papou,' Vaso said, 'I will help him finish getting dressed.' Papou protested - after all he was only 87, he didn't need anyone to get him dressed or sit with him while he worried. Vaso shushed him.

It wasn't very far, just up the donkey track almost to the big house, turn left and she'd be there. The Priest's house was small and ramshackle, surrounded by his garden and tumble-down hen and goat sheds. Connie had seen him tending to his vegetables and animals, always dressed in his black robes, his hair in a ponytail and his beard in a plait incase it got tangled, or nibbled by a goat. She had never spoken to him. He seemed too remote, too strange.

The villagers talked about him all the time and it wasn't always good. They couldn't forgive him for not being their old Priest who had been with them for many, many years. Pah! they moaned, what does this one know about anything? He is too young. He knows nothing of the world but prayer. Pah! He is from Athens. What does he know of Makrigialos? There is more to this village than God and praying. Papou and Yanni defended him - hadn't they sat in his garden with him many times, enjoying a glass or two of his homemade wine and talking long into the night? Give him a chance, they insisted, he is a good man. After all, he can't help being young. He'll grow old in time, just like the other Priest.

She pulled her coat round her. The wind was coming from the North, blowing out to sea and churning the waves until they were as grey and high and wild as any that surrounded England in winter. Papou called this wind 'Boreas', he is shaking his cloak at us, Connie, he said, and this is just the start of it, soon 'Vorias', the biggest wind of all, will chase little Boreas away and bend the trees till the tops touch the ground, and bring the mountain snow. Whatever it was, Connie thought, as she pushed on up the hill, it was cold; she hurried on, past the fork in the path and avoided looking up to the big house.

The Priest's house was of the same golden stone as the big house. Vaso thought it must have been stables, when the rich people lived there all that time ago. It wasn't quite falling down but it was in need of some repair, windows were cracked, tiles had fallen off the roof and the door didn't quite fit its frame. Perhaps Priests didn't mind, perhaps they had to suffer a little to be good Priests.

She knocked hesitantly, then a bit harder, and strained to hear any noise from inside, any shuffling of feet or turning of keys. All was silent. Oh, dear. Maybe he wasn't in. She would have to go back empty handed. Oh.

'I saw you coming. I was in the garden,' he said. Connie nearly jumped out of her skin. His voice was rich and deep with a resonance that made it full, but soft. A velvet voice. It was quite beautiful. And unexpected. 'They tell me your Greek is quite good, or would you like me to speak English?'

'I can manage in Greek if you don't talk too fast but I go back to English when I can't think of the right word or I get confused or I don't know the word I want.' She felt afraid of him and that fear made her speak too fast, and too much. She managed a brief smile.

'Well, in that case we will speak English. Mine is very good.' He didn't return her smile. There was no twinkle in his eyes. His brown eyes were expressionless and didn't seem to be quite looking at her. She told him what had happened and why she was here. He nodded. He went inside to get the papers - to her surprise he shut his door and left her standing outside in the cold wind. She was pleased. She didn't want to go in his house.

They walked down the track together and all the time Connie felt uneasy, unsure. Planning how she could get away from him if he … if he came too near …if he … if he … If he what? Suddenly he spoke, his voice so close to her she thought she could feel it vibrating right in the middle of her chest.

'I have been told what happened to you in the big house. And about your troubles. And your plans.'

'Emm, yes.' The sound of his deep voice had broken her train of thought for a moment, the dark imaginings creeping around the edges of her mind were scattered away into the wind. He didn't say anything more. They picked their way through the mud and stones in silence. When he lifted up his robes to keep them out of the dirt,

Connie caught a glimpse of big, black wellingtons. It made her want to laugh.

The wind was getting stronger and blew harder into her back. She had to stop herself from letting it push her, faster and faster, down the muddy hill. The Priest's robes fluttered and flapped and billowed all around him. He was like a huge crow against the grey sky, his cloth - feathers rippling and ruffling with the wind under them, his thin, white crow-legs visible above the wellington tops as his robes blew higher and higher. He strode on, making no attempt to hold the flapping, black cloth down. She tripped and stumbled along beside him.

'I am sorry. I walk quickly. You must be careful not to fall I think.' He slowed down. 'Here, hold onto my arm, the wind is vicious today.'

'Thank you,' she said. 'I have the wrong shoes on for this track, I should have worn stronger shoes.'

'Yes. Wellingtons would be best.' His chuckle rumbled between them. Was he laughing at her? She took a sideways glance at his stern profile but saw nothing registered there, he was looking straight ahead, no rise to his lips, no crinkles round his eyes. His beard blew up and his face was lost in a mass of swirling hair.

She was pleased when they got down to the main road and she could leave loose of him. The skinny, bony arm had begun to feel hot under her hand. It troubled her that she was touching him. Why? Because he was a Priest? Because she was scared of him? Because she thought he might hurt her? But why would he hurt her? She pulled her hand away from his arm. He took no notice.

She had started to think some strange things since … since the big house. She tried not to acknowledge these things that crept into that head of hers. But they scampered around and kept her awake. She worried that people were watching her, talking about her or planning to do terrible things to her. One dark and quiet night she heard a scuffle outside and wondered who was coming to get her. No matter that she told herself it would be a lizard escaping from an owl, or a bird on the roof settling back down to sleep. No matter at all. In that black instant she cowered and trembled under her sheets, because it was a man intent on no good.

One morning she filled up her bathtub and wondered if someone had drilled a hole in the wall, a tiny chink in the stone he could watch her through, peer at her as she had her bath, naked and alone. She took a picture down, pulled out the hook, hammered it into the place where she knew the spy-hole was and hung a towel on it to stop his prying eyes from seeing her.

A group of people outside the bakery, chatting about this and that, were really planning to kidnap her, lock her somewhere dark with no chance of escape. Somewhere no one would find her and they could do anything they liked to her. She crossed the road so they couldn't catch her as she went by.

Sometimes, when she was standing next to a stranger in a shop or at the bus station, she wondered if he - because it was always a 'he' - was suddenly going to hit her, kick her or push her down onto the floor.

She didn't tell Vaso because the thoughts weren't always there, they just sneaked into her head without her bidding. She could shake them away, think of something else to keep herself safe from them. But they kept coming back, again and again, when she was least expecting them, or asleep. In a flash, or in a nightmare. It sounded like madness.

Poor Connie. You don't know that this is normal for people who have had such terrible things happen to them. You don't know it has a special name. It will take a war in a far-away desert to give these
reoccurring thoughts a name and until then they are your secret.

Outside Papou's house the Priest turned to her, his voice low and gentle. 'Before we go in, I want to say this. I think you are brave. I think you are too brave. I think if you want to talk to me anytime, about anything, please knock on my door. I will listen.' He turned away and pushed open Papou's door, boomed a happy greeting, and she was left standing outside in the cold wind again.

There wasn't much Vaso and Connie could do about the men in suits. They could only hope, as they went from house to house, that people were as determined as them. Everyone welcomed them in and promised - absolutely promised. Promised not to sell - on my mother's grave, they said and crossed themselves.

When they got back to Papou's they were frozen stiff, feet and fingers ablaze with the pain of the cold, but they were pleased with themselves. Happy that all their friends were going to stick to the plans. The Priest and Papou were huddled close to the stove, talking and
laughing companionably and they shuffled their chairs along to make a space for the two women to sit next to them and get warmed up. They

both took off their shoes and wriggled their toes in the heat until the feeling started to come back, the coffee pot bubbled, the dog snored and the air was thick with comfort.

'Well,' Papou said, 'I hope that is enough. I hope our friends will be sensible and wise. I think we will have another meeting in the spring, and make a plan for the new venture I have in my mind.'

Connie and Vaso stared at him.

'Ah, yes,' the Priest nodded, 'a new hotel of our own, perhaps. It is a good plan and will keep everyone busy.' He rubbed his hands together and patted Vaso's knee. 'Don't look so shocked, what do you think we talk about? Do you think all we talk about is God? We don't talk about women so what else is there but business and money?' His rumble of laughter filled up the room,

'Perhaps a new hotel, a coffee and ice cream shop and a modern supermarket.' Papou said.

'But ... but ... the money? Where will we get the money?' Vaso said, 'there is no money in this village for all those things. Who will build them? Who will pay for them? Who will own them?'

'Vaso, Vaso, you have no faith. No faith at all. There is more money in this little village than you would imagine. Oh, and didn't I tell you, my brother is a bank manager in Athens. He has helped many people build hotels in Spetses and Santorini.'

Spetses! The island of the rich - affluent and pretty, only a short boat ride from busy and crowded Athens, perfect for the wealthy. None of them, except the Priest, had been there, but they all knew about

Spetses and its tourists. No, not tourists, visitors. Since the earliest days rich Athenians had flocked to Spetses to enjoy the sun, build big villas and exclusive hotels that only those with plenty of money could afford. And Santorini! The place the rich foreigners went to for the beauty and the ancient history. Santorini, the ancient island of Atlantis so the old story went, with its volcano and white, sugar - cube houses.

Vaso burst out laughing, 'You are a dark horse,' she said to the Priest.

He nodded, 'I know,' he said and laughed some more.

Connie had missed huge chunks of the conversation once it turned to buildings and bank loans. Her Greek vocabulary didn't go that far and they chattered so fast they forgot to translate for her. She had started to doze off, her hands resting lightly on her growing belly and her thoughts beginning to drift. The voices in the room faded away, she could only hear her heart beating and her steady breaths in and out. She

wondered when the baby would start to move, wondered if it would be a boy or girl, wondered if it would look like her. A sudden image of a man's face thrust itself into the spaces between her cosy thoughts and she jumped. The Priest's voice chased the picture away, 'I must go, I have animals to see to, goats to milk, and we have talked enough. If I sit here much longer, I will be in danger of falling asleep. Come Connie, walk home with me.' He shook himself free from the warmth of the fire.

She stood up too, stretched out her legs. She could do with the fresh air. They pulled on their socks and shoes, heaved on their coats, kissed everyone goodbye and braced themselves for the wind and cold outside. The Priest encouraged her to hold on to him again. And this time it was fine. In the last hour or so he had become a good man, not a stranger anymore. She could feel his kindness inspite of his rugged face and impenetrable gaze, and as they walked, heads bent against the weather, she thought she could like this scrawny, bearded man with his calm manner, unexpected laugh and soulful voice. Maybe he would be a good friend.

'Connie, I said that you are brave, perhaps too brave. Did you understand what I meant?' he said.

'No, not really.'

They were coming to the fork in the path, she kept her eyes down and looked at the muddy ground to avoid catching sight of the big house.

'There. That is what I meant. You can't look at the house. You can't think about this thing that has happened, or even where it happened. You don't say anything about it. Who it was. How you feel. Do you think your bravery in doing this on your own might be misplaced? Might be the wrong thing to do. Might not be brave.'

They carried on walking. She kept silent. They were almost at his door before she said anything. 'I don't know. But I am scared to think about it. I shouldn't have been up there. I shouldn't have been wandering around on my own. Timos said so, I think he was right.'

'No. He was wrong. You didn't know anything about Roula, you had no reason not to go up to the house. Someone did a bad thing to you. You did not do it. Why don't you come in? We can talk about it. I can make some tea. I like English tea.'

Connie shook her head. It was a trick. Vaso must have put him up to this. To get her to tell him things. Who it was. After all, Vaso had tried, over and over again, to get her to talk about it hadn't she? She was suddenly furious. She didn't want to go in to talk to him or drink his damn tea. She managed to smile a little and keep her voice reasonable and quiet. 'Another time. I should get back. I am going to Irapetra later with Vaso. We have Christmas presents to buy.'

He nodded, telling her to come and see him any time she wanted, any time at all. And then he was gone, into his house and the door shut tight.

She stood for a moment staring at the rotten door hanging askew on its old hinges. No. This was unfair. How dare they gang up on her to get her to talk, to get her to think about it, to get her to tell those things she never, ever, ever wanted mentioned again. How many times had she told them? She raised her hand - she was going to thump on that door and demand to know what Vaso had said to him. The Priest would have to explain to her what they had been saying to each other. He was a Priest. Don't they have to speak the truth all the time? Over the sound of the wind she heard him clanging buckets of feed and calling for the goats - come on girls, come on pretty girls, he shouted, and the goats bleated in reply and their bells jingled as they ran towards him. Her shoulders slumped and her arm fell back down to her side. She turned away, angry and sad. Her eyes blurred by wind and tears, she tripped and stumbled back along the track. How dare they? Maybe she would shout and scream at Vaso when she got back to Papou's house. But she didn't. She turned into the courtyard, went to her beautiful, peaceful goat shed, lay on the bed with Puppy and cried. She couldn't trust anyone.

Everyone was intent on something. Some other hurts were planned for her, she was sure of it. There was only the dog she could rely on. Only the black, long-nosed dog who pressed his skinny body alongside hers, thumped his tail against her feet, and stared deep into her eyes. He watched her lids droop and settled himself down against her warmth.

Oh dear, the secrets are strengthened. The secrets of who and why and what to do. They gather in the farthest reaches of your soft and gentle soul and tie themselves into hard, numb knots of self-doubt and mistrust. Attach themselves to all the confusion and turmoil already part of you. Suspicion and wariness are forging strong links with the

apprehension and uncertainty that already hide inside you. Secrets. They are no good. They are the spiders of the heart and mind. They wrap up all the trust and faith and hope in their cobwebs. When the webs are done, they suck out all the truth, confidence and spirit. They leave

behind a dry and empty heart, a husk that cannot be refilled with all the joy and love and life that you deserve. They will lie in wait, Connie, lurking just beneath the surface of your everyday. You will never be free of them. Oh, you will try to shake them off. By forgetting? That is not the answer, never the answer. You don't realise this yet, you aren't ready to listen to anything, except the voice that tells you to ignore and forget. And when you think too much, or are caught unawares, then in they will come, the crawling spider - whispers of those terrible secrets. Whispers that remember and remind.

Crikey, Ed says, when they all step onto the airport tarmac, it's a bit hot. And it is. The local newspapers are already full of dire warnings about the terrible hot weather that is to come. But they know nothing of this yet - they just puff and pant and keep fanning themselves with their passports.

The kids are grumpy after being cooped up in the plane for so long. They pester for drinks and sweets and want to know what they should be doing, where they should be going. Ed rummages in his holdall and gives them a packet of mints to share out. He doesn't have a clue what happens next, Connie always did the sorting out for them, kept them right - follow them, he says, pointing at a man wearing a Newcastle football top and his big, blonde wife and 3 big, blonde kids. They keep their eyes on the black and white stripes and are pushed onto a bus, crowded in amongst the grannies, Stags and Hens, teenagers, and the mams and dads holding beetroot - faced babies and whining kids. Ed warns them to stay close to him, clutches Claire and James' hands tight, tight, tells Stella to hold onto the back of his shirt. For goodness sake, Dad, she grumbles, I'm not going to get lost on a bus. Honestly. But she stands close behind him. The bus crawls away from the plane, slowly, slowly creeps and bounces towards the terminal and empties them out again. They stay with the crowd and are jostled and shoved into the terminal. It's jam-packed, Ed had never seen so many people in such a small place. And there is only one small kiosk, with only one small man in it, to let them all through passport control. Great clouds of cigarette smoke billow over them as the smokers, deprived for so long, suck the innards out of their fags. The little man barely looks at them, or their passports, and then they are shoved into another huge room stuffed with people.

People cram as close as they dare to the great black carousel as it grinds and clanks and spits out suitcases, bags, pushchairs and packbacks. Pushing and shoving and growling at each other, they want to get closer and closer, arms stretched out and hands grabbing at their bags. It is so frantic. Ed makes the children stand back - we will wait, he says, because this is awful. The bus for Makrigialos won't go without us.

Another good Dad-plan, and in a few moments, like corks popped out of bottles, they end up in the arrivals lounge. Breathless, but with suitcases in hand. A girl with impossibly high heels and immaculate makeup, ticks their names off her list and directs them to their coach. It hasn't been as difficult as Ed thought, it's only taken twenty minutes; no one got lost, no one cried, no one exploded in a fit of bad-temper, and they've managed it all without Connie.

The big glass doors swish open. The full force of the Cretan heat hits them again. And the noise. Honking, tooting, people shouting for taxis, the rumble of wheeled suitcases. Everything enveloped in the haze of cigarette smoke. What was that strange horror film Connie had made him watch years ago? It was in Italian. He'd complained he didn't understand it and it wasn't his sort of thing, but she had made him watch it anyway. Suspira or something - just watch it Ed, she'd said. He had tried, he really had, but he couldn't make head nor tail of it. The only part he could remember was a girl getting a fright when the doors in the airport opened and all the noise flooded in, or perhaps it was out. But this trip isn't going to be like a horror film. Connie would be all right, she would be happy to see them and ready to come home. And

everything will be back to normal.

The girls leap up the steps of the bus and pick the seats right at front. They want to be able to see as much as possible out of the big windows. It takes ages for everyone to get on the bus and it gets hotter and hotter. The holiday rep counts heads until she is satisfied they are all present and correct and eventually the driver starts the engine, the air-conditioning comes on and the coach jolts and sways out of the airport into the traffic. All the buildings are run down, the trees are grimy and dusty and huge metal sheds line the pot-holed and bumpy road. Not what Ed had imagined at all – oh well, airports are always near the roughest parts of the cities, it was bound to get better and prettier.

The excitement fades and they settle down and become quiet. Poor things, they're tired, they've all been awake for a very long time. James has fallen asleep, his skinny legs curled up on his seat and his head and shoulders across Stella's knees. Claire is almost asleep next to her Dad, her head resting on the window. Stella strokes her little brother's hair and thinks about her mother living here, all that time ago, all alone, without little brothers and little sisters to look after, no mam and dad to help her. Stella feels sad for her. It makes her want to cry. The Greek world passes by.

The bus noses through the traffic, out of the rough part and into the centre of Heraklion - still nothing much to see - and out on to the coast road. Now the blue sea comes into view. They pass through strings of seaside villages, crowds of people walking along the roads, cars
going where they want, stopping when they please, and always the glint from the sea in their tired eyes. The bus swings and turns, leaves the coast behind and up, up it goes into the high hills, struggling and crawling its way through the bare mountains, then winding down and down to valley floors, passing far off villages and far off, unknown lives. Even Stella closes her eyes now, still thinking of her mother who doesn't know they are coming, and wonders what she is doing as they inch their way towards her.

Another coast comes into view. Empty. Vivid blue sea. A sparse shore with tiny resorts - nothing more than a few seaside villages.
Sometimes the coach stops in one of these small places and a few people get off, rumbling their cases along beside them as they go into their
hotels or apartments - soon they will be rested and sitting round their pools with beers and snacks.

Then it's their turn. They have arrived. Only the four of them clamouring to get off, all in a rush and all in a fluster. The bus driver is handing them suitcases from the belly of the bus. Welcome, welcome, the manager says, shaking their hands, welcome to the best hotel in the whole of Makrigialos, welcome to the best kept secret in the whole of Crete.

It is lovely. The reception area is cool and light, the chairs and sofas are modern and pretty. Stella likes it. Crumbs, says Ed, this is nice, but his head is already full of where Connie might be, how will they find her, who will they ask, when will they ask. He wants to go and get her now, this very second, he has missed her so much, he is so worried about her. He will have to wait. He will have to wait till they have unpacked their cases and got themselves sorted out. What if she doesn't want to see him? What if she is angry and upset that they are there? What if she doesn't want to come home? What has she come here for?

'Dad, Dad, come on, I've got the room keys. Come on.' She shakes them at him.

'Right. I'm coming.' He follows the kids up the marble stairs. 'This is nice,' he says, again.

CONNIE'S PLACE, 2000

The black dress feels beautiful against her skin - soft and smooth. It reaches right down to the floor, unusual for a woman of her height and this alone is enough to make her feel glamorous. It wraps and swathes and flatters her out- of- shape body with all its shimmering loveliness. She looks in the mirror and watches herself twirling round and around, the dress swirling and billowing. If only Ed was here to see her. He thought she was lovely even when she was pregnant and fat and spotty - you are the most beautiful girl in the world, he would say as he rubbed her back and massaged her feet. He had never seen her in a dress like this, never seen her in anything so fancy, not even on the day they got married. She had worn a purple suit and he didn't have a jacket because his arms were too long for the only one they could afford. He got married in his shirt sleeves and an overcoat. A Register Office wedding, then off to the pub for sausage rolls and sandwiches for. They had been happy and surprised at themselves.

The posh frock needs more than just a hurried slick of lipstick to do it justice. Thank God for airport shops - her new make-up bag is bursting with all sorts of expensive creams and powders. She settles down onto the stool to do the best she can with a face that hasn't seen this much make up for a very long time. She studies herself. She hasn't really looked at herself like this for years.

There has always been something about you that is quite extraordinary, Connie. Stunning. Did you know? Have you forgotten? Is it those green eyes? Is it that thick hair? Is it that clear skin? What is it? Is it the way you hold yourself so tall and straight? Head always up, eyes always ready to look directly into those which might be focused on you. Is it the way you use your elegant hands when you talk, not afraid to punctuate your conversations with movement? You are an
Amazon warrior, Ed had said one night long ago, as you lay in bed, you are fierce. Can you remember that, and how hard you had laughed?

Once upon a time, you had wanted to be a cute, little kitten of a girl - one of those tiny, thin blonde ones who always look pitiful and in need of protection. But it was too tiring and difficult to be that girl and you gave up trying.

Yes, from time to time, you have been a scared and quivering wreck, or too brittle and harsh and unable to keep up all that vitality and vigour. But aren't we all like that sometimes? Don't we all forget, as the years go on, who and how we were? Underneath all the hurts you wanted to bury and keep away, there has always a bearing and power about you that is admirable. You have no idea how many women have looked at you and wished they had just the tiniest smidgeon of your spirit and essence. Isn't that the way with people like you? People who have spent half their lives inventing a persona they can hide in, and
eventually it becomes them. It might have been theirs from the

beginning, they just didn't know or didn't allow it to flourish.

You are a confusion of beings, often sad and weak, sometimes tough and full of strength. We can be all those things, some of the time. The trouble is, you have no capacity to forgive your mistakes or weaknesses, to forgive the things you have no control over. But all that beauty that is in there - real beauty. The beauty of being so much more than that pretty, little kitten-girl. When you took the money from the jewellery box, slammed the bedroom door on that old life, perhaps you had forgotten who and what and how you can be. Maybe you had given up on yourself for too long. Had it all become too much to bear – only you know. But, look, here you are, staring in the mirror and you are starting to remember, aren't you? Yes, you are only wondering which eyeshadow to wear and whether to do cat - eyes with the eyeliner, but it's a start.

Come on, Connie. You were always a wonder - with or without all these concoctions - you've only forgotten. If it helps you remember, then get the brush in your hand and do it. Take that soft, sable brush and push it into the golden powder in that expensive, little pot. Take that kohl pencil and make that bold slash of black against your emerald eyes. Come on.

She steps into the room and she feels beautiful and brave, excited and happy, but alone. The throng of people are talking and laughing amongst themselves; children are running about, little boys slide on their knees across the marble floor and the little girls twirl their pretty
party dresses around themselves. Just as she had done not twenty minutes ago.

She recognises almost everyone, even the youngest ones look like their families. Except for that young man standing with his Greek mother - Connie sees how different they are. He is taller, his skin is paler and his hair is lighter, and she knows his eyes are green. Her boy. Holding his Greek mother's hand. And beside them is Timos. Still handsome, his floppy hair still full and dark, and at his side a long-legged, black, skinny dog with its pointy nose held high in the air to catch the smells of food wafting around him. For a split-second Connie thinks it is Puppy. Poor Puppy. Puppy was long dead. He was a good dog. She had missed him so much after he was gone.

Oh, and there is Iakchos at the bar. Her breath quickens a little. She can dare to think it now, say it perhaps, her first love. Oh, he is looking her way and standing up, smiling and waving, his brothers are jumping off their stools and coming towards her.

Every living being in this room is connected, all parts of one big, loud, happy, excitable and loving family. And here she is, in her posh frock, wondering how on earth it has happened that all these people are part of her life, have helped to form her. How could she possibly have left them? She is crying now, because she is not so alone. Not so by herself as she made herself think. Oh. Is it too late to reclaim them all? Is it too late to love them all again?

Vaso sees her and runs over - no, no, there will be no tears, today is a happy day, you have come back to us, she whispers as she throws her arms around Connie and hugs her as tight as she can. Connie can't speak for tears. Her breath and lips and tongue won't form any words at all, but her heart is full of words. All the words she wants to say but can't, all the words she has lost or hidden or thrown away. Vaso tenderly wipes away the tears and takes her hand - come on, lips up, she says, and leads her into the crowd of smiling people.

It is the time to celebrate. They hug her and kiss her and shake her hands. They talk so fast her rusty Greek ears and tongue can't keep up. They giggle at her mistakes, they pet her, tell her she looks wonderful. Oh, they are so joyful, so delighted. And she is happy to see them too. Iakchos twirls her round and whistles through his teeth – Connie, you are beautiful as ever, he says, and she blushes and slaps him, telling him to stop. She talks and smiles and says a million hellos and all the time she is moving closer and closer to her son. He is on the other side of the room, waiting until she can push her way through the throng and reach him. He is watching her. They look into each other's green eyes and know this time has been too long in coming, they know there is forgiveness and love in both of their hearts.

Timos watches too. His own heart is torn a little, he has his secret worries. His time in Australia - oh, so long ago - made him miserable, and sent him home to Vaso after a year that seemed to last forever. Sent him home to his wedding, his new wife coming with a ready-made baby boy, a boy he loved with all his heart. Since the very moment Vaso told him Connie was back, his thoughts had raced into a black hole and wouldn't come back up to the light. Will the boy want to leave them? Will the boy love her more than them? What if they don't get along? What about the other children, all the new sisters and brothers to fit in? And what will happen when she goes away again? He has said nothing to Vaso - it would cause an argument. She only sees the good, the happy and the best. She knows everything will be perfect, she is so certain everything will work itself out because it is the right time. She has already said all of this, he dare not disagree so he keeps quiet and worries that his son will want to leave them.

He knows what he should do at this moment as Connie gets closer - it is the right thing to do and he will do it now. 'Come on,' he says to the boy, his only son, 'you have waited long enough.'

The crowd parts to give them space to hug and cry and kiss each other's wet faces, and everyone claps and whoops and cheers. Connie's head is bursting with the noise. Her heart begins to glue. She can feel it. Feel the pieces righting themselves, moving and turning into the places they need to be - the places that will make it whole again. It is painful and exhilarating. Her never forgotten child - here and real in her arms - and her smashed heart become one in that glorious instant.

And Stephanos? What is he thinking as he holds his English mother close to his heart and feels himself soak into the warm and soft embrace that is her? At last. Over her shoulder he sees his father and mother holding hands and crying. He loves them so much. He puts a hand out and tugs at his father's arm, pulls them all closer and closer until they are huddled together in one mass of heat and tears. It is finished. It is right.

The party is fun, everyone is happy, drinking and singing long into the night. When it gets too much for all the little children and they become fractious and tearful, they are settled down to sleep in one room. All piled in together - brothers, sisters and cousins - with Vaso's old mother to watch them, ready to croon them back to sleep if they wake up and wonder at the noise. Connie talks and talks. Throws her arms around everyone she knows and some she doesn't. She dances with

Iakchos time and time again, enjoying the feel of his hand on her waist and the look in his eyes.

'I missed you,' he says, 'missed you so much, I do not have the words to tell you how much. I thought I would never to talk to you again. Sometimes I even pretended you were dead.' He pulls her close.

'Oh, Iakchos. I missed you too. I didn't know I would be coming back. I wanted to, so many times, but I couldn't find a way. There were too many things stopping me. I couldn't get through the mess, I was stuck.'

'And now look at us, we are old and married and life has come full circle. We have met again and it might be only yesterday since we sat in the bar, talking and talking and teasing those brothers of mine.' He laughed and twirled her under his arm.

'I hope you're not going to dance with her all night, you devil.' It was Timos, he took her from one pair of strong arms and held her in his own. She was afraid for a moment. Afraid of what he might say.

'Connie, I am not so glad you are back but I am happy to see you.' He was struggling to keep his emotions under control and it showed in his handsome face.

'I know, Timos. I know. I am frightened you hate me. We were not the best of friends when you went to Australia and I was sorry for that.' She stood still in the middle of the floor, her dress swirled against her legs and rested gently on the floor. He pushed her away from him.

'Look at you in your grown-up clothes and all your make-up. To me you are still that half-grown woman, so pretty and so sweet, I cannot believe you have come here to cause any trouble for us. Am I right
Connie?'

'Oh, yes, Timos, you are right. I just needed to see the boy. I have needed to see him for twenty years. I have no idea what's going to happen but I don't want to upset anything or anyone.'

'Good,' he says and pulls her hand up to lips, 'thank God for that, now we can get on with the party.'

She smiles and laughs and soaks in the love that is effervescent in the room. The love that bubbles and pops and flows around them all.

Much later, they sit outside - Vaso and Timos, Connie, Roula and the Priest - all together as if it has always been this way. Stephanos lies full length on a sofa and falls asleep, overcome by too much beer. They are tired and relaxed by wine and food and drained emotions.

Everyone else has gone home, their raised voices and their singing disappearing further and further away up the road, then drifting back to them on the warm breeze.

'Father, you have aged well.' Connie says, 'you look as handsome as you always did. When I came through the big village on the bus I saw a Priest in the bakery, I didn't realise it was you.' She giggles and hiccoughs slightly. The wine almost has the better of her too.

'Ah, Connie. You are kind. Who can believe all these years have passed by?' His voice as rich and deep as ever, his expression not as inscrutable as she remembered. He has grown into the village, just like Papou and Yanni said he would. He has been taken to the hearts of most who live in Makrigialos and the big village up the hill. Only one or two people avoid him these days - people with dark hearts and thoughts.

'I know. I am so sorry. So sorry for the time wasted. So sorry for leaving and never coming back … until now …' her voice breaks.

Vaso interrupts her. 'No. I said no crying and I mean it. There is time for that later when we are sober and the light of day is shining on us. We can cry tomorrow. Tonight we will drink a little more Metaxa and bask in the night sky and shining stars.'

The Priest takes Connie's hand and pats it. 'Don't worry, you had troubles. We knew you did. We wondered how you would survive them. Perhaps surviving was all you could manage and that's why you were kept away. I thought you were too brave.'

'Or not brave enough.'

'Well, that could also be true. You are here now. That's all that matters.'

Everyone nods and repeats the words …. all that matters. Matters. All that matters. Here now. Here.

Roula stands up with a sudden flurry, announces that she is tipsy and she must go. She's the only one who hasn't spoken to Connie very much. Yes, she said hello, smiled and fluttered a dry and powdery kiss on her cheek, but no real conversation has passed between them. They had never been friends. Connie calls after her. 'Good night Roula. I am pleased to see you.'

'Are you, Connie? Are you? Well. That's good. I'm not so pleased to see you, but that is my fault. Not yours.'

They all gasp. They are shocked. What does she mean? Vaso tuts and stutters to speak, unable to get any words out.

'Connie, you are reminder of bad things. I look at you and all the bad things come flooding back. I didn't think they would after all these years, but they do.'

Vaso jumps up, ready for a fight, the Priest shushes her and tells her to sit down. Timos hangs his head in his hands. Stephanos sleeps.

There is nothing to be said. Wait. No. There is plenty to be said. Roula is wrong to do this now when everyone is happy. She is wrong to do this now when she doesn't know this Connie. This older, tougher, harder, more brittle Connie. This Connie, emboldened by wine, this Connie who shoots up from her seat and runs after her, suddenly sober and full of anger.

'You were always a mean woman, Roula. Full of self-pity. And jealous.'

Vaso chases after them and catches her by the arm. 'Not now, Connie, not now,' she says. But it's too late, Connie takes no notice and shrugs her hand away.

Roula turns around, her eyes hard and black, her face is blank but her tongue is sharp. 'And you were always stupid, Connie. My troubles were not like yours. My story was not yours. No one wanted me to speak, to tell the truth. No one cared about me. But everyone wanted to look after you and still you pushed them all away. You wouldn't let anyone help you. And then you ran away. Of course I was jealous. I couldn't run away. I have lived all my life in this place knowing that people think badly of me. You have lived your life surrounded by people who worry about you and care for you. All these people here,' she waved her hand around the people who were staring at her open-mouthed, 'your husband and children in England. But you threw them away. You might as well have spit in their faces. And now you come back here like the prodigal child and everyone forgives you and loves you all over again.'

She points at Stephanos still sleeping on the sofa, 'That boy, the one you left behind, even he will forgive you. He should know the whole truth, you should tell him everything. Would he forgive you after that?'

Connie crumbles, no, she deflates like a balloon. 'No, Roula, he doesn't need to know anything more. He has a mother and a father who love him. I could never have looked after him like Vaso and Timos have done. I left him here, where he was safe. After everything that happened I couldn't even look after myself ...'

'Pah! You talk of self-pity. Listen to yourself. Grow up. There's no need for such nonsense now. Look around you. You are welcomed back. You will always be loved and you will always be looked after. You are protected like some precious jewel. Isn't that enough for you? What more do you want? Pah!' Roula shakes her hands free and walks away, leaving Connie ashen-faced and shaking.

Stephanos hasn't moved - is it possible he is still sleeping through all the shouting and the tears? His eyelids flutter, his breathing quickens. Is he waking up? Can he hear the words his English mother and spiteful Roula throw at each other? Timos places his hand on the boy's head and strokes his hair, just in case he is stirring.

The Priest is the first to speak. 'Vaso, I think we will have some coffee, would you and Timos go inside and get the pots prepared. The boy is fast asleep. Come on, Connie, we'll have a walk on the beach and when we come back the coffee will be ready.'

He takes her hand. 'Well. What do you think of that Connie? Do you think she was right? Do you understand why I'm asking?' His voice is soft and gentle, her hand is warm in his. The sea caresses the sand, the stars are bright in the dark sky and from somewhere up on the hill, she hears the pair of Scops owls hooting.

'Do you know, Father, I do. I think Roula is right. I've been so caught up with fear and guilt, I couldn't think straight. I've wasted all this time hating myself and thinking I was hated. And look – so many people love me. And I understand why you asked. That's why you told Vaso to hush. You wanted me to hear what Roula was going to say. It's as if you knew.'

He chuckles. 'Ah, yes, but I only guessed, I didn't really know. From the moment you walked into the room her mood changed. The more she watched you, the angrier she got. I saw her face grow darker and darker as people welcomed you back with so much love. She was itching to speak her mind. I know Roula well. Her life has never been easy. When she finds things difficult she broods on them and then there is a fair chance she will explode. Perhaps if you had not spoken to her she would have gone home and it would have passed. Ah, well, it is done now.'

'I have made such a mess, done such terrible things. She is right, I don't deserve all this love.'

'I think you have always tried your best and that is all that can be asked of anyone. You have not been cruel and unkind, you have been scared and hurt, and made mistakes. It is forgivable. Did you do these things on purpose to make everyone unhappy? You know what we say here, in Greece? We say 'I made a salad, I made the sea'. Do you know what that means in English?'

Connie shakes her head.

'It means a big mess, like lettuce leaves thrown into a bowl or waves made choppy by the wind.'

'But, what shall I do now? How will I fix it? How will I make up for all my mistakes?' She rakes her fingers through her hair, her face looks drawn and tired in the moonlight.

'You can't make things different. Leaves are only leaves and the sea is only the sea. Mistakes are only mistakes. Things are what they are. If you think you can fix things then I'm afraid you are going to make another battlefield inside yourself. Let things be what they are. Let things find their own resting place. It will happen. It is happening now.'

'Oh, God.'

They are back at the bottom of the steps. Vaso and Timos are bringing a big tray with coffee pots and tiny cups and sugar bowls to the table. Vaso shakes Stephanos by the leg and Connie sees him sit up, stretch, and rub his eyes.

'How could I have done this? It is terrible. I have hurt everyone. Oh.' She tugs a flower from the nearest pot and tears it into pieces.

'Look at them. Have they had awful lives? Are they angry, sad, do they hate you? Roula was right. You are loved and will always be loved. The only thing you can do to make it better is forgive yourself. And the only things you have to forgive are mistakes.' He sits down on the step and pats the space beside him. She sits. 'A long time ago, I told you that I would always be there to listen to you, I even bought some English tea in the hope you would come to me and we could drink it together. You never came and you turned away from everyone. Then the baby arrived. Remember how shocked and frightened you were. Vaso heard you crying night after night and she told us, we all knew. We talked about it amongst ourselves. We watched you struggle to even look at the baby. We saw how hard it was for you to hold him and feed him. You let Vaso do too much for him and we knew this would be no good. Did we do anything to stop it? No, we didn't. Don't you see? Don't you think we have all made salad and sea, all made our

own mistakes? And aren't they just as terrible? Don't you think we find it hard to
forgive ourselves too? Do you understand?'

She let the torn petals scatter onto the sand and picks a fresh flower. She tucks it behind the Priest's ear and kisses the top of his head.

'Perhaps I do.'

The villagers stuck to their word. They waited for the men in suits to knock on their doors and they shook their heads, said no to them in strong, loud voices. Every day they wondered if they were doing the right thing, but they had promised. It was winter, the fields were bare, the hens had stopped laying, the goats were waiting for their kids to arrive, money was tight but they stuck together. The men in suits went away with their briefcases still full of cash and fleas in their ears.

Christmas came and went, the winds blew, the rain fell and the sea raged. One day they woke up to find a flutter of snow on the beach. A good sign, Vaso said, it means we will have a long, hot summer.

Connie grew fat and lazy and the bigger she got the higher she held her head. Defiant and proud, she smiled and chatted with those who patted her swelling belly, and ignored the ones who looked away as she passed them by. Good for you, Iakchos said. Thank goodness they were friends again. He stopped worrying about her; she seemed so happy. It didn't enter his head that there could be anything amiss. He was furious when he thought about what had happened to her, but there she was, right infront of him, a grin on her face and a giggle in

her voice. She was fine. Of course she was, because everyone loved her and was
looking after her.

Vaso had a letter from Timos, all the words she read out to Connie were contrite and sad. He can be sorry a little longer, she said, and put it away.

Soon the days lengthened, the sunshine was a little warmer, the wind dropped and drifted up from the south, a hint of Africa on its tendrils. The men in suits were definitely gone. Everyone knew they would be back next winter unless there was a plan, unless they made some changes, so they gathered in the village hall again under Papou's watchful eyes. They listened, talked too much, shouted each other down, kissed and made up, and the plan was thrashed out. And in the middle of all this, on a spring day when the goats were jumping on the hill and the trees had started to build their buds, Connie came home from
hospital with her baby son. A little boy with eyes that changed to the same sea-green as hers, and a soft covering of golden hair on his tiny head.

The ease of his birth surprised them. She woke up in the early hours with a stabbing pain and a trickle of water soaking into her slippers. Another pain came and went and she walked across the courtyard to Vaso's door, the dog whining at her feet, sensing something unusual. The knocking was loud in the dawn's quiet and Vaso appeared at only the second rap. Connie was calm, Vaso was not. She screeched and chattered and ordered Connie to do this and that. She ran to Papou and woke him up too, despite Connie's protestations, and they all went to the hospital together. By 10.30 in the morning the little boy had arrived. Connie still calm, and much, much too quiet.

Later, when it was over and they were back in the café, Vaso told Papou how worried she had been. Connie hadn't uttered a word, she said, not made a single sound. She watched the midwife, her eyes wide and full of fear, followed her instructions and in a single slither the boy was born. And then she closed her eyes, turned her head away and waited. Not a sound, Papou, not a word. Silent all the time. The midwife cleaned him up, wrapped him in the blanket and gave him to her. She had to pull her arms open and make them fit around the baby. Connie looked at him with such an expression! I have never seen anything like it, Papou. And then she tried to give him to me. She said she was tired, too tired to do anything and would I give him a bottle. Me! Then the nurse shouted at her and told her to breast feed him until he got the things he needed. She wrestled and pushed the baby onto her until he sucked. It was awful, Papou, awful. It was as if she didn't want to feed him. I thought she was scared of him. Poor little thing.

Papou nodded - it is the shock, he said, she'll get used to him. I have seen this with the goats. Sometimes the new mothers are too young. They want to walk away from the kids and we have to force them to look after them. After that, they are fine. It will take a little time and then she will love the baby. She won't be able to help herself from loving him. Vaso hoped he was right.

Connie stayed in hospital a week. She was healthy and strong and recovered well, the baby was thriving. She had visitors every day, they brought presents for the baby and sweets for her. They fussed over the boy - he is so pretty, they said, with his golden hair and his peachy skin. Who does he look like? A hush fell over the room. Oh dear, their mouths had run away with them and they were sorry, but the words hung there. He is a beautiful, like his beautiful mother, someone said to fill up the silence.   When the visitors went home,

Connie put him in his little cot and stared out of the window with tears pouring down her face. He slept.

Vaso packed a bag with some clothes for him, a hat and one of Yanni's pretty blankets. She was excited to be going to collect them and bring them back to the café. She drove all the way with the window down and the fresh, spring air filling up the van with all of its fresh goodness. Connie was dressed and sitting on the edge of the bed, the baby wailing in the cot beside her.

'The baby, Connie, he's crying.' Vaso said and picked him up to soothe him, 'I have brought some new things for him to come home in. He can meet his new family in his best suit.' She laughed and crooned at the boy. 'Isn't that right, little one?'

Connie turned around to look at them. 'Vaso, you will be such a good mother, you love him more than me already.' Her voice was dry as dust.

'Connie, you will love him in time. You are just a child yourself. And after … after everything that's happened perhaps it might take a little longer. Look at him, he is beautiful. He looks like you. He is so tiny. It's not his fault Connie.' Vaso pushed the tip of her little finger into his searching mouth, he sucked and stopped crying.

'I know. I know. Is it my fault, Vas?'

'No, Connie, it is not your fault. Enough of this. You are tired. Come on, take your baby. You'll feel better when we all get home. Believe me, you will.'

But she didn't feel better. She felt worse. As soon as she could, she bought him powdered milk and bottles. Breast feeding was too painful and at least with bottles, Vaso could help her. He was a good baby - he didn't cry much, he was happy to feed and sleep. At night, when she was on her own, it was she who cried and cried.

You were like this after the birth of every other child - silent and crying. Every birth reminded you of this first one. Every new baby reminded you of that little lost boy, who sucked from his bottle and searched for his mother's eyes even though she was always looking the other way. Oh yes, you let them tell you it was post-natal depression, even though you knew otherwise and they were wrong. You let them give you bottles of tablets to help you feel better. And they did help. They blunted the harsh and piercing pain of remembering that green-eyed baby who was so far away. They dulled the memory of that golden-haired child and you locked him inside your head and heart for ever, with no escape.

In Crete, in that first long-ago time, Connie had no name for what she felt. At night when he snuffled and wriggled and started to stir, ready for his milk, she felt heat rise in her, felt it fill up her chest and her head. She heard herself begging - don't wake up, please don't wake up. But he always did. She would stumble out of bed and get a bottle for him. She fed him silently - no soothing whispers, no lisping baby words, no rhythmic rocking to settle him back to sleep. There was no love there, there was nothing. Poor baby. She would put him back in his cot and lie on her bed, hugging the dog close. He didn't mind, he only shook his head when too many tears fell onto his ears. She didn't tell anyone. More spider-secrets to creep and crawl around her head. More secrets to scuttle close to all the others and build another web.

But Vaso heard. Papou, she asked, can you die from crying? Leave her be, he said, she will need to cry as much as she can. She can't speak the words to us, so maybe the crying will be enough.

Night after night Vaso listened to the sobbing until she thought she couldn't stand it anymore and might dissolve in tears herself. She wanted to help her; she wanted her to love the baby, cuddle the baby but Connie wouldn't talk to her. Vaso despaired. During the day Connie seemed all right, a little quiet perhaps, but she came to the café and helped Vaso with the things they needed to do to get ready for the new holiday season. The baby lay in his carry cot and slept and ate. He was fat as butter, content and easy. Vas thought he could feel that his mother was scared of him. She asked Connie one day. Connie looked at her and shook her head - no, I'm not scared of him ... the words trailed away. Vaso waited, thought she would say more. But she didn't. She gave him to Vaso and went to get the tablecloths out of the cupboard - we must check all these for stains and rips, she said.

People came to see the baby, placed money under his pillow and a drop of honey on his lips. 'Na sou zisei' they said - may the baby have a good life.

There were so many things she must do and must not do. They filled her head with all the traditions she must follow to keep the baby safe from harm. He will not have his name until he is baptised and that will be months away, so you must call him 'baby' incase the evil fates find him.

You should stay in the house for 40 days, and then you must go to Church for your blessing.

You must never cut his hair and don't let the evil spirits get his finger or toe nail clippings, burn them.

Never dry his clothes outside during the night.

You must put this charm on him to keep away the evil eye.

All nonsense, Connie said, old wives' tales and she laughed - Pah!

No, it is the truth, the real truth, said Vaso, offended. No good will come if you don't listen.

When the visitors left, they gathered in a huddle on the corner and wondered.

That girl will go mad with this. Did you see her face?

Who is the father? Who? Will he turn up and claim that child?

Of course he won't. He is long gone. One of those hippies passing through, that's what I think. Poor girl.

Yes, that baby will be hard to love, and such a sweet little thing.

Then they shook their heads and went back to their own worries.

Roula never came, but she stopped Vaso in the street and asked her questions, her voice hard and her eyes expressionless. There is jealousy there, Vaso said to Connie later. That is why you stay in the house for so long, other women will be jealous of your baby and they will cast the evil eye on you and him. Connie just tutted - for goodness sake Vas, that's enough!

No, I tell you, that is what happens, it does.

T he afternoon is dragging and dragging, the time passing ever more slowly. The kids want to explore the hotel, find the pool, and see what is where. Ed is fit to burst. He wants to find his wife. He has made a plan – of course he has - he'll ask at the front desk where the address on the letter is and they'll know and they will tell him. Then he'll bundle all the kids in a taxi and go there straight away. Straight away. His Connie will be there. And she will be thrilled to see him. Happy he has found her. They will come back to the hotel and she will stay with him in his room and they will be happier than they have ever been. And when they wake up in the morning everything will be perfect.

At this very moment, as the kids oh and ah, and he thinks about her, his wife is sitting on the veranda of "Connie's Place" talking to her son.

'I was so sad all the time, Stephanos, looking at you made me cry. I tried not to look at you at all at first.' She holds his hand tight in hers. 'Vaso was so good with you, she loved you so easily. Everything was too hard for me. I was too young. Oh, now I sound silly and sorry for myself.'

'Mama has helped me to understand,' he frees his hand and stands up, 'do you know I have some photos of you?' He fishes in the back pocket of his jeans for 3 small dog-eared and worn photos. She looks at them and laughs. There she is, trying to turn her face away from the camera, smiling, hair blowing in the wind and sand drying on her bare feet. She peers at herself, not quite sure this girl is her. How can it be?

'That girl doesn't even look like me. She is so young … just a child.'

'You haven't changed, Connie.' She raises her eyebrows at him. 'No, look. Same smile. See, and you are smiling now.'

'Yes. Smiling at this child in the photo who looks so happy and free of everything.'

In a photo of a crowd of friends, it is ourselves we look for first and want to stare at. Then we can decide if we are too fat, too thin, too old, too young, too ugly, too happy, too sad. We can hold our old self up against our present self and be filled with longing and regret and grief over those selves we have lost. Maybe we look and are overjoyed that the young self, and the life that went with it, has gone, is over. Or wonder how and why we were ever like that old self.

A photo reminds us of everything, everything that came before, during and after the shutter clicked. We can smell the air, feel the breeze and hear the words that surrounded us in that moment. And here it is, all sealed up in one small, square of glossy paper.

'Mama gave me these photos when I was very young, I have looked at them every day. Sometimes I've been angry, sometimes I've been sad, but I have always looked at them.' He taps his finger on the largest of them. 'See this one, this is my favourite. The one I like the best of all.'

It is just her face - she is staring straight into the lens, the sun lowering behind her and the rosy glow of sunset spread all around.

'You look like an angel. And I see myself in your face.' He is quiet for a few moments. She wonders what he is thinking - this boy is so open and straight-forward, she hopes he will tell her everything. He is like Vaso - truthful and honest and clear in thoughts and words. Oh, it's wonderful that he is this way. He has been so brave, so sensible after everything that has happened to him. Not like her, she thinks - a coward, scared and tied up in all the cobwebs that are her own doing, held tight in that tangled, chaotic snare of misery and fears. If she were like him, she would have cut herself free. If she were like him, her world would have been so different and the sunny-faced girl in these photos might not have disappeared.

'Mama always told me I looked like you. And then I got taller and taller. They laughed at me at school because I was so tall.'

'Me too, I was head and shoulders above everyone. They made me stand at the back in school photos.'

'Me too.' They both laugh together and the world is better. And somewhere in her heart one of those whispering spider-secrets comes crawling out of the box, curls up its creeping legs and dies.

'And my name. They kept my English last name. Mama told me that on the day of my Baptism, the Priest said that my name would help me learn who I was, who my mother was. He was right. I have talked to him about you many, many times. He told me all sorts of things Mama didn't. He told me about the dog and …'

'Ahh, there you are, the pair of you. Come on, I have coffee ready and Timos needs the boy to get some work done. We will have people needing meals soon,' Vaso slaps the boy on the back, 'come on, lazybones.'

She picks up the photo of Connie's face. 'You've been looking at the Angel photo. He called it that when he was just little - Mama, show me the Angel photo, he used to say.' Vaso kisses the top of his head. 'This is good for you both and I am pleased for you. But now it's time for work.'

Stephanos stands up and slips the photos back into his pocket, 'I will see you later, Connie.'

'You kept my last name for him, Vaso.'

'I did. And don't you dare cry. It is too early in the day for tears. Maybe later.'

Connie asks if there was something she can help with, Vaso shakes her head. 'We are going out, she says, we are going to see something.'

Spring had crept up on them. The flowers were nodding their heads in the fields again, the sound of goat bells tinkled around the hillside, and Yanni brought Connie another present. He had been clearing out his sheds and right at the back, amongst the sacks of feed and bales of hay, he found a pram. Now it stood in the courtyard, washed and painted, its white rubber wheels scrubbed clean. They all came out and stared at it. He looked at Connie expectantly.

'It was my daughter's,' he said, 'all my grandchildren have slept in that pram. I was so happy to push them around the village for everyone to admire. The hood is a little worn but maybe it will be useful.' He looked so proud and pleased with himself, his eyes misty at the memories tied up in that old battered contraption. They shuffled their feet and didn't quite know what to say. It was an ugly thing, it looked like something the Queen would use, or the nanny.

Papou started to laugh. 'You can't put the baby in that,' he said. 'What are you thinking? It must be 25 years old. Honestly, Yanni, I wonder about you sometimes.' He slapped his hand on his thigh, chuckling to himself all the time. Even the dog was amused, growling and letting out little yaps as he jumped around. Vaso shot Papou a warning glance and he shut up.

Yanni lowered his head. 'I just thought it might come in handy,' he said, a blush rising. Connie was sorry Papou was making fun of him, poor Yanni.

'It is beautiful, absolutely beautiful,' she said, 'take no notice of Papou, he's only jealous because he hasn't brought me such a fine present. Wait, I'll get the baby and we'll take him for a walk.'

The boy was asleep. Lying on his back, his little arms flung out wide, he was almost too big for the carry cot now. He didn't stir as she picked him up. She carried him out and laid him in the pram, put his blanket over him, took his chubby hands and tucked them in under the soft wool, patted them in safely. Come on, little one, she said, we are going for a walk with Uncle Yanni. The world came to soft and gentle halt. In that still, quiet second, she couldn't take her eyes off him.

Vasou elbowed Papou in the ribs and they all watched her. It was as if she was seeing the baby for the first time. As if he had just appeared from nowhere and suddenly, there he was, ready to be loved. She lifted her hand and stroked his hair, slid a finger down his cheek; he opened his eyes and locked her into his green-gaze. Without a sound she fell to her knees and crumpled to the ground. Papou almost caught her but all he could do was he help her up. She was crying. Really crying and

crying, snot and tears running down her face, her chest heaving with ragged sobs. They fussed and cooed over her - oh, Connie, poor Connie, Papou whispered, his old man's voice soothing and calm. Vaso took her arm and they walked her into the café. Yanni pushed the baby in his huge pram.

'Connie, this is the best thing. Let all this out and you will feel so much better,' Vaso said. There was no whispering or soft words from Vaso, just common sense. At last, she thought, at last we will get to the bottom of this and we we'll know what's going on in this girl's head. And once we know, then we can help. She brushed the hair out of

Connie's eyes - tell me, you can tell me, she said.

Many more tears were shed and much more weeping was to come before Connie could even begin to speak. She was so consumed with her wretchedness there might as well have been nobody there, no one looking at her in her despair. She laid her head on her arms and cried and cried. They could only stand by and watch as her body was racked by one great sob after another.

She was crying for everything. Everything. For the baby and all he had missed, and the guilt and the shame because she didn't love him. No. Because she couldn't love him. Despite all those promises she made to herself she hadn't loved him. Until now. Until that glorious look had pierced her soul and thrust the green of new beginnings into her very depths.

They waited - Papou and Yanni and Vaso - they sat still and quiet, casting little glances between themselves that needed no

explaining. They were so sad for her and angry too. That this thing was happening to her was wrong. Would she would ever get over it? Just because she had cuddled the baby once, started to speak to him, didn't mean all was well and it was over. Even this deluge of tears didn't mean she would be better, that the black thoughts would be washed away

forever. Vaso knew that much as she sat and listened to the weeping.

When Connie was able to speak, the words came in short, rasping outbursts, barely audible. They listened without a murmur and let her fumble and search for the thoughts and feelings she had kept inside for all these months, without interruptions. Even Vaso kept silent. Of course, she wanted to speak, wanted to comfort her, tell her everything was all right and not to worry, but Papou held her hand and squeezed it every time she opened her mouth and drew in a breath.

Out it all poured. They understood everything she said to them. They knew everything now. Except the name of the man. And when there was nothing left in her to utter another word, the baby woke up. Vaso didn't jump up at his cry, didn't pick him up and whisper softly in his ear, or brush her lips against his hair. Not this time. She left him to cry. Connie stirred herself and went to him, pulled him up to her face to kiss him with her own mother-lips, and soothe him with her own words. They breathed a collective sigh. The coffee pot was put on to boil, Yanni and Papou took themselves into the bar for a reviving Metaxa, and

Connie sat with the baby held tight in her arms and stared at his little face.

'Come on, drink this. You will feel stronger.' Vaso handed her a cup of coffee, ' that is enough for today. Anyway, we have things to get ready. Visitors will start arriving in one month. There is lots to do.'

'Vaso, do you realise I have been here for one whole year.' Connie said.

Vaso laughed. 'Of course I do. One whole year. And look where we are. Watching you cry yourself to death. Well, it is over now and we can finally live again. Can't we, Connie?' Her question was more of an order. That was Vaso, so certain and sure of herself, the world around her, and the people in it. Oh, to be like Vaso. How easy those spiders would be kept at bay. Vaso would just flick them away or squash them underfoot. Connie looked up and smiled at her.

'I love you, Vaso. You and Papou and Yanni, and everyone. I won't ever be able to make it up to you. Or thank you enough.' Her voice trembled.

'Oh, shush, you silly donkey. We are family now, and we will always help each other. Now you have started, you will need to keep talking. Drink your coffee and pull yourself together. You have a baby to feed and then, when he sleeps, you should have a rest. Later, I will make you a lovely lunch and we can talk some more and maybe you will feel even better.'

She lay on her bed, the baby snored slightly next to her and Puppy grunted at her feet. She was exhausted and drained. All the fears and troubles that had poured into her head and circulated round and round, getting darker and stronger, were trickling away. In the quiet and warmth of her goat shed, she imagined them seeping slowly away through the soles of her feet.

The air was so still. The only sounds floating in through her window were the buzz of a passing insect and the rumble of thunder in the distance. She sat up and looked at the sky. It was bright blue but on the horizon, way out to sea, a line of sickly yellow and black clouds bubbled high above. A storm was coming. A big one. Oh, well. She fell asleep as the afternoon hummed on and didn't see the first, far-off flash of lightening. The dog lifted his head and whined.

'Connie, Connie.' A loud bang and a crash as the door was flung open. The wind flew in, setting the curtains flapping. Vaso was wet to the bone. 'Quick, quick, get up. Bring the baby and the dog. You must come to the café. The storm is terrible and the sea is very high. It will be safer up there in the café, off the beach. I must go and get Papou.'

The baby screeched at the noise and started to cry, his eyes wide, terrified at all the commotion. Connie jumped up and closed the window, the wind inside the goat shed calmed a little but the door still slapped against the wall, every crash another thing to scare the child. She ran to it and hauled it shut.

Vaso was gone, running across the courtyard, illuminated by a great flash of lightening as she tugged and pulled at the heavy gate. The rain jumped and leapt around her feet, bouncing up as high as her knees. A bolt of lightning hit the sea with a crack and the thunder growled overhead.

The sea was too loud, not the gentle 'shuuuuush' she was used to. It roared like a monster tearing and eating its way through the sand and pebbles. It was too close. God. Oh God. She grabbed the baby and pulled her coat on, wrapped him in a blanket and clutched him to her chest, held the edges of the coat over him and zipped him in. Come on Puppy, she shouted above the noise of the rain and the wind and the sea. Puppy, Puppy? But he wasn't there. He was gone. Run out of the door when Vaso had come in.

She was soaked through in the ten second dash to the cafe. The thunder was booming right above her now and the flashes of lightening were almost at the door. She ran around slamming all the shutters and winding in the blinds - there would be nothing left but tattered rags tomorrow. He was still crying when she unzipped her coat. Thank goodness, he wasn't wet under his blanket. She rocked him and quietened him as best she could. The noise was so loud, the café shook against the onslaught of the wind and rain and he kept on crying. Don't worry baby, don't cry, Mummy is here. Look, I'll make you a nice, warm bottle and we'll sit here and wait. It'll be all right. Just you and me, warm and cosy. She hadn't said that many words to him in his entire life. In his 3 months of existence she had never uttered such a lulling of

murmurs. He shut his eyes and rested his head against her shoulder, snuggled the top of his head under her chin. Oh, little one, there, there, there, here we are, safe as houses now. She started to sing as she made the bottle, a nonsense song about nothing, just a soft string of sounds. When she sat down and curled him into the crook of her arm to feed him he was fast asleep.

But, the dog, where was the dog? He had run out of the door, scared by the noise and the great streaks of light that burned down through the sky to the sea and the sand. He ran and ran, his head down and his tail between his legs. He ran without thinking, without knowing where he was going, because he was only a dog and he was frightened. The single thought in his doggy head was to get away from the terrible sounds and the wicked lights. So he kept running. Past the café and up the hill he ran until he came to the big house and forced his skinny, wet body through the undergrowth, pushed his way inside where he would be safe. He found a warm, dry hidey-hole and lay there, curled himself into a ball and whined. From his velvet head to his skinny tail, he was a ripple of shivering and shaking. And because he was only a dog, he couldn't think of Connie worrying about him as she rocked her baby. And he couldn't wonder what was happening as the house was buffeted and lashed by the worst spring storm Papou had ever seen.

Because he was only a dog, he couldn't tell the difference between the noise of the storm that terrified him so much he dared not move a muscle, and the creaking and groaning of the old staircase as it began to crumble and fall.

The storm screamed and howled around them. They huddled in the café whilst the fierce wind threw stones against the windows. Connie was excited by it, she stood close to the glass watching the rain lashing down and the claws of white light slashing across the sky. She wanted to run out in it, feel the electricity all around her and the pelt of the huge drops on her skin. She would feel really alive, out there, in that weather. She would be whipped by it and left with cold and stinging skin to
savour. She could take comfort in that pain and it might dissolve away all the other pain she sensed but couldn't touch. That other pain was not like the hurt of rain and stones and flying sand.

Ah. Connie. This might be your future now. To want to feel real, physical pain and blot out the agony of the intangible, the lost or the thrown away. Your love for the baby is growing but there will be times - even when life is good - that too many spiders will crawl and writhe, craving your attention. Your need for a reminder of real pain might overwhelm you until it is fulfilled and released. You might starve yourself and then you might eat and eat and eat until you're sick. You might try a tentative slash of a razor blade on your arm. You might

befriend untrustworthy people who might encourage all sorts of things you were always warned about - drugs and stealing perhaps. You might find yourself standing on the bank of a river wondering what it would be like to jump in and disappear. Maybe you will wade in up to your knees, then decide the water is too cold and that is enough for tonight - maybe
tomorrow.

'Come away from that window, Connie. What if a stone comes through?' Vaso was terrified. She didn't like these huge and wild storms, it was lucky they were only once in a while. Connie dragged herself away and settled down by the stove with Vaso and the baby. His eyelids fluttered at every rumble and crash of thunder, every blast of lightning. She watched him breathing peacefully and marvelled at the blueness of the blood in his eyelids, the pinkness of his cheeks, the gold of his hair, and his fingernails - so tiny - like pale shells.

There was a rattling at the door. The Priest burst in, soaking wet and dripping. 'My goats,' he said, 'they've all run off. Frightened by this weather, I've tried to round them up but it's impossible. I thought you would all be here, can I join you until this is over?' He shook the water off his useless umbrella.

'Come in, come in, I'll put the coffee pot on,' Vaso said and dragged a chair up to the stove for him. He sat down and pulled off his wellingtons and his socks, rubbed his hands in front of the heat. Steam began to rise from his wet clothes.

'Ah. The baby. I have not seen this little one yet, since I have been away to see my family in Athens. Such a wild day to meet a new member of the village.' He leaned over to look at the boy. 'He is a big one,' he took the chubby hand in his and shook it up and down, 'I am pleased to meet you, my boy. Welcome.' He mumbled a prayer and touched his cross to the baby's lips.

'Thank you, Father,' Connie murmured, in spite of her misgivings about the cleanliness of the Priest's hands and the crucifix.

'And you, Connie? How are you?'

She hesitated. How was she? She didn't know. She had barely got over all the weeping this morning, and now this storm. 'Oh, I'm feeling much better …'

Vaso interrupted, unable to contain herself. 'She has cried all morning, Father, she has had us frightened half to death, in fact, she has cried every night for 3 months. I heard her from here. Sobbing and sobbing.'

'Vaso, that is the nature of this thing, I think. It would be unreasonable to expect Connie not to cry,' he put his hand on Connie's, 'isn't that right Connie?'

And she supposed it was.

The wind howled and the rain lashed down for the rest of the morning and on into the afternoon. Connie hoped Puppy was alright, poor dog, out there in the driving rain, all alone. She kept going to the door and shouting for him but his name was whipped away by the fierce wind. Vaso huddled next to the stove and grumbled every time she opened the door. Papou and the Priest were in the bar worrying about the goats and the rising tide. The baby lay in his cot and gurgled. Happy and smiling, waving his fat hands about - not asleep for once. Connie watched him. Stretched a hand over to tickle his round tummy. Felt his soft skin under the brush of her fingers. He was the prettiest baby in the world, of course he was, pretty as a picture. She bent down to him and breathed in the powdered smell of him. It set the tears

springing in her eyes again. Tears she couldn't keep away. Tears she didn't really
understand.

Vaso tutted, 'Please don't, Connie. It will be alright now, you'll see. Everything will sort itself out. Please don't cry anymore.'

Connie brushed the little seeping's of tears away and smiled at her friend. She would have to try.

There was another flash of lightening. She counted the seconds 1 … 2 … 3 … 4 … 5 then came the crash of thunder. It was moving away. 5 miles inland now. She went over to the window and peered out to the sea's horizon. The blue sky was coming back. The Priest pulled his wellingtons back on - it was time to go out in the last of the rain and search for his goats before it got any later. Connie said she would go with him and maybe she could look for Puppy, if it was OK for Vaso to watch the baby. Vaso nodded - it was fine, the boy would be happy with Aunty Vaso.

The world looked clean but shattered. The storm had been fierce enough to flatten the flowers and grass; leaves and bits of branches were scattered everywhere. Pebbles, stones and sand left where they had no right to be. The edges of the path up to the Priest's house were washed away. The rain had cut deep into the soil, water and mud was gushing down the hill in these fresh gullies. Hundreds of ants tumbled one over the other to escape the water flooding into their nest-holes. Poor little things, thought Connie as she splashed through puddles and squelched through mud.

'I see you have wellingtons on now, Connie. I think they are too big.'

'I borrowed them from Papou.'

The sun had come out and suddenly it was far too hot. The air was thick with moisture and the smell of wet vegetation hung heavy all around them. Intense and unpleasant. She felt weighed down by the atmosphere and the sucking mud around her feet.

'This is horrible,' she complained out loud to no one in particular, 'really horrible.'

'What did you say Connie?'

'I said it wasn't very easy walking in this mud in these stupid wellingtons.' She heard him chuckle. It was broken off in mid flow and he pulled in his breath.

'Look, Connie. Look!' He was pointing up the hill.

A whole corner of the big house had crashed down into nothing but a pile of stones and shattered beams of wood. The treads of the staircase hung askew from the exposed wall. The ivy and great tree canopy were tangled and entwined amongst the rubble. The remains of the balconies, twisted into rusty spikes, sat on top like a crown. She could see the inside the bedroom - the beautiful birds and flowers open to the air and the fireplace adrift with no floor to hold it.

'Oh, my God,' the Priest muttered into his beard, 'Connie we must go back and phone the Mayor in Irapetra to let him know. They will have to come and see. This is not safe. Come on.'

Connie barely registered the mud splashing up the backs of her legs as they ran back to the café. My God. The house. She was glad. Perhaps they would come and pull the whole lot down and bulldoze it into oblivion. It was avengement.

But is it, Connie? The house did nothing to you. You loved that house, you liked to visit its dusty interior; you enjoyed that calm as you wandered through its discarded rooms and felt the essence of those left-over lives. Does the sight of this twisted stone and wood and metal, felled by wind and rain and lightning, really make you happy? It is the flesh and blood you need to raze to the ground. Not the stones and wood. Evil given for evil done. Are you are still too kind and sweet and gentle for that? Will you seek your revenge, search for your retribution? Or will you turn all that hate and hurt and anguish inward and store it away in your head? Will it come out one day? Of course it will. In drips and drabs, in broken skin on the palm of your hand, sudden sharp words, unexpected cold shoulders and hasty fury. And it will be aimed at the wrong people - the people who love you the most. They will wonder how someone like you, someone so kind and lovely, can sometimes be so

furious and mean. But they will forgive you, time and time again. Because they love you totally, even though you hate yourself. It is almost too deep to reach, that other love - that love for yourself that will make you feel clean again. Almost.

The goats were found and herded home. The mayor was phoned and news of the big house spread like wildfire through the village. Even in all the excitement Connie could only think about the poor dog. She called and called, listened and looked, but there was no answering bark, no streak of black running towards her. No sign of him at all. Everyone assured her he would come home - once he is hungry, they said. They would all keep an eye out for him and fetch him back if they found him. Hours and hours went by. Connie fretted about him, poor dog. He would be frightened and lonely out there all alone. Rubbish, said Vaso, he's a dog, he'll be off chasing rabbits and making friends with new people. You'll see. He'll come trotting back tomorrow as if nothing is wrong, without a care in the world. That's what Greek dogs do. Stop worrying. But Connie couldn't stop worrying. He was a home-loving dog, not a street dog and she knew what happened to the street dogs and cats in Athens and Heraklion. Poisoned. Maybe it was the same here. Pah! Vaso snorted, not here, silly. He'll come home. Connie went to bed that night wishing he was there, lying on her feet.

A dogless day passed and the workmen turned up to start work on the big house. They came in a lorry and the whole village turned out to watch them drive it up the hill. Never in a million years, they muttered amongst themselves, will they get that thing up there. Too muddy. Too steep. They cheered and whooped encouragement as the lorry slid and swerved and lurched across the wet ground. They clapped when it
managed a foot or two. The lorry belched out thick black smoke and the stink of burning rubber filled their nostrils. It was impossible. In the end, a long chain of people wound its way up the hill and every piece of debris was passed, hand over hand, down to the lorry. It was the only way. They left the biggest and most useful stones in a pile - someone might want them. It was going to take weeks.

Another dogless day opened up, fresh and bright. She had struggled to sleep, the hooting of the Scops owls hadn't even been able to lull her into a slumber. She had tossed and turned, rearranged her sheet, flipped her pillows over and over to find the coolest spot. She got up and went to get a drink; her hair was annoying her just hanging there so she tied it up and sat on the doorstep to feel the cool air on her neck. The baby woke up for his milk. She carried him to Papou's pine tree and sat on the sand, comfy amongst the roots. He sucked contentedly on his bottle and she listened to the sea. It was peaceful there under the branches, watching the sun wake up the new day. Her little life snuggled against her, his eyes shut and his tiny fingers entwined with hers. Flakes of dandruff were in his hair. She pulled them out. He had a crust of milky snot on the end of his nose. She rubbed it away. His socks were falling off. She pulled them up. And the sea shushed and lapped against the sand and pebbles, wrapping them both in the swish of its swirling kisses. If only the dog was there. If only lots of things.

No wonder you can't sleep, Connie. Is it the dog? Is it the imaginings of his fate that are stopping your eyes from closing, stopping you from drifting back into the sleep you need? Or is it those spiders of yours thumping and bumping against the lid of their box? Never mind. You can think about the dog and it will take you away from the other things. The dog will be your diversion for now. It is only a different pain to enjoy.

There was gloom stuffed in her head like wet cotton wool when they got back to the goat shed. Far better to be outside in the fresh air on a day like today. No use bothering Vaso this morning, it was still much too early. She wrapped a long piece of striped cloth around them both and slung the baby on her hip, the long tails of fabric tied tight under his bum. Vaso thought it was ridiculous to carry the baby this way - you look like a peasant, she had complained, it's bad for his legs, he should be lying down. Connie had just sighed and hoisted him higher up on her waist - I can't push a pram anywhere round here, she said, and what did they do before someone invented prams? After that she carried him everywhere with her, tied tight against her and blinking his green eyes against the sunlight. Today she would have a walk up to the big house, it might blow the cotton wool away. She hadn't been up there for a while and it was the only topic of conversation in the café from dawn till dusk - she might as well see what was happening up there.

Workmen were milling about, smoking cigarettes and drinking coffee, people from the village were watching, a few were sifting through the remains to find something useful. Connie stood a little way off, careful not to get too close and stay out of danger. Roula was there, watching from the other side of a patch of shrubbery. Connie didn't want to go over and talk to her, she didn't really like her very much. She found her unfriendly and sharp, her whole manner was unpleasant and her voice was hard to listen to, so whining and petulant. It grated on Connie's nerves.

Roula had seen her. Oh God, she was coming her way, purposeful and intent on speaking. Connie pulled the wrap higher around the baby, covering his head and pushing his arms in. There might be nothing in all those old wives' tales Vaso had told her but she felt troubled that Roula would be looking at her baby. She might even try to touch him.

'Ah, Connie. You are here too. Watching this place be torn down. It's good, yes?' Roula laughed. Not like the gurgles of Vaso's happy giggles. There was much in Roula's laugh that told of misery and anxiety, it was a laugh born from sadness and anger. The laugh of witches and wicked step-mothers and evil queens. Ghastly and grim. She didn't even glance at the baby.

'I think it is a shame.'

'Then you are a fool.'

'No, Roula, not a fool. Just more forgiving than you.' Connie turned away from her. The malice in her voice was too much to bear.

'No, Connie. There should be no forgiving for what has happened to us. No forgiving at all. What is it they say those fancy head doctors? They say "denial". That's what you are suffering from Connie. Denial. All your silence will not make it go away, Connie, you cannot make it be forgotten. You want to pretend it didn't happen? Yet you remember every time you look at that baby. Do you know that the man who did this to me is standing in this crowd?'

Connie was rooted to the spot, there was no getting away from Roula now. She couldn't help scan the faces of the people standing around them. She recognised the men from Makrigialos, the big village and the surrounding farms. There was the Priest talking to Yanni, there was the goat keeper from up the hill, the shop keeper from the big village, the baker's husband, the schoolteacher and a couple of his older pupils, the rug-maker, the veg-man, the German hotelier and some of the waiters, all the local wine makers and the olive growers, Georgos and his father in a huddle with the Goat Lady's husband and the crazy son.

'Yes, you look at them Connie. Isn't the baby's father here too?'

'Leave me alone, Roula.' She started to walk away. There was a taint of the disturbed around Roula, she didn't want it spreading to her - like mould or scarlet fever.

'He is here, isn't he Connie? Isn't he?' Roula grabbed her arm with those scrawny fingers that made Connie think of forests of thorns, crumbling turrets and spinning wheels.

'Get away from me, Roula.' She raised her voice, pulled her arm free and pushed Roula as hard as she could. 'Go away.' Heads turned and looked their way. Yanni muttered something to the Priest and they both started to walk towards her.

Roula saw them too. 'Ah. Connie, the knights on their white horses are coming to rescue you. But what of the Ogre? What of the Beast? Will he come this way too? Come and admire his little boy? Will he come and say he is sorry?'

Connie screamed at her - screamed at her to leave her alone, she never wanted to speak to her again, she was mad. Roula started to walk off, laughing and laughing. Everyone was looking now. Everyone.

Connie was overcome by something unexpected and unknown to her. She caught up with Roula, swung her around by her shoulders and slapped her across the face. As hard as she could. It wasn't enough to make her feel better. She pushed both of her palms against Roula's chest and shoved her down onto the ground.

'Don't you ever come near me again, do you hear? Never speak to me again, ever. Do you hear me?' she shouted. Looming over her like that, Connie imagined herself kicking and kicking that haggard face
until the terrible laughing stopped, blood flowed and bones shattered. The Priest took her arm and urged her away just in time, before she lifted her foot and acted on her imaginings. Yanni helped Roula up, tried to wipe the mud and dirt from her clothes but she shoved him away and ran back to Connie, her face twisted with rage and spite. The

Priest put his hand up to ward her off - it was no good, even he couldn't stop her.

'He is here, isn't he, Connie? He is one of these handsome men. Look at them. Look. You can see him now, can't you Connie? The
English virgin's monster is here. He is watching you, Connie. What do you want to say to him?' Roula was screeching now. The faces of all the men were turned towards them. No one moved. Even the bulldozer was silent. Every word echoed around the hillside. Loud and clear for the whole world to hear. And Connie's world had started turning upside down and inside out. The grass and sky and trees and people were
spinning, round and round in slow motion with Connie at the centre. The Priest was pulling her, talking and talking in that calm and soothing way of his. She could see his mouth moving but couldn't understand a word he was saying. Roula's witch-red slash of a mouth was flapping up and down, her hands waving this way and that. Then Roula spun away from her and she saw the man. He was staring at her. Only a few strides away. She took a dizzying step towards him, just a step.

Now, Connie. Tell the Priest. Do it now. Take three more steps. Go over to him and point your finger. Say it. Here he is, Father. Here he is. This is him. The man who did this thing to me. The man who hurt me. Take another step.

There was a shout. A workman – hey, I've found something, it's a dead dog, looks like it hasn't been here that long, and it's got a red collar. The others crowded around to look. One of them pushed at the long, skinny body with his steel toe-capped boots - yes, definitely dead.

The world turned again. The man smiled at Connie and sauntered off to chat to the workmen. He knew her moment was wasted. He was safe now.

They brought the dog's body home. The Priest carried him as carefully as if he had been a person. Connie's grief was quiet. No tears, just wide-eyed disbelief. She couldn't be consoled. She sat silently by the stove with the baby on her knee and stared into space. Vaso wanted to say - thee mou, it's only a dog. Not a child. Only a dog. But she held her tongue, even hard-nosed Vaso knew this would be the wrong. No matter that she thought this was the only sensible thing to be said. She had no conception of pets and how some people could love them so much. No one did. Except the Priest who once had a little dog of his own. Ah, little Bella. He pictured her now, as he told Connie they would bury poor Puppy up at his place, in the garden amongst the flowers. Bella had been run over trying to follow him to work one day. He had thought of that little dog many, many times over the years. How trusting and loving she was, how she liked to have her ears scratched and her belly rubbed, how lovely her fur smelled and the feel of the little pink pads on her paws. He understood Connie's sadness. He sat next to her while Vaso carried on with the chores.

There was no need to say a word, Connie could trust him - he would not to try and take away her grief with hugs and platitudes.

They took the dog to the Priest's garden, dug a hole and placed him in it as gently as they could. Vaso picked bunch of spring flowers and laid them on top of the mound of earth - she thought Connie would like that. Yanni brought a small square of stone he found up at the big house - the perfect size with the dog's name and the date painted on it black. There, we will never forget, he said to Connie as he pushed it into place and patted it down.

It was a beautiful day, the sun was warm, the breeze was balmy, it was definitely spring. Vaso held the baby and put an arm round
Connie's shoulders. She had never seen anyone be so upset about a dog. Of course, there had been that fight with Roula which was bound to be making her feel unsettled. Fancy Connie slapping Roula! She wanted to hit her sometimes too. Honestly, what a crazy woman that Roula was, and all this just when Connie was getting herself together. Now she would fall into pieces again. What with the dead dog and everything. The Priest hadn't told her what the fight had been about and, as usual, Connie was keeping silent. She never thought Connie had it in her to do something like that. To hit Roula! Unbelievable! She would get to the
bottom of it, perhaps she would visit Roula later and ask her and remind her - no, she would tell her - to keep away from Connie. The poor girl did not need any more agitation. She jiggled the baby up and down as he grumbled, and rubbed Connie's shoulder absent-mindedly.

The Priest chanted a prayer for the dog to hasten his way to Heaven. What harm could it do? Connie believed the dog would go to sit with God and that was enough for him. She was English after all. They all went back to Papou's house. For tea and cakes.

Vaso is right - who would have thought you had that in you? But, of course you have. It's simmering and bubbling under the surface. How can it not be? How can all this be happening to you and you not be full of rage? Oh, you hide it well. You think of lost dogs and Scops owls, of cleaning and working and the mundane. You make the margins of your life narrower and narrower to contain it. When was the last time you walked through the village to the German's hotel, when was the last time you walked up the hill to the big village, when was the last time you passed the time of day with anyone other than Vaso, Papou and Yanni? How long is it since you have seen the people you call your friends - Yiota, Iakchos and his brothers? Those kind people who invited you for coffee and teased you about Georgos. And Georgos? When did you see him last? Was it the day in the autumn when you lay on Papou's sofa, snoozing in the heat and chatter, letting your bruises heal? Was it that day? Was it?

'Well,' said Vaso, 'that is the end of it,' and carried on with her cooking. She didn't have time to worry about the loss of an old house. No, not at all. Only a big pile of stones marked where the corner of the house had been. The rest was still standing. It looked naked. The trees and climbing plants had all been taken away leaving just a bare carcass of stone. The windows had been stripped of their dangerous metalwork that might have fallen down at any time. The last of the glass had been broken and carried away. The inside had been ripped out - all the floors, all the staircases were gone. There would be no more wandering around that old house any more, for anyone.

Connie shook a table cloth out and smoothed it over the ironing board. She liked the smell of red hot cloth, the hiss of the water she sprinkled under the iron as it sailed and smoothed its way across the cotton waves. It was a satisfying job. She didn't want to think about the house today. The iron sailed on.

The baby was propped up with cushions and surveyed his little world of trains and teddies with a smile on his face. There was his mother and his Aunty Vaso, both talking and full of busy. Both of them ready to entertain him at any time, always ready to pick him up and cuddle him at a moment's asking. He was such a good boy, happy to sit and look, and play with anything that came his way. Happy to eat his food, drink his milk and take his naps. Vaso thought it was a miracle he was so contented, considering his start.

He had his name now. Connie hadn't been able to wait any longer - calling him 'baby' was silly, she said. She went to see the Priest and told him she had picked the name 'Stephanos' and he could be
baptised any time. The Priest had um'd and ah'd and pulled his beard through his fingers as he thought it over. There had already been no blessing after forty days, but he had chanted a prayer over a dead dog, so he could do this for her couldn't he?

'Please, Father,' she said, 'it will make Vaso happy.'

'Well, Connie. In that case, I think we will baptise him on his Name day, December 27th is St. Stephen's Day. How does that sound to you?'

'Wonderful. He will be 10 months old. Perfect.'

Connie wasn't concerned one bit about him being baptised. It was Vaso who mentioned it all the time - if something terrible should happen to him, God forbid, the angels would not be able to find him, she said. Connie had given her a withering look. Vaso grumbled - I know, I know you think I am old-fashioned, but it is tradition and he is a Greek baby so he must follow tradition.

Connie was sure Vaso would be furious when she got home and told her the baby would be called Stephanos from now on.

'Mmmmm, Stephanos. Stephanos. A very good name,' was all she said, then, as she went into the kitchen, she turned around and added, 'the first Martyr. Are you sure that is the best name you could think of?' Connie rolled her eyes and they got back to their work.

With the ironing finished, the baby fed and the lunchtime snacks over, it was almost time for a little nap before the afternoon's work. The days were longer and warmer but no tourists had turned up yet, only the villagers were drifting back to the café, there would only be a few meals to make for later and the bar to stock up and clean.

Vaso sat down with a sigh and puffed out her cheeks. 'I am tired, Connie. You must be too,' she smoothed her brow with her hand and pulled her apron off, 'I have a good idea. Do you know what we should do, Connie?'

'No. But I'm sure it's going to be a good idea.' She laughed. 'Go on, tell me your good idea.'

Vaso frowned, she still didn't quite understand when Connie was being funny. 'I think we should go swimming. Take the baby in.'

'Vaso, are you mad? It's too early for swimming. It's only May. The water will be freezing. Anyway, you hate swimming.'

'I know. We could paddle. It's really hot today. His skin will have to get used to the sun, he is a Greek boy.' Vaso stood up. That must be it, settled. 'Come on, get some things and let's have a play in the sea before we have a nap.'

Vaso was right, little Stephanos would have to get acclimatised to the heat and the sunshine. This time next year he would be running about, brown as a berry and used to splashing in and out of the waves.

Don't wish his life away, Connie. There is plenty of time for wishing.

The water was cold, but not as horrible as they feared. Bracing, Connie said and tried to explain to Vaso what it meant, without any success. She hadn't been in the sea for months. It felt lovely. They sat on the sand with the baby between them and he screamed and squealed every time a tiny ripple splashed over him. He didn't like it. He stretched his hands up to his mother to be carried away from this terrifying new thing. She lay him on her legs and laughed at his pet lip, and when she laughed Vaso laughed and then the baby laughed. Papou heard all the noise and came out to join them. He had his old box camera slung around his neck - come on, he said, I will photograph you all. And the sun shone all around them and the waves burbled in time to their
laughing and they smiled and played and posed and sang with sheer gladness at those beautiful moments.

A handsome man stood behind his kitchen curtains and watched them playing on the sand – look at them, without a care in the world. If he went outside he could stop their laughing in the blink of an eye. With a snap of his fingers. No one should be happy today. No one. He watched her every morning when she went for her walks with that baby. That was his baby. She would never let him see the boy. He knew that. He sipped his hot, black coffee. His life was not what he had expected it to be. He was not what he had expected to be. He put down his cup of bitter dregs and spat into the sink. One day he would speak to her. One day he would stare right in her eyes and tell her. This is your fault. Yours. Pah! She is another one who has ruined his life, another one who … who … made him watch her, made him seek her out, made him touch her. Another one who remembers. But they always remember. Next time he will put a stop to the remembering. Next time it will be different.

The Priest is back. Come on, hurry up. He's got news.'

Connie opened her door, Vaso was running across the courtyard shouting and waving her apron at her. Vaso's excitement was a good start to this day - another day of sun, and another day to see who

clambered off the bus and stepped out into the holiday-time.

It was early. Early enough for the air to be crystal clear and cool. Connie and the baby had already enjoyed their morning walk along the beach - him wrapped and slung on her hip, and she, wearing flip flops and a coat over her pyjamas. They hadn't seen a soul - the sea was quiet, the sky was waking up, the air so fresh and new her skin shivered at its lick. On mornings like this it was easy to tell that it was going to be another hot day - the sky was pale and big and the horizon far, far in the

distance, the sun shimmered and dazzled on that sharp edge of the world, ready to melt away the chill. She could smell the heat coming, smell the day getting ready to envelope them all in its brilliance in spite of the snap in the air. As she walked, she talked and sang to her little boy - threw the darkness that lurked in her head to one side with every step and every nursery rhyme. Yes, it was easy on those mornings. And now, here was Vaso, full of joy and a flurry of chatter to keep Connie's mind from straying too far towards the dark.

She hurried over to the café, the baby chuckled as she bounced him along in her arms, his fat - baby smile dimpling his cheeks. Connie was excited to see the Priest again - it had been weeks. She ran in and hugged him. He kissed the top of her head and they all sat down with coffee and toast to hear the Priest's good news.

His brother, the bank manager, had organised a loan for the whole village - they could pay it back, he said, a bit from this family, a bit from that. They would form a cooperative and they would build a new supermarket and a café for ice-creams and the like. After that was done and the bills were paid any left over money would build something else - a hotel perhaps or apartments. His brother, the lawyer, had drawn up special contracts for them all to sign. Vaso clapped her hands with delight. Connie was bewildered by all this talk of contract and buidings and went to put the coffee pot on - she didn't understand any of it.

'What a jolly little thing he is,' the Priest said when she came back with the tray, 'so pleasant. We have been playing.' He hid his face behind his hat and pee-po'ed at the boy to make him laugh. Connie beamed at him - she had missed him. When she went up to his garden to put flowers on Puppy's grave, she was always sorry when he wasn't there. She often rested a little up there, sitting next to the dog, listening to the goat bells, wondering what the hens were squawking about and stopping the baby putting all the grass and soil in his mouth. It would have been nice to talk to the Priest on those days, but the moments had passed.

'He is, isn't he? He likes everyone.' She looked down at her son and wondered if she had ever been like him. So happy and easy in his world.

No, Connie, you weren't like him at all. Can't you remember what a reserved little thing you were? Quiet and sullen, with no ready smile. All the photos of you were staged studio portraits - no caught-in- the- moment snaps. Look at you, your mother used to say, you'd think there was someone behind you ready to beat you with a stick. She used to laugh too - look at your face, what a worry-wart you were. Well, maybe that was how you felt all the time, worried.

It was no wonder you looked so sad and worried all the time. You can remember the day your Dad left home. You came in from school and he was in the front room packing a suitcase, his clothes laid out in neat piles on the yellow nylon carpet. Mother was in the kitchen. I'm going to live somewhere else, he said, snapping the locks shut. He walked out of the door, down the path, into his car and was gone. Didn't you run to the window, push back the net curtains and watch him drive away, pressing the palms of your little hands on the glass? Daddy, Daddy, you said, your lips touching the cold window-pane. He didn't come back though, he didn't even turn around, did he? And then mother called you into the kitchen for your tea. Where's Daddy gone, you said. I don't know, eat your food before it gets cold, she said.

You lost everyone that day, not just Daddy - Granny and Grandpa, aunties, uncles, and cousins. A whole family wiped out with his one sentence. Poor you, only left with Mam and Grandma. How old were you, Connie? Eight. That's right - only eight, and you didn't see him again until you were fourteen. He was a drunk by then - a wrecked man with another shattered family to call his own.

And what happened next? Just as life had settled down with Mam, along came Daddy, drunk and maudlin, and told you all about your dead sister, didn't he? Slipped into an icy pond on the way home from school; only found when her cardigan floated to the surface as the weather eased and the ice softened. He told you how all the other children had run home, shouting and shouting for their mams and dads. Everyone in the village had searched, helped, consoled. But the little girl was drowned. They brought the dripping cardigan to him first. An hour later a man in a rubber diving suit carried his dead child to him and placed her in his arms. He stood there, cradling the sodden body of his little girl, his world falling away with every drip. And his wife howled beside him, clutching the other little girl to her chest - a left-over little girl whose life would change forever because those broken parents would never mend. Daddy said there wasn't a mark on her, perhaps the hint of a bruise on her left cheek, and he rubbed away the tears on his own cheeks as he talked.

And all the time you had grown up with the photograph of this unknown and smiling child - a pretty little thing, wearing a tartan dress and red ribbons in her blonde hair. It had always been there hadn't it - on top of the piano, sometimes on the sideboard, sometimes on the

radio-gramme? Fancy that, you have known her all your life. How many times did you ask mother who she was? How many? And what did she say? That's Lillian. And turned her back on you. You knew not to ask anything else. Just like you did when she told you to eat up the day that Daddy drove away.

You were glad Daddy told you but you couldn't bear to think about him crying and drinking his life away. Couldn't bear to think of your Mother unable to touch the child again, never able to reach out for one last hug, never able to smell the hair, feel the skin of her lost child. Never able to talk about her ever again.

And now, here you are in Crete and only four years have passed since your Daddy told you about Lillian; only four years since he dropped down dead getting out of his car, felled in an instant on his way to buy a birthday card. Surely there has been enough grief and misery in your family, enough torment, enough ... enough ... it must end

sometime. Life could only get better, it must. Why not today? On this sunny and exciting day when the Priest has come back with good news, when Vaso is full of plans, and you and your baby have had a lovely walk on the beach. Perhaps you will put an end to it, Connie, with your beautiful boy.

The Priest picked the baby up and let him pull at his beard,' How old is he now, Connie?'

'He's five months.'

'Connie, I think you are doing a good job with him. How are you?'

Connie wondered if she should tell him how she really was. How she tossed and turned every night, how she dreamed about men with moustaches catching her, how she dreamed she had turned into a doll, how she wondered if dying would help her mind rest. 'I'm fine, Father, really, I am.'

He lifted one eyebrow and smiled his gentle smile at her. 'Well, that's good.' He didn't believe her at all. She looked a little too thin, the skin under her eyes was a little too black. He watched her as she gazed at the child on his knee. It did seem she had turned a corner with the baby - yes, she had fathomed out a way to love him. She had been able to make a love exist for them, one they could share, and that could only be a marvellous thing.

'Father, I'm afraid that must be enough for now,' Vaso said, 'the bus will be coming soon and we have some work to do, food to prepare, bed sheets to wash, so we must get on. Go and talk to Papou. He will be excited.'

The Priest handed the wriggling baby over to Connie. 'I am back now, come and see me anytime you want. I have the English Tea remember.' He took her hand in his, Connie liked the feel of his cool and bony fingers and she grasped them tight. 'I will,' she said.

Before they knew it the summer was fully upon them again and every day was the same - hot and hectic. Work, sleep, work, more visitors and more work. There were more tourists than last year, the new bus drove all the way up to the German hotel to drop people off right outside the door this year - no more moaning about walking up the dusty road.

They were kept busy and the baby grew and grew, he sat up on his own and they clapped and cheered - no need of cushions to prop him up now. He spat his food all over the family table and upended his cup all over the floor. He laughed and gurgled and chattered in his own baby way, entertaining everyone with his antics. Somewhere between February and now, he had turned into a whole person, a real person with a mind and nature all his own.

There were more meetings in the village to discuss the work that was planned for the winter - building the ice cream shop and a supermarket. Everyone spent their days talking and talking about all the good things that were coming for their futures. It was exciting.

Grass started to creep over the remains of the big house and people forgot.

It's all right for people to forget someone else's troubles, it's what people do, even the best of friends. Lives carry on and new things replace the old worries. But you didn't forget. You invented a new game for yourself. Every time the memory-spiders flexed their creepy-crawly legs and ran amok inside your head, you opened the magic memory-eating box and swept them in. Pushed down the lid and left them there. The lid bounced and pitched as the hairy spider-feet tried to shove their way out, and the sound of a thousand scrabbling tiny claws made the bile rise in your throat, but you trapped them in there with all the other ones. Oh, yes, there were spiders there already. A fine collection - those tarantulas you got from Daddy and the false widow spiders from Mam. Those giant house spiders that tormented you during your lonely little-girl days and nights were the worst.

Life was hard for you when you were little, wasn't it Connie? So quiet. No emotion allowed - no crying, shouting, laughing, because Mam couldn't stand it could she? All those days and nights with no one to talk to, imagining you had been left in that house by the golden-haired, bareback rider from a travelling circus. Imagining that one day the circus might pass through the village again and the woman, in her spangled costume and huge feathers in her hair, would come to claim you. While you waited, you imagined the feel of the broad rump of the dapple-grey horse rocking and pitching under your feet as you pirouetted in the spotlights, and the crowd ooo'd and ahhh'd as you went cantering past. Or you read book after book. Any book you could lay your hands on was fair game - fairy-tales, encyclopaedias, Mam's Mill's and Boon, anthologies of poetry you didn't understand, any book from any book shelf in the house. Suitable or not, no one cared, you just read them. Little Connie, getting ready to grow up into goodness knows who.

The forgetting was easier for Connie too as the village got busier and busier with tourists. She didn't get a chance to go out very much, but that was all right, she didn't mind. Her friends came to see her.

Iakchos brought his lovely, pretty girlfriend to see the baby. Connie liked her and ignored the stab of jealousy in her heart and pushed it right into the box with the spiders.

Vaso complained almost every day - we need to get out of this café, take a night off, we need to see more of the girls from the village, we need some time to chat and giggle and have some wine, she said. Connie laughed – there was no time to do anything other than work and sleep, and there was the baby to look after. Anyway, she liked being in the café or in her goat shed. Now she was so tired by the end of the day she went to sleep quickly. She didn't have a moment to listen for the little Scops owl hooting his lonely hoot before she fell asleep, sometimes she didn't even hear Stephanos as he grumbled and whimpered himself awake in the mornings. She was too tired to lie awake thinking about that man, his hands, and his face too close to hers.

The dawn was beginning to break when the baby started to squeal and shout for her on this late August morning. She struggled to open her eyes, it was an unearthly hour to get up. She was lucky to have that quiet beach on her doorstep to wander along, the gentle sea to

paddle in and Papou's tree to sit under; they could go for a walk and have a cuddle under the branches whilst they waited for the rest of the world to wake up. She didn't go far, only up to the tree or down to the old harbour. Seven hundred yards. Nothing could happen to her in seven hundred yards, could it? She was safe there on the open beach. No

monsters to get her, no one to leap out on her - she pushed the spider-feet back into the box.

She felt stronger and braver and better than she had in a long time. It didn't matter that she only had seven hundred yards to feel better in. Who knows what she would feel like, what she would do, if she was too far from home. But time was on her side, winter would come around again and she could worry about everywhere else when it was quiet and dark again. Yes, she thought, there's plenty of time to practise being brave. Baby steps. She laughed to herself. Silly me, she said to the baby as she opened the door.

... It was greyer today, the sun shrouded with wisps of cloud, the air damp. It would be hot later. Once the sun had shed that misty cloak of his, he would split the trees with his heat ......

It was the mother they felt sorry for. Poor woman. It was nearly two weeks until there could be a funeral, what with the police and everything.

Poor Georgos to end up drowned like that. Such a young and handsome man to die in such a terrible way, they said in the church hall after the service.

Connie didn't go to the funeral. A few other women from the village made their excuses and stayed at home as well. Strange, said Papou.

When Roula found out that Georgos had been pulled from the sea - dead and swollen with the salt - she had laughed and laughed and laughed until the tears streamed down her face and they thought they would have to take her to the hospital. We thought she had gone crazy, Papou said. Trelos. And he twirled his finger at his temple.

No one knew where Georgos had gone into the sea, the beach was flat and smooth, sheltered in the two arms that made its crescent. The sea was shallow inside those mountainous arms - Connie could walk out for half a mile before her toes started to lift off the sea bed and she needed to swim. When she looked back to the shore it was full of teeny-tiny people and miniscule umbrellas, it was so far away.

There were no cliffs to jump from, no craggy ledges to fall off. How did he end up there? Dead on the sand in front of the café. Papou said he must have fallen off the harbour wall when he was drunk. Everyone knew he was too fond of the drink, like his father.

'Or he jumped. Maybe he was pushed,' Vaso said. Connie looked at her from underneath her lashes and kept her head down, pretending she was absorbed in the baby's toenails.

'Why did you say that, jumped or pushed?' Papou asked. 'Why would a young man like that jump into the sea? And there are no murderers in Makrigialos. Pushed! Pah! Who would push him?' He glanced at Connie but she absorbed in the baby, head down and concentrating on his fingernails now.

'Oh, I don't know. It was just a thought. Everyone has secrets, maybe his were too much for him to bear any longer, or maybe someone found out about his secrets and didn't like them. But, you are right, he probably slipped, you said yourself he liked a drink. The stones are wet on the harbour wall what with the nets and all the fish scales and stuff, aren't they?'

She went into the kitchen and they heard her clashing and banging the pots and pans about. Papou mouthed at Connie, 'Vaso is looking for the teapot.' That meant only one thing - English tea and a serious conversation. They both knew she only got the teapot out if Connie was ill, upset or needed talking too. Oh God, what was Vaso up to?

Connie grabbed Papou's hand. 'Did you tell her?' she whispered.

He shook his head and crossed his heart - no, of course he didn't, he would never do something like that to Connie, he was much too loyal. Vaso came back in and sure enough she had the tea - set and a plate of biscuits on a pretty tray. Connie and Papou looked at each other. No, this was not good, it could only mean one thing - Vaso knew, she knew about Georgos, knew he was the man and she was going to make them talk about it. Talk about what he had done.

Connie stood up. 'I must get this baby down for a nap. It's been a long day.'

'Sit down. I will talk to you now, because this is over. He is dead. No need for secrets any more. Don't you see? It's finished.' Vaso poured them all a nice cup of tea and, as Vaso talked, Connie tried to think of all the animals that began with A, then B, and then C, then the flowers and then the actors.

Vaso asked if he had been the one that did this terrible thing to her. Connie nodded. Vaso told her everything Roula had said that day at the linen van. And now he was dead, she said, there would be no need for anymore worries, no more bad dreams, no more turning out like Roula. Perhaps even that poor woman would be able to make a better life for herself, now he was gone. Isn't that right, Connie? Good.

Oh, Vaso, it is finished for you and you think with a curl of the waves and the pouring of tea, it is finished for Connie too. You think you have all the answers. How can it ever be finished for Connie? All the talking in the world isn't going to get rid of the feel of him, the smell of him, and the weight of him. All the tea in the universe isn't going to get rid of that baby boy. Connie has too many things to think about. And she is only up to the letter J. Jack-rabbit. Jasmine. John Wayne.

Christ. Connie. Your monster. Drowned and washed up the beach, right at your feet. Did he fall, did he jump? Was he pushed? Did an unknown assailant watch him and creep up on him in those early hours - barely light, barely day? Who shoved him so hard he toppled down into the water and did not get out again?

Was it you, Connie? Did you sneak up behind him as he walked along the harbour wall, hiding behind this boat and that boat until he found snug place to sit and watch you as you strolled along the beach with your baby? His long legs dangling over the wall and his grey sweater pulled up across his nose to stop his breath from billowing into the cold, early air.

 Did you slip back to the goat shed and pop the boy in his cot for five minutes, cut behind the café and hide behind the boats yourself?

 Did you slip off your flip-flops and creep along the length of that fishing boat and, when he turned around, did you kick your size eight foot into his surprised face?

 And what happened when he fell in the sea, Connie? Oh, that's right, he couldn't swim, and did you laugh as he scrambled and scrabbled to get a finger-hold on the disintegrating, slimy wall, falling backwards time after time into the grimy and oil-slick harbour waters? Until that last time. And then he was gone. Disappearing into the depths right under your nose. Did you catch his eye as he gulped in that last breath? Is that what happened? No Priest to stop you, no Yanni out there on the harbour wall to hold your hand and wipe away your tears. Was it you who watched a handsome, wicked man sinking and sinking into the dirty sea? Evil given for evil done.

 You love the water, don't you Connie? It cools and cleanses and washes everything away. And it kills.

 And you, Vaso? Up and about unexpectedly early, opening the blinds in the café, who did you see? Oh, there was Connie strolling along with the baby strapped to her hip in that ridiculous cloth. Wait a minute, who was that inching stealthily along the harbour wall? Keeping his head down, slipping behind the boats and piles of rotting nets, sly and furtive until he finds his place to sit. His place to watch and wait, letting his long legs dangle over the wall, his toes only an inch above the water. Hidden from Connie's view, but not yours.

Was it you who tip-toed across the sand, edged between the boats in your slippers, holding your breath, watching your step?

Did you get so close to him that he never knew who pushed him in, never knew whose hands thumped against his back and sent him face down into the sea.

You knew he couldn't swim, didn't you Vas? You knew.

But you didn't push him in, did you?

Water spiders, so small and insignificant, have a bite that is harmless, they can't really hurt, and definitely can't kill something as big as your monster. Unless the monsters are caught unawares and have an unexpected reaction to the venom hidden in the spider's tiny fangs. Those spiders live in a bubble of air and carry it with them down into the depths of their watery hunting grounds, it keeps them protected, breathing, and alive. You can put them in the box with all the others now.

Oh, well, perhaps we will never know how Georgos ended up in the sea. Perhaps it is best not to know.

They don't have to pick their way between pebbles and stones now, the path is smooth black tarmac, easy to walk on. This one won't wash away in the rain. Vaso is taking her to the big house. There isn't much else up here she'll need to see, she follows her without a word.

'So, Connie, how are you getting on? With the boy, I mean.' As if she could mean anything else.

'Vaso, he seems such a lovely boy. Well, man really.'

Vaso eyes her carefully, weighing up what she is about to say. Connie laughs. 'Just say it Vas, it's not like you to hesitate. Just say whatever you want to say'

'So, I have done a good job with your baby?'

It isn't the question Connie expected and it hits her right in her guts, hard as a fist. She stops walking and they both stand still amongst the bright new grass and flowers. Two grown women regarding each other with a myriad of thoughts and words wheeling in their heads. The world goes on around them as they watch each other, neither one knowing how to say all the things they need to say. The sun shines down on them. It doesn't care. The goat bells jingle. They don't care.

For a split - second Connie is angry. How could she ask such a question? There are too many layers to those few words. A good job?

How could she answer this? Was it a good job to bring up this baby and help him be a man? Was it a good job to help him see how his missing mother had struggled? Was it a good job to help him make sense of his loss? Was it a good job to ease his anger and his pain at being left

behind? Was it a good job not to turn him into her son? Was it a good job he had not been brought up by Connie, in cold and far off England?

Connie sits down on the grass. Her head is pounding. Vaso has done a wonderful job. A fantastic job as far as she could tell. Was it just a job? She looks up at the blue sky and the fluffy clouds floating past, wishing she could speak, wishing she was at home, wishing she hadn't come, wishing she had never left. Vaso comes closer, her shadow is thrown over Connie and is as big as the world.

'Will you take him away from us Connie? Will you take him back to England? Will we never see him again?'

'Vaso, I can't take him away. He's too old. He'll do what he wants. I can't make him come with me, any more than you can make him stay here.'

'I know this. Timos said you had not come to take him away. But we were worried.' Vaso shakes her head, 'I couldn't let you take him Connie. I couldn't. He is my boy.' She sits down next to her. 'I am not ready to forgive you yet, not ready to let him go. I'm sorry.'

'I know, Vaso. I know. Listen, you might never be able to forgive me for what I did, but I'll understand.'

She puts a hand out to her friend. Vaso takes it and presses it to her heart. 'Feel here. It was broken when you left. I didn't know what to do. Everyone told me to forget all about you. But I couldn't. I missed you so much and I was worried about you, scared for you. The baby won't remember her, they said. Papou said you would have to come back one day, you wouldn't be able to help yourself and it would be much worse if I lied to the boy. Much worse. So, I told the boy the truth. But I couldn't tell him why you didn't come back. All I could say to make him feel better, was that you were so young and so confused, that it wasn't his fault, or yours. There were times, many times, it wasn't enough and he cried and got angry with me. Sometimes I thought we would all break into pieces.'

'Vaso, it was me he was angry with. Me. Not you. He told me. I promise I will not try to make him leave here, leave you. I promise, Vaso. Look, we need to get through this and we need to forgive each other or we can never be friends again, we'll always be wary of each other, wondering what we are going to do next. I don't want that. Do you?'

Vaso leaves loose of Connie's fingers and lets them drop. She gets up and walks away without answering the question. 'Come on. I want to show you the big house.'

'I'm not sure I want to go all the way up there. I saw it from the bus. Just a glimpse as we came down the hill, it looks different but …' Connie's words trail away in to the warm air, her head begins to fill with jumbled thoughts - memories are already crawling into any little crack.

'Don't worry. I'm here with you and I remember too. We will be fine, we will look after each other. You will be happy to see it, I promise. It will chase away all those demons you have kept in your heart for so long.'

Connie is surprised. Vaso had been so determined, so right, so sure everything would be perfect after Georgos was dead. It had been the answer to everything. Burying him on that hot and sunny day, so long ago, would put a stop to it all, she said. No more nightmares, no more demons, no more worries that someone will catch her, hurt her, kill her. Push the monster into the sea or under the earth, it makes no difference, he has gone and the rest will go away too. It will. Yet here she is twenty years later telling Connie she knew she would never forget about the demons.

'I was wrong Connie. When you didn't come back I knew I had made a mistake. I have hated myself for it. You would have come home if I hadn't been so right all the time. Timos said I should have let you speak that day when you found Georgos. Every day I have thought how I should have helped you, but all I did was try to make you tough. Like me. I made you scared to come back.'

'No Vaso, you didn't …'

The sentence remains unfinished. They have turned the last and steepest bend in the path and the house is in full view.

The house is stunning. Complete. Rebuilt. The balconies are painted a soft pale green, the honeyed walls glow in the sun, the huge windows are open wide. White voile curtains waft in and out with the breeze. The house is breathing.

The garden is neat; tidy grass and rose bushes galore, their dark green leaves thick and lush, buds already forming, some about to burst. The path is paved with golden stones, an arch of clematis frames the carved front door. The remains of clumps of primroses are hunched in terracotta pots. Drifts of lavender flow right up to the steps.

'Ah,' Vaso sighs, 'he uses so much water in the summer but he keeps everything growing and growing. He has many books about your "country gardens". Beautiful, isn't it? An English garden for his English mother.'

'My goodness.' It's all she can say.

Vaso pushes the door open - still no locked doors in Makrigialos. Inside it is awash with light, quiet and hushed, but full of that gorgeous light. Connie stands in the hallway. She can see into the main room - no brown apple peelings in that fireplace, no fallen roof tiles smashed on those rugs. The stairs are in front of her, polished and shining - no

broken treads, no splintered, crushing timbers here. The smell of lemons is all around her.

'Vaso, it is beautiful.'

'I know. Isn't it.'

'But how and when and who?'

'Stephanos. He has saved up every penny since he was 14 and started working in the café. He worked and worked and saved and saved. When he finished his National Service and came home, he decided he wanted to be a gardener. He looks after everybody's gardens in the

village, and all the hotels and the fancy villas up in the hills. One day he sat us down and said he had bought the big house.'

'But no one knew who it belonged to. Not even Papou. And there was nothing left of it.'

Vaso laughs and taps Connie on the arm. 'That boy of ours is a genius. He spent hours and hours looking up the history of the house anywhere he could - libraries, the church, that new internet thing. I heard him typing hour after hour and talking on the phone night after night. He never told us a thing, just tapped his nose and said we should mind our own business. And the Priest helped him. He had a lot to do with it. That man has so many brothers, all those lawyers or bank managers or some other useful thing.'

Connie smiled, "that boy of ours" Vaso had said, had she noticed too?

'He paid very little money, but now, look at it.' A proud mother standing in the house a clever son has rescued.

Connie turns around in a slow circle, admiring the sweep of the stairs, the sheen of the mellow wood, the beautiful rugs on the gleaming floor. If she wasn't standing here in the flesh, she would never have believed it was possible. There had been almost nothing left, just a pile of grass - covered stones and the gaping wreck of a house.

'Day after day he poured over drawings and plans and pictures. Never showed us anything. And little by little the house started to grow. A wall here, a door there, a window here. It was like a miracle. I told Timos he was building it for you, maybe when the last stone was laid you would appear from nowhere …' Vaso looks over to Connie, just a brief ghost of a smile, '… and look … here you are.' There are tears hanging on the tips of her lashes. The sunlight catches them and they sparkle like tiny gems. 'Look. You are here, in the house.'

And now the tears fall and slide down her face. Connie has nothing to mop them up with, no apron to dry them, there is no old man here to distract Vaso from shedding those tears and stop their dripping. Connie lets them fall - it's the best way.

'So, who lives here? Just him?'

A shiver of her shoulders and a rake of the hair off her face and Vaso is recovered. 'Of course not, we all live here. It's too big just for him. And there is still plenty of room, enough room for another whole family to move in and we would still not bump into each other.'

Connie goes to the foot of the stairs. 'Can we go up?'

Vaso nods and leads her up the shining wooden staircase.

And at the very moment Connie places her foot on the first stair, Ed and the children are about to leave the hotel. He is waiting in reception wishing they would hurry up and finish buying those sunglasses. God. It is all taking so long, they are so slow. His brow is furrowed with the effort of trying not to get irritated with them. He wants to go. He feels like a bit of knitting the dog has played with, limp and damp and tangled up in knots. Oh, hurry up, he wants to shout, bloody hurry up for God's sake. The receptionist looks up, catches his eye and smiles. A smile full of friendliness and happiness. He wishes he felt so happy. Perhaps he could ask this young woman about the café. Perhaps … if he wasn't so scared she couldn't speak English.

Just ask her Ed. Just ask. Go on. You can do it. You've come this far.

'Excuse me, do you speak English?'

'Of course. How can I help?'

'Oh good.' He fumbles in his pocket for the scraps of letters and shows her the name and address. 'I'm looking for this person, Vaso

Papadakis.'

He holds his breath without realising. Holds his breath and looks into the brown eyes of this woman - her answer might hold a key for him.

'I know her. She is Vaso Angavanakis now. They have the last apartments in Makrigialos, right next to the harbour - Connie's Place,' she smiles and gives him back the letter, 'you will find her there.'

Has he remembered to breathe? "Connie's Place"? What does she mean "Connie's Place"? His Connie? Before he has a chance to say anything else, the kids come running into reception waving their new sunglasses in his face - look, Dad, look. The two youngest skitter about like lambs in the sunshine. Stella saunters along behind them like a film star, all long golden hair and the blackest of black Ray - Bans. His breath comes back. Fake Ray-Bans. What a waste of their holiday money. That's Ed, he's practical. The impact of the receptionist's words is taken away by the matter-of-fact. Fake Ray-Bans for goodness sake.

He takes Stella to one side while the others jump about and fuss with their new purchases. 'I've found her, Stella. Found Vaso. She's still here. Don't say anything to the others, just in case your Mother isn't with her.'

Stella raises her eyebrows, he can see them over the top of the damn fake sunglasses. 'Oh, Dad. Are we going now?'

He nods. 'Yes, right now, I can't wait any longer.'

He shouts for the others and they walk out of the German hotel and into the sunshine; into the 'now'.

Claire and James jog ahead, pointing at this and that, calling back to their Dad and big sister - look at the sea, when can we go in? Can we? When? They seem to have forgotten what's brought them here. Ed and Stella talk quietly together. Ed is worried but Stella is a sensible girl - if mam isn't there, she tells him, this Vaso woman will know where she is.

Half way down the road James spots a track, it turns through the bushes and salty edges of the beach where the land is neither sand nor soil, and winds down to the sea. The kids want to walk this way, get their flip-flopped feet off the hot tarmac and dabble them in the water. Can Ed bear the walk to take a bit longer? Yes. They have got this far, another few minutes till he sees her again won't matter too much. He can give them that.

Cool water laps over their feet and they wander along, glad they are here, on this beach, in this sunshine and walking towards their mother. Ed thinks he knows why his Connie is here, thinks he understands why she wanted to come back - look at this place, everyone is smiling. And there are the photos, those ones tucked in Stella's bag, Connie looking so relaxed and carefree here in this little seaside place. The photos show a Connie he has never caught sight of in the flesh. Maybe that Connie had been left behind here, maybe that's why she has come. To find that Connie again. He thinks he understands at last, and he is happy.

And where is Connie as her family splash along the shoreline, taking in the views and feeling so content? She has made it up the stairs.

The bedroom takes Connie's breath away with its simple prettiness. Billowing white curtains, a white tiled floor casting pools of sunlight all around them, one wall bursting with the same blue and green flowers and golden birds she remembers. The bed is plain and simple with its virginal covers and plump pillows. It is beautiful - no dust, no dead leaves, no handbag left abandoned in the middle of a rotting rug.

'Vaso. I can't believe it. I can't take all this in. The wallpaper? It's impossible.'

Vaso laughs - the old gurgling giggle that had been missing until this very moment. 'I knew you would like it. I knew. He saved a scrap of the paper and had this made, but it is all fresh and new. There is
nothing left in this house to remind us of anything bad. Can you remember how I hated this house? How many times did I tell you how much it scared me? Then … what happened to you … And now, we live in it. Sometimes, I can't believe it myself.'

'Is this your room, Vas?' There is silence, for a moment Connie thinks Vaso hasn't heard, 'Is this…'

'No.' Vaso points to the table by the bed, to a photo in a silver frame. She hands it to Connie. The photo is of her - back to the photographer, head turned slightly so her smiling profile can be seen and, looking over her shoulder, his mother's lips pressed against his cheek, and his green eyes staring straight out into the world, is her baby son.

'This is your room, Connie. This is the room he made for his mother. For you, when you came home.'

She sits down on the bed. There are no words. Not even lost or hidden ones. No words at all.

Connie, this is what your "now" is. It is shock and pain and regret. It is hope, elation and realisation. It is those terrible spiders scuttling out of the dark and into the open - writhing and twisting and struggling to scramble back to cover where they'll be safe. Time to chase them out now, Connie, time to brush them away, maybe even stamp on a few. Not all of them will go, you'll never catch all of them, but the ones left behind will be afraid to come out into the light again. You'll always know they are there, you might catch a glimpse of them as they run from dark corner to dark corner. You'll even think about them from time to time and force a few more of them out into the open. But they'll never frighten you as much again and their cobwebs will be flimsy and easy to break. Now.

Vaso sits down beside her and puts her arm around her. Tears drip onto the photo.

'Come on. Don't cry.' Vaso's voice is soft and gentle. A mother's voice. 'He wanted you to come home and we let him do this for you. It was to make you happy. Not sad. I wondered if this room would be the right room … after everything that happened here. I couldn't stop him. I couldn't tell him. I wanted to, but I never found the right words, and then it was done.'

'It is the right room, Vas. It is the perfect room.' And at that moment she means it, really means it, because the spiders are tumbling out, like those ants on the path on that terrible stormy day so long ago.

How can you mean it Connie? How can you look at this room, even with all its new freshness and beauty, and not feel the crawling of the past running up and down your spine? Do you think about it as you admire that pretty wallpaper, that crisp white bed? Do you think of those hands on your pristine skin, that mouth on yours? Do you remember how you tried to fight him off, tried not to let him overpower you? Fought and fought until your strength was gone and you tried to lie still and pretend you were dead. Do you believe what you have said? You do, you must.

'Come on, I will show you the rest of the house. You need to see the kitchen. It is a wonder. I know you will love that too.'

'Oh, Vaso. I hope you remember I'm only good at peeling vegetables. My cooking has never got any better.'

Vaso links her arm and they leave that beautiful room, shut the door on the peace and quiet. Shut the door on the girl she was, lying there on a mouldering rug, eyes shut tight, thinking of circus horses and hearing nothing but the tearing of her clothes and the breathing in her ears.

There is such a lot left to say. There is such a lot already said. It hasn't been as difficult as Connie has imagined for all these wasted years. Her son is overjoyed to see her. He has planned and prepared for her coming to find him because he wanted it so much. Vaso and Timos have made it easy for her and she is grateful. They had sat together one cold night - a boy's lifetime ago - and talked long into the darkness. It had been a hard conversation. Many tears were added to the floods that had already poured out. The child was almost two, he ran and laughed and jumped and sang the whole day long. He was cheerful. But his mother was not coming back. There were no more letters and no more places left for Vaso to look. His mother was gone. That winter night, so long ago, as he slept, tucked up tight in his little bed, his teddy snuggled in his arms and a photo of his mother on the bedside table, they decided what was best to do. As the stars twinkled and the bright moon shone down into the boy's bedroom, they promised to always tell him the truth, no matter how hard, or sad it was. From that night he couldn't remember a single day when he didn't know about his lost mother, who loved him so much she left him there to be safe and happy for ever and ever.

Splashing and jumping through the frills of waves doesn't take them as long as Ed feared and he's enjoying it. They pass the apartments, cafés and the shops full of tourist things - no, he says, you are not buying any more rubbish. They try not to tread on people toasting themselves on the hot sand. They nod politely and smile at the Greek man with the hairy chest like a doormat and avert their eyes from his impossibly tiny trunks. Ela, Ela, he shouts, calling for his kids to come here, stop this, let's do that - his plump and pretty wife trails along behind him carrying the picnic basket and towels.

The smell of roasting coffee beans and sun tan lotion and the salty tang of the seaside drifts on the air all around them.

'No wonder Mam wanted to come here, Dad. It's really nice.' Stella says, up to her knees in the sea.

'I was just thinking that. I wonder what it was like when she was here before.'

'There wasn't much here, just a few houses and a café. They all got together and decided not to allow any high-rise buildings or outsiders to take over the land. The whole village stuck together for years and years to keep the place for themselves. Apparently, there was a Priest who had a lot to do with it. They pooled all their money and did things bit by bit to keep it perfect.'

'How do you know all that, Stella?'

'There's a book in the reception, it's full of photos too. I was reading it while the kids were picking their sun glasses. It mentioned Mam's friend, Vaso, and her Grandad. And some big house up the hill.'

They both look up, they aren't quite in the right spot to see the house from the beach, but another few hundred yards and they will be able to catch a glimpse of it. If they look again. And if they peered hard enough against the sun, they might see their mother coming back down the hill.

'Well, fancy that. I'll have to read it later. When we get back.'

He is wishing he never has to read that book. His wife will tell him the story of Makrigialos because they will be together. Sitting in a café, holding hands and watching the sun go down.

James' voice carries to them on the breeze, his whooping and shouting rises above all the other sounds of seaside holidays, he's waving at them and jumping up and down. 'I've found it. It's here, Dad.' He points to a white building with bright blue balconies, a wooden veranda running its full width, flowers overflowing from their pots and tumbling down each step to the beach. Oh, so it is. "Connie's Place" is right here in front of them. The wooden plaque bears his wife's name. They can do nothing but stand and stare.

Meanwhile, up the hill, what is Connie doing? The very moment her husband and children think they have found her is passing her by as she and Vaso walk to the Priest's house. It won't be too long, not now.

The dog's resting place is there for anyone to see, anyone who might want to come and visit, might want to spend a few minutes contemplating life and death. Anyone who wants to pass a little time, on a too-busy day, resting on the dry grass with only the bleating goats and the squabbling chickens to keep them company. The Priest has kept the little grave neat and tidy, he has cleaned the footstone and made sure the name and date are always readable. There is a great heave in her chest. Poor Puppy who helped her out of her goat shed when she wanted to stay in there forever, or die. Poor Puppy. That smooth, non-descript stone reminds her of so much more than just a skinny dog she loved so much. It brings alive pictures of Yanni and Papou sitting close together, heads bent towards each other, sharing a laugh, Papou holding her hand when she was sad, Papou reading the news headlines to her every

morning … oh, too many pictures. She bends down and pulls out a weed or two and pats the bump in the grass as if she is patting the dog himself.

'Come on, I think this is enough for today.' Vaso interrupts her memories. Connie agrees, it is time to go back to her room for some contemplation of her own.

'Before we go, can I ask you something? You can tell me to mind my own business if you want.' Vaso nods. 'Why didn't you have any other children?'

'It just didn't happen. Can you imagine? None. We tried and tried. We had many tests, but no doctors could find anything wrong. It was God's will. I even asked forgiveness for all the bad things I had done but He punished me anyway. I couldn't bring new lives into the world.' Her face crumples for a second, Connie thinks she is going to cry but she pulls herself together in a flash. 'Come on. Let's go.'
The conversation is over and they head back to the café.

Stella might as well be in a dream as she stands there staring at her mother's name. Glued to the spot at the sight of it, afraid to move in case it fades away and she's deserted once more. The world drifts away from her and Stella is flooded with her mother's essence. Her mother's voice calling her to get up and get ready for school. Her mother holding her skinny 6-year-old leg and sticking cartoon plasters on a scraped knee. Her mother shouting at her that night she wanted to go to that awful party and her mother's arms hugging her tight when she came home again, drunk and sick. The smell of her hair, the feel of her hand stroking her forehead when she can't sleep. Oh God. Please let her be here. Please.

Come on, Ed says, she'll be surprised to see us, that's for sure. He walks up the steps. Stella is uncertain, not sure what will happen, fearful that she won't be there, that she has never come here at all.

There's no one at the reception desk. All is quiet. Not even the buzzing of a bee to disturb the calm. The outside world is muffled and far away. Bang. Bang. Bang. They jump. Well, someone is about, somewhere - come on, Ed whispers. Stella laughs - stop whispering Dad, you idiot.

'Hello. Anyone here?' she shouts. James and Claire start to laugh too and all of a sudden it is just a sunny day on holiday again.

'Hello-ooo.'

'All right, Stella. That's enough.' He is a bit frightened to disturb the calm, afraid to find out what the next few minutes will bring. The banging stops, a door opens and a tall young man steps through, wiping his hands on the back of his jeans.

'I'm so sorry. I am hanging pictures. My mother would normally be here but she is out with her friend.'

Ed has rehearsed this a thousand and one times in his head. No, a million and one times, and now his tongue is stuck to the roof of his mouth, his lips are frozen. Oh God. He can't think where to start. Stella knows exactly the right words to say. Clever thing.

'We are looking for my Mother. She came here the day before yesterday. Her name is Connie. If your mother is Vaso, then we think she is your mother's friend.' She smiles back at him and meets his green eyes with hers.

The young man hesitates before he speaks and brushes his flop of golden hair out of his eyes to give himself a moment before he answers. Only he knows he needs that split second to keep himself composed, to stop himself from saying too much, too soon.

'Yes, she is here. My mother is Vaso. They have gone for a walk to see our house. I don't think they will be long. What are your names? I am Stephanos.'

They don't register anything at the sound of his name. He is not surprised they don't react and rush into his arms, they don't know. He didn't know until yesterday. They will all have to wait a little while longer to get the whole story.

Ed introduces them one by one, Stephanos shakes the hands of his new brother and sisters, checking their faces for any sign that they are like him. The eyes. The oldest girl has his eyes. The mother's eyes. They all have the same luxurious golden hair. They are all too tall.

'I wonder if we could wait for her. Maybe outside on the veranda.'

'That will be fine, would you like some drinks? I have no idea how long they will be, but they have been out for quite a while,' he says, still smiling.

'Can we have ice cream?' they all chorus together, 'can we Dad?' He nods, yes, he will organise some nice treats for them; the two little ones are happy and scamper off outside to sit in the sun. Stella hangs back, she wants to stay with the grown-ups, but Ed shoos her off to sit with the others. He has an important question to ask this young man and he doesn't want Stella to hear his deepest fear spilling into this glorious moment full of sunshine and ice-cream.

'Could you tell me something?' Stephanos regards him with a careful look, unsure what the question will be. 'How did Connie seem to you? Was she all right? You see, we didn't know she was coming here. She just upped and left … we were worried she might not be happy … was she anxious or upset?'

'I was talking to her this morning and she seemed fine to me. A very nice person. She will be happy you are here.' Stephanos laughs a little, 'don't worry, all is good. I will go and get those drinks and ice creams now. Maybe a beer for you?'

'Oh, thank you, I've been worried about her. I've realised I don't know very much about her at all. She told me she lived here when she was young but other than that nothing. I've got no idea what made her come back here like this – not telling us and running away. And a beer would be just the ticket.'

'I think there is lots you will learn about your wife today.' The boy reaches out and pats his shoulder.

Nice bloke, Ed thinks as he goes to join the children. His head still feels full, the huge jumble of knots is still in there, but thank God she is here and thank God she's not crazy or anything. Oh, he is looking forward to seeing her. He can't wait. He really can't wait.

And what is Stephanos doing as his mother walks down the hill and his siblings are waiting for their cool drinks? He is in the kitchen.

He is leaning against the door, his shoulders are shaking, he is crying. No wonder. First the long-lost mother appears out of nowhere and only two days later, a new brother and sisters and a step-father arrive. He's a sensible boy, he is, sometimes too sensible, but this is almost too much. He lets the tears fall until there are no more and when his sobbing has died down, he runs a tea towel under the cold tap and holds it to his face. He wipes his eyes, stiffens his back and draws himself up tall and takes a coffee pot down. Yes, like Vaso, he can pull himself together in an instant.

Well, Ed, it won't be long now. Connie and Vaso are just coming around the corner by the supermarket, their feet are about to walk on the sand. In a matter of seconds Connie will be able to see someone familiar sitting on the veranda. Someone she loves and needs and could not have survived all these years without. You, Ed.

When Stephanos brings the tray of snacks and drinks he is himself again. He wants to speak to them, sit down beside them, find out everything he can and tell them who he is - of course he does. Oh yes, he has had a happy life and he loves his Mum and Dad with all his heart, but he is not their flesh and blood. He's not like them, not dark and short and Greek to the very ends of his fingernails. This little family sitting here in front of him, laughing together as he serves their drinks, are his blood. His flesh is almost as light as theirs, his hair the same gold and always those green eyes to give his heritage away. He has noticed that the boy has green eyes too. The middle one has blue eyes like the Dad, but her hair is the blondest of all, almost ginger in the strong sunlight. They are talking the afternoon away as he wrestles and struggles to keep himself in control. He must contain himself until his mother comes back, it would be the wrong thing to do to speak out. Poor boy. So much to take in, so much to think about, so much to get used to.

The women bump into Yiota coming out of her beautiful shop. It is crammed full of summer clothes in all shades of pastel colours, blowing a soft and gentle rainbow around them in the sea breeze. Connie gives her a hug. Yiota was always a kind woman, Connie had liked her. Connie's Greek is still rusty and she struggles to catch the drift of their

conversation, as they chatter she makes her excuses and wanders on by herself. She is tired. Exhausted. There is so much to think about. Her mind is tumbling over itself to make sense of everything, the thoughts are rushing and somersaulting around in her head. She needs to lie down and rest. When she is asleep maybe it will sort itself out.

Oh, there is her boy outside the apartments - he is so tall and handsome.

Wait. Who is that? Who are those people sitting on the veranda? That man looks just like Ed.

No … But ... Hang on ... Isn't that Stella?

Connie starts to run, shouting at them, calling their names.

Oh, my God ... Oh, my God...

They look round and then they are running too. Down the steps and into her open arms.

My God...

They cling to her. She looks over their heads and Ed is coming towards her, his face split into a great beaming smile. She cups their faces in her hands and kisses them over and over again. Stella is laughing, the younger ones are crying and Ed is just smiling and smiling and smiling. Stephanos watches them and feels a stab in his heart, the swift pain of jealousy jabbed into his very core. But it won't be much longer now, then he will meet them properly and he can hug them too. He walks down the steps and waits, quietly and patiently, for something astounding to be said.

Connie apologises again and again... I'm sorry, I'm sorry. I'm so sorry. Ed puts his arms around her. The comfort of her warmth against him, the pull of the years together – stronger than the pull of the sand under her feet - the strength of his love for her, the ache in his body and heart for her are all unleashed in his tears. His legs threaten to give way with the relief and a surfeit of love.

'Jesus, Connie, you bloody scared me. You really bloody did.' He pushes her hair away from her face. 'Christ on a bike. Thank God you're here.' He pulls her to him again. She doesn't speak, just holds him tight. Oh. What to say, what to do, what, what, what?

'Connie,' Vaso is calling her, 'Connie. Thee mou... Connie. Is this your family? It must be. Silly me. Oh, my goodness.' And in the blink of an eye everyone is hugging and kissing and jumping up and down and screeching and crying. It is a moment of joy. No one knows who is who, or what is what, but the fusion of so many emotions is exhilarating.

At last. At last you have them all here, Connie. Now what? Is it too much to ask for the truth? No secrets now. Not now. Not now. Come on, it is time for you to speak, time to stop kissing and hugging and time for all the talking that must be done. That 'now' you have been wishing and searching for is here. The mood is right, the happiness is palpable, and all these people are waiting for you to make the first move, say the first words. Don't let them down.

Vaso recognised the handwriting. Connie hadn't had a letter from her mother since before the baby was born, this was a surprise. She turned it over and looked at the address on the back. Yes, from the mother. She left it on the table. No rush to give it to Connie because she wouldn't be too bothered. Vaso couldn't understand Connie and her mother - they didn't seem to like each other at all. Vaso missed her mother all the time. It was almost a day trip to get to Heraklion to see her, she went as often as she could and it still wasn't enough. That new road would make a big difference, it was going to be a nice straight road, blasted right through the mountains but goodness knows how long it would take to get started, let alone finished. She consoled herself with the thought that Mama would come home one day, and they would all be together again.

'Letter. Mother.' Vaso shouted from the kitchen when Connie came over to the café with the baby. Connie plonked the boy down on his play-mat, he picked up a brick and started to suck it - another normal morning, sunshine and work to do. Mmmmm, Connie murmured, what is this one going to say. She opened it without much hope for it to be a happy letter. They never were. Vasou was chopping onions, the coffee pot was bubbling, almost ready for their breakfast, and the baby was sitting on his blanket trying to shove a toy car in his mouth. All was well with the world on this ordinary Makrigialos morning.

'Oh God. Oh God. Vas.' Vaso looked up from the onions, Connie's face was white, her hands were shaking. What on earth?

'My mother is ill. Cancer. She says she hasn't got long and I must go home. Oh God.' Connie held the letter out to her. It was just a note, only a few words scrawled on a sheet of lined paper torn from an exercise book.

'Oh God. What will I do, Vaso?' The baby squealed and laughed at the wobbly clown rolling round and round on his blanket.

'You must go, Connie. She is your mother. You must go. You will have to go. You won't forgive yourself if anything happens to her and you're not there.'

That was true. She would have to fly back to England and watch her mother die. Vaso gave her a cup of coffee and went to get Papou. He would know exactly what to do. There would be flights to organise, Connie wouldn't have the money for that. Papou would sort it out.

They sat around the table talking and talking, trying to think what to do for the best. There was no option. A flight home and however many weeks it took, that was the way it was. Let each day come and go, Vaso said, and then you'll cope, then you'll know how to manage.

Oh Vaso. Brave and tough, so sensible and so right. How could you be so wrong this time?

Papou rang the Priest. He came down from his little house to talk to her. She wanted Vaso to go with her to England but it was impossible, could the Priest come? Could Papou come? She knew the answers. You are scared Connie, the Priest said, that's all. It's fine to be scared when things like this happen. It's normal. The best thing to do is ring her from here and talk to her, make a plan with her. Papou agreed. It was months and months since she had spoken to her mother. When she heard her voice crackling through the wires, tinny and far away, Connie broke down in tears. Yes, her mother said, I have cancer and there's nothing anyone can do. I suppose it serves me right for smoking so much. She had croaked a laugh out from somewhere. Come home, Connie. Please. I need you.

There was no one else. No one at all. No aunties, or uncles or grandmas to help. No friends, no husband, no - one. Just Connie. So, that was that.

The Priest said she didn't have to go if she didn't want to, they could arrange a hospital - after all, people who lived on their own got sick and died all the time. Vaso and Papou looked so horrified at the very idea that someone could leave their mother to die alone, Connie didn't dare say she thought it was the perfect answer. The moment passed and it was decided. Papou would pay for a flight, the Priest would take her to Heraklion and she would go home to England to be with her mother. It would be a terrible few weeks.

But the baby, what about the baby? Should she take him? No, she would leave him with Vaso. It would be better, he was too little to go all that way in a plane. He was too little to be with a dying woman and, in her heart of hearts, she didn't want to take him. Why? Because she didn't want her mother's wretchedness and loneliness to contaminate him, to taint him as it had done her. No, far better to leave him here with his Aunty Vaso, in the sunshine and the joyfulness that was his home. Far better because she wouldn't be away for long, a few weeks, a month perhaps. They tried to talk her out of it, tried to make her take him but she was adamant. No, it will be bad for him, she said, there will be too much sadness and pain, too much grief. No. Better he stays here with you because you are his family as well.

She flew home to England three days later. She hugged and kissed her little boy goodbye. Cried and cried as the Priest drove her to the airport. Cried and cried as she waved him goodbye. Cried and cried as the plane took off. She peered out of the window at the tiny speck that was Crete disappearing in front of her eyes. Clutched in her hand, so tight it cut the already broken skin of her palm, was Vaso's golden brooch. Bring it back for my wedding day, Vaso said, bring it back.

Brave Connie. You didn't have a clue, did you? But there was no clue. There is no instruction manual for life. You only do what you can do with the information you have been given.

Your mother took five months to die. You rang Vaso every day, talked to the baby down the crackling line and cried and cried. Your mother faded away and you faded with her. With every week that passed you retreated, further and further away from your mother, away from yourself and away from Crete. And away from the little boy you left
behind. *And when it was over you lay on your little-girl bed in your mother's house and didn't know what to do. And you stopped crying.*

You were only a girl yourself, how old? 18 or 19? A short lifetime of hurt upon hurt, of not telling anyone, not talking to anyone who could help you lift those burdens from your skinny, young shoulders. And the spiders came back and wrapped you in their multitudes of cobwebs, their layers and layers of soft fleece protecting you from any more pain. You shut the box, slammed the lid and walked away. It was for the best, you said to the spiders - get in there, be quiet and never come back. I never want to see you again. They huddled in the dark and waited, whispered and scuttled and bided their time.

But they did come back. No matter how many times you slammed that lid, those spiders bumped and pushed at it, poked their legs through any crack, and one day the box broke. There wasn't a big enough box, Connie. That was the problem. No box in the world could keep them hidden forever. And then? Well, then it was time for something big.

And what about today as you hug your family and wonder what to say? You are here, today, in the 'now'. Today. What are you going to do about it? They are waiting Connie - Ed, Stella, James, Claire, Stephanos and Vaso. They are waiting for you to tell them, waiting to find out what their futures will be.

Connie reaches into her bag, pulls out the old brooch and puts it on the table in front of them. The emerald spider is the colour of those eyes. The delicate golden web is tarnished and blackened.

What's that you said, Connie? Speak up.